DOG DAYS

DOG DAYS

Mavis Cheek

WINDSOR
PARAGON
THORNDIKE

This Large Print book is published by BBC Audiobooks Ltd, Bath, England and by Thorndike Press®, Waterville, Maine, USA.

Published in 2005 in the U.K. by arrangement with Faber & Faber.

Published in 2005 in the U.S. by arrangement with Harold Ober Associates Inc.

U.K. Hardcover   ISBN 1–4056–1133–2 (Windsor Large Print)
U.K. Softcover   ISBN 1–4056–2124–9 (Paragon Large Print)
U.S. Softcover   ISBN 0–7862–7802–1 (Buckinghams)

The text of this Large Print edition is unabridged.
Other aspects of the book may vary from the original edition.

Set in 16 pt. New Times Roman.

Printed in Great Britain on acid-free paper.

British Library Cataloguing in Publication Data available

Library of Congress Cataloging-in-Publication Data
Cheek, Mavis.
    Dog days / by Mavis Cheek.
        p.   cm.
    "Thorndike Press large print Buckinghams."—T.p. verso.
    ISBN 0–7862–7802–1 (lg. print : sc : alk. paper)
    1. Divorced women—Fiction. 2. Mothers and daughters—Fiction.
3. Dating (Social customs)—Fiction. 4. Women dog owners—
Fiction. 5. Dogs—Fiction. 6. Large type books. 7. Domestic
fiction. I. Title.
PR6053.H4334D64 2005
823'.914—dc22   2005010231

For Clive,
who introduced me to word processors

May all the Brians of my acquaintance, and the many more out there living useful lives, forgive me . . .

CHAPTER ONE

One of the things that I had *not* considered in the traumatic change from family status to single parenthood was dogs. Many things had crossed my mind and scarred my heart during the bitter days of deciding that my marriage was at an end, many things both tremendous and trivial, but of these, undoubtedly, dogs were not one. Not even a fraction of one. Indeed, on the Richter Scale of Emotional Considerations, dogs did not even appear on the graph.

In fact, I loathe them. Or rather—to be fair, since I have learned in all issues to try to be fair—I loathe not them but their owners. The dogs themselves I have merely distaste for. They are but crap on legs, beleaguerers of the sandalled foot on a summer's eve, providers of that little pile of excrement right where the honest citizen walks by, scratchers in grass and sniffers of personal places as their vile progenitors exhort you to enjoy the experience for they are simply 'trying to be friendly . . .' My best friend, to my certain knowledge, has never lifted my skirts with her nose to establish rapport. I see no reason why a dog should expect such a privilege. Their owners belittle the language, a heinous crime. They say 'walkies' when they really mean 'shitties' and they call exercise what the rest of the world understands quite plainly as urinating up against lampposts. I have long thought that a good curse would be 'may you be a tree in a nation of dogs'. I might use that one day.

However, when one is deep in a pit of guilt because one is wresting one's only offspring from happy dual-parentage into the uncertainty of living with Mother, one is prepared to make sacrifices. Rachel's woeful blue eyes took on a certain cunning (a ten-year-old's morality is mercifully uncomplicated when it beholds a fissure in an adult's armour).

'If I can't have Daddy,' she said, 'can I have a dog?'

And in that first gush of relief that she had not altogether turned her back on me for being, apparently, the only evil doer, I agreed.

I do not know how Gordon felt about his daughter settling on one of the canine breed as a father substitute. Such Freudian discussions were not high on the agenda. But it certainly influenced *my* choice.

Rachel is a good child. My criteria for this description are purely selfish in that she is fairly self-sufficient, not given to tantrums, and she is of a loving disposition. She also has an understanding and maturity which I think she was born with but others might say came as a direct result of her being an only child. And a girl. Girls are notorious for maturing early and for being 'easier' than boys though 'easier' seems a kind of double-speak for 'amenable'. Rachel is certainly easy and amenable and it seemed to me a small price to pay to agree to getting a dog to keep her that way.

We went to Battersea Dogs' Home. This is a good place to visit, like hospital waiting rooms, if you wish to be made ashamed of your own petty problems. When I looked at all those sad, wet eyes and desperately wagging tails, it did occur to me that my troubles were light by comparison. After all, so far no one had said to me that if I didn't get sorted out within a week I'd be snuffed out. I don't know if this kind of brisk caninicide is practised there or not, but I certainly felt as if I were looking upon a group of condemned souls. I had a difficult five minutes with my daughter when I had to explain that we could only take *one* inmate home with us—but, like I say, she is persuadable, is Rachel, and after I had mopped her eyes and blown her nose and patted her head a few times, she began to look about her realistically. I must say children are very good at coming to terms with things quickly and practically. She put the whole idea of Rachel-the-saviour-of-the-doggy-world behind her quite soon and developed a chilling reversal in her appraisal of the goods on offer, dismissing this one and that one with a Mengele flick of her finger.

Eventually, with considerable effort on my part, we selected the weakest and wettest of

3

mongrels in the pound. Rachel wanted the racy little cross between a Jack Russell and a something (a very something), but it had far too many of Gordon's traits for my liking. Small and wiry with bright snapping eyes; a prominent, urgent profile and—I could sense—totally selfish motives behind its cocky, winning ways. I had lived with one like that for too long in its human form to burden myself with another, albeit four-legged and linked to me in animal slavery. Whereas the wet-looking mongrel had not an ounce of spunk left in it.

'Look,' I said to my daughter, who was kneeling and stroking the Gordonesque creature and smiling delightedly. 'What about that little thing hiding in the corner?'

'Thing' was apt. It was small, thin, and its short coat was the colour of Co-op gingersnaps (though I approve of the Co-operative ethos entirely they do always manage to make everything seem just that little bit duller than all the rest. Who else would splash headlines all over their shopfronts announcing a special offer of one penny off Jacob's Cream Crackers—possibly the most boring biscuit in the world . . . ?) and somewhere along the line this dusty-looking creature had encountered a bit of spaniel. Its wet brown eyes and curiously wavy ears said this, but it had none of the spaniel's dignified composure. It just lay in a bony heap, looking up at us unmoved. It had to be called Brian.

I could tell it would have been just as happy to stay there and die quietly from lack of love—and probably would have too. Rachel saw nothing in it to appeal and was still hanging close to the Jack Russell by-blow which had the light of triumph in its beady little eyes. I almost heard Gordon's voice saying 'Feed me, scratch me, keep me', which was too much.

'Rachel,' I said, pointing to the heap of despair, 'this one's hair is the same colour as yours. Look . . .'

It was about as true as comparing Titian's beauties to a carrot-haired Brueghel peasant, but it worked. She began to look more favourably on him.

'And Daddy's too,' I added quickly.

Rachel's hair is one of her beauties. A deep auburn, long and thick, and one of the better legacies from her father. It makes up a little for the other major legacy which I can do nothing about—her preoccupation with money. Gordon's meanness, which may or may not be to do with his Scottish origins and that apocryphal northern trait, was deeply felt and sincerely manifested. What he called being careful I called tight-fisted and Rachel seemed, potentially, to have that same great flaw. From a very early age she never spent her pocket money, she just counted it and put it back in her Dumbo money box with a small smile of contentment. Gordon did much the same, only he didn't have a Dumbo money box and his financial reticence was altogether on a grander scale. You can forgive people many things if they are generous. Dickens was right with his Squeers and his Quilp—'from meanness' fount do other poisons flow'—and though Gordon was neither vile nor vicious, his lack of generosity made him less and less lovable through the years. Rachel had it in embryo and I would have to do something about it once all the current familial upheavals had been dealt with.

She was still havering for those snappy, bright Jack Russell eyes which, sensing victory, had begun to dart and flicker in anticipation while its body exercised a sideways waggling that I, personally, found quite obscene.

'It will grow very big,' I said in desperation. 'And it will cost a lot to keep. Remember, we are not going to have much money when we move. Still, if you want it I suppose you can help out with some of your savings . . .'

That worked. The amorality of children is astounding. We are the sentimentalists, not they. She dropped the idea at once. 'Will this one be cheaper then?' she asked, pointing to Brian the spunkless.

'Oh yes,' I said, fondly looking upon the creature which appeared to roll its eyes in fear of being plucked from its happy slide into morbidity. 'This one will be much cheaper . . .'

'Why?' she asked.

I have always encouraged her to question things, so good for her intellectual development, so good for her educational understanding, so annoying when the questions are turned upon me.

'Because,' I said, thinking suddenly of Gordon and his antithesis, 'because it will be *grateful* . . .'

She allowed this and Brian was ours.

My guilt was eased, but only slightly. If I could have achieved the same effect by providing six ice creams a day or a poolside holiday on the Costa del Sol, I would have done it. Nothing—not sugar-rotted teeth or kiss-me-rapido hats—was too much to pay for a little relief from guilt. But Brian it was and, unlike those other palliatives in which I could have taken a little vicarious pleasure, he was entirely a sop for Rachel. For me he was merely a trial, an anathema called Dog. And, in the journey out of my relationship with Gordon, I was to meet many of those and most of them walking around on two legs.

CHAPTER TWO

It is a curious phenomenon, since men are generally judged to be the active and women the passive in their life-roles, but solicitors and marriage counsellors and their kidney will confirm that most often it is the woman who confronts the failure of a relationship, it is the woman who usually ends up taking the legal action required to bring a marriage to an end.

A man may watch from the sidelines while his wife cavorts off every night wearing expensive French scent and not much else, saying she is going out to her pottery class and don't wait up; a man may find himself in a separate bedroom without his ironing even being considered as part of the domestic routine let alone a say in the nightly choice of telly programme; a man might even be aware that he and his wife have not, actually, spoken for five years—but he will do nothing about it. He may even, in rueful mental privacy, think it would be nice if things returned to status quo, but most of the time he will wait for it to happen naturally. An optimism born of years of ascendancy perhaps. But a woman who finds a pair of knickers in the glove compartment of her husband's car which, so far as she can remember, do not belong to her, or a woman who has spent twenty years attempting to explain that half a minute of foreplay does not constitute an orgasm, or who suddenly realises that apart from 'pass the marmalade' she and spouse have had no conversation for a decade, will act.

And that, in the end, is what I did. Overcoming, as I have said, that most profound fear of all, that fear which should make cowards of any parent bent on separation, that fear of how Rachel would react.

I knew that she had no idea of what the reality would be. It is one thing to be told one day that your parents are separating, but it is quite another to experience it first hand. And Gordon and I were laggards in making any great waves while we still lived under the same roof. Cowardly or protective? I do not know.

But after the decision was taken, after I told Gordon the decision was taken, we continued together for another four months with little perceptible change—as far as Rachel was concerned—in our outward lives. We went on sharing the same bed. He never offered to go into the spare room and neither did I. We had slept next to each other, pure and sexless, for three years, so why pretend that the double bed in which we sweated and snored our way through the night had any particular symbolism attached to it now? It was no more meaningful than sitting next to each other on a settee. Difficult for those who share their bed lovingly and erotically to believe, but so it was. We went on as before and I knew that our daughter had not really grasped the meaning of living separate lives, because I knew that we had not. It was all abstract. After the first emotional flush of Declaration Day things just continued as before and it was no good trying to talk to her seriously about it. I realised that

9

after a very few weeks when she said to me one bedtime: 'Mummy, I've inherited all Daddy's bad traits, haven't I?' And I realised that all I had done was to open my wounds and pour out the plethora of disloyal invective that had been hidden for too long. When she left her bedroom untidy (*really* untidy—almost gold medal standard) I would tell her, in my crossness, how very like her father that was. If she was lazy at her piano practice, preferring to watch television or doodle at her drawing books, I would call her idle and cite that as another of Gordon's specific frailties. If she ate the last cake or apple or banana without asking if anyone else wanted it, I would say that such selfishness was paternal. And so on. I soon realised that this was not the way. That I had to keep my feelings hidden still. After all, he was her daddy, she loved him and he loved her. What was my anger compared with her need for that? So then, even disloyalty to Gordon was denied me and therefore our lives went on very much as before.

Even the househunting was abstract until Gordon found his new home. There was simply no point in my going out with Rachel and finding the perfect place for us, if he was still ruminating and dismissing everything he saw. The only level on which things became different was when I refused to vet his viewings. He found this quite monstrous, since for all our married life (eleven years of it) I had always dealt with the practicalities. He was like a child when he came home from seeing a flat here, a bijou res there, a three-storey dump somewhere else. He would look at me accusingly as he sank into his chair and he would shake his head and look sorrowfully neglected, and say, 'I can't live in a place like that.'

I would go on with the washing up, or reading my book, or ironing (yes, of course I still did his—how foolishly confrontational it would have been not to), and say, 'Really? Oh well, never mind.' And try to sound kind but disinterested, though every nerve-ending in my body would be shouting out that he should and he must because I was desperate, desperate, desperate . . . to begin finding a new home for myself.

On the whole I won the battle of Gordon's mawkish house-hunting: he got more and more frustrated, and more and more outrageous, as I got, apparently, calmer and calmer, as disinterest appeared to give way to uninterest . . . The final straw was when he came home one night and described an *enormous* flat, with *huge* rooms, a *lovely* garden, *just* the right price, *perfectly* positioned. Some instinct told me that he was winding me up and that, despite all its perfection, he was not going to buy it. After he had finished the eulogy he stood in the doorway watching me with that same kind of

11

sly wonder with which a cat observes its potential prey.

'Jolly good,' I said, which was, really, unforgivably hearty. I went on painting my toe nails trying to keep the brush steady, which was not easy. And I waited.

Gordon was grinding his heel into the carpet and, metaphorically anyway, grinding his teeth. 'Well?' he said eventually. 'Don't you want to ask me something about it?'

'Um,' I said, thinking, you bastard for putting me through this! I asked the first thing that came into my mind. 'Has it got nice wallpaper?'

'A typically bourgeois question from my typically bourgeois wife.'

Not for long, I thought.

'All right,' I said, smiling. 'Are you going to buy it?'

'No,' he said.

'Well, then,' I said. 'There's no point in my asking you anything about it. Is there?' I began on the left foot.

Gordon began to pant. His red hair is a true indicator of his temper and, despite his absolute control when he is singing, his breathing goes all over the place when he is angry. 'Don't you want to know why I'm not going to buy it?'

I summoned up every ounce of cool left in me. Fortunately, when Gordon gets to the panting stage this is quite easy. I have always

12

found myself contra-suggestive. Must be infuriating really.

'Well, no,' I said. 'There's not much point if you're not going to live in it. Anyway, it hardly has anything to do with me—'

'My God, you are selfish!' he said.

'All right,' I said evenly. 'Why are you not going to buy it?'

He looked at me, the sly wonder enhanced by triumph. 'Because it's too perfect . . .'

Well, it had to be something stupid like that, didn't it?

'Oh,' I said, putting the last touches to my ten little piggies. 'Well, that's that then.'

I was glad Rachel was in bed. The thought of the meal he would make with *her* over *that* was too awful to contemplate. I knew his argument. It was that as a singer he needed some *Angst* in his life. I translate this for the layperson: as a singer, Gordon needed something to blame if he was not always up to the perfection he sought. He just could not bear people coming round to his new place, wherever it was, and saying things like 'Well, you've certainly fallen on your feet here, haven't you?' Or worse, actually envying him. No. His new home where ere it be, must have flaws. But let us not get too one-sided in all this. Out of such confused masochism was born a great voice. If he had been tall, dark and muscularly built he might well have ranked among the best in the world. Being more like a wiry Rob Roy than a hulking Pavarotti his need for a flaw was inbuilt. Even with his hair blackened and his complexion olived he would never pass muster as Don Giovanni or Figaro—minor roles must always be his, though he play them exquisitely well. If he had only been born Welsh and not Scottish things might have been different, but there we are—he was not.

So that was what that little dialogue was all about. Gordon had found a flat that was absolutely right and so he had rejected it. I kept my head bent low over my toe nails while my stomach grew knots and knots upon the knots. If he had known how desperate I truly was he would have gone on like that for years. To suppress my feelings was all in this game and the only hint, on that particular night, of how angry and despairing I felt was that I put salt in the stewed apple instead of sugar. It was a small consolation—but passing fair—to watch Gordon's face as he discovered this.

'My God!' he said after he had spat the mouthful (rather neatly under the circumstances) back into his bowl. 'She's trying to poison me now . . .'

For a moment—*Just* for a moment—the idea appealed.

Rachel was desperate too. Given that she did not really understand the full meaning of our separation, she was child enough to be excited at the prospect of moving house. She talked of big gardens, an enormous bedroom for her (despite the largeness of our house she was in a very small room—Gordon had the two best upstairs ones for his music) and lovely kitchens where she and I could cook together. With that same amorality that she would bring with such unburdened effect to the choice of her dog, she was keen to get on and get started in a new house. And it was hard for me to tell her what I continually had to tell her, that we must wait until Daddy was suited. Gordon grew angry because she would bring the post up to our bedroom each morning—piles and piles of estate agents' brown envelopes—and open it all for him, reading out and discarding as she saw fit. He saw it as my keenly worked conspiracy that she should be so cavalier about his new home and worked quite hard at the 'poor me' image. But Rachel only paid lip service to this.

'Yes, yes,' she would nod, reading through the literature, 'but we'll find you something nice that I can come and stay with you in . . .' And she would read out: ' "Large living room with french windows on to patio garden." Oh, Daddy, doesn't that sound *lovely* . . .' And he—torn between being a good father (which, on the whole, he was) and making us all suffer (which, on the whole, was *plus ça change*)—would show a kind of huffy interest in what she was reading out.

*   *   *

Gordon really did not want the separation. Like the majority of men he would have been contentedly discontented to go on living the absurd lie of happy families. I can understand it. And, really, at that time I had no real perception of why I could not. There was no one else in my life, no one whose arms I longed to be held in, no one to whom I wanted to rush in a joyful throwing off of the chains of disharmony. And I was leaving a cultured, financially secure stable (albeit hampered by Gordon's desire to spend as little as possible) for empty pastures new. The uncharted waters of insecurity, of fending for myself, of total responsibility for both me and my daughter—for I knew that no matter how much Gordon loved Rachel, he would, like so many divorced men I knew, soon come to an easy, untrammelled lifestyle where she was concerned.

Because of his characteristic difficulties about finance, and not wishing to rock the boat more than I had to, I agreed to maintenance for Rachel only, despite my solicitor's urging that I should, and had the right to, get something for myself. The solicitor was a nice man with nicely balanced ideas about fairness and the law. We sat in his plain white office which had just enough personalia—photographs of a pretty young woman getting her degree, a young couple with twins, a cartoon of a very seedy-looking judge, a water colour of a lake somewhere—for his clients to have something to hook their eyes on to as they poured forth their most intimate stories of failure. He probed for quite a long time to find out exactly why I wanted a separation.

'Did Gordon hit you?'

'Not often . . . Scarcely ever . . . Never seriously.'

'Did Gordon womanise?'

'Not at all, so far as I knew.'

'Did he keep you short of money?'

'Not *seriously.*'

'Did Gordon behave properly towards his daughter?'

'Absolutely. Kindly and properly.'

'A good father?'

'A good father.'

I could see the solicitor was perplexed. What were my grounds?

Why did I want to take my daughter out of a happy, secure family home? Why did I want to take myself out of a happy, secure home?

'Because I can't go on living under the same roof as him.'

The solicitor, Mr Pownall, raised his hands fractionally off his desk and gave a little resigned sigh which said, quite eloquently, that on my own head be it.

'I think,' I said, 'that if I have to continue

17

like this, I shall go mad. That's all I can say, really. It's the quality of my life that is suffering. More than that—well, there isn't really anything more than that, is there?' I looked at the photo of the smiling girl with the degree and my eyes filled with tears.

Mr Pownall coughed. The cough said that he had made up his mind. 'Very well,' he said with kindness, and he began taking notes.

When he got to the bit about maintenance I froze, imagining Gordon's face. I knew very well that it would take every ounce of persuasion to get him to part with money for his daughter. But to part with money for me?

'Oh no,' I said. 'Just for Rachel.'

'Mrs Murray,' said the solicitor, 'eleven years of marriage add up to something. Eleven years of being your husband's secretary and housekeeper and mother-at-home have their worth in the market place. Career loss, no pension, little prospect of making that up while your daughter is so young. You have a right to something for yourself, as well you know.'

Tell that to Gordon, I thought.

'No, no,' I said, calm and resigned. 'Only for Rachel. I shall get part-time work at something . . .'

'At what?' he asked, politely interested.

'As a telephonist, or in a shop . . .' I hazarded.

I could think of little else. Marriage and

motherhood had put an early end to my plans for a career. Rachel arrived right in the middle of my becoming a mature student. During the first ten years after leaving school I had been flighty in employment terms. A barmaid, a market researcher, a typist in an estate agency, never settling to anything. Then I met Gordon. We met in a Chinese restaurant—well, eating house might be more appropriate—where a bunch of us young women from the market research agency had decided to eat after a hard day's street-questioning of Soho-ites about their tastes in toiletries. I ordered crab with ginger sauce and, tackling a large claw with the nut crackers, managed to shoot it with balletic perfection right into the lap of the red-haired young man sitting at the next table. He looked up from his book with a kind of disbelief and stared at the ceiling, and then, the disbelief turning to crossness, he looked down at his ginger-and-oil-soaked crotch. One of the girls at my table, a raunchy Amazonian from Mauritius called Wanda (whom I still see occasionally), let rip with her wit.

'You sure got your claws into him, Patsy!' she yelled.

And I, who had been hoping for some kind of miracle of British sang-froid on the red-haired young man's part whereby he would pretend *not* to have noticed a crab claw in his groin, could do only one thing. I leaned across the aisle and picked up the offending item

19

from its very personal lodgement and was about to say 'So sorry' or some such useful phrase, when Wanda, to whom restraint did not come easy, spotted the juxtaposition of my hand above Gordon's lap. 'Careful she don't take more than she's owed,' she roared.

Our eyes met, his blue and hard, mine blue and supplicating, his softened, mine fluttered (you could still do that in those days), and I said, 'You must send me the cleaning bill.' Which—being Gordon—he did. Only he *had* written on the bottom that he would like to see me again. I invited him to spag bol at my flat, he arrived with a bottle of red wine and wearing a plastic apron, which I thought was terrifically witty. And there we are. After that we went steady for two years and his career developed well. I began to feel dissatisfied with work (I was twenty-seven by then, and Gordon and I went to enough music parties for me to feel embarrassed and increasingly frustrated when I was asked what my profession was and that glassy glaze came over people when I replied that I worked for an estate agent in Putney) and so, when I saw an advertisement in the *Guardian* for mature student degree courses, I applied.

I think I had never been happier. The arts course was a wonder of discovery, both of the academic and of the self. I went at it like a chunk of blotting paper for the first year and, truth to tell, I found my relationship with

Gordon got in the way a bit. We were, as you might say, on the way out, and not too acrimoniously either. My academic star seemed to be set and there was already talk of a further degree later. Gordon was doing well too, and then, in the summer vacation, he suggested we go to Cologne together. He had some work there and the organisers had made a mistake in thinking he was married. They had paid for two tickets and a double hotel room, which, as Gordon so characteristically said, it would be a pity to waste.

Performing artists get extremely high on their work. At the end of a night of giving their all to an audience they cannot slink off home or to their hotel and just curl up in bed with a Frederick Forsyth. They need to expel their highness somehow. And Gordon, who was on liberal expenses, did it with German beer and sex—and I, who happily had nothing to do at all, joined in the orgy. We got drunk every night, ravaged each other's bodies afterwards, and slept it off until lunchtime the next day. And at the end of the week we crawled home to London and I was not at all surprised to feel rather ill for the following weeks.

That was Rachel.

I remember ringing Gordon one golden September morning—we had scarcely seen each other during the six or seven weeks since our return—and arranging to meet him at a pub by the river. I sat there on the terrace, looking out over the glinting water, waiting for him, knowing that no matter what the outcome of our meeting, I would never go back to college because of the child in my womb. Beyond that I had no idea what was going to happen. I just wanted someone else to make the decisions for me. Already those embryo-protecting hormones were sloshing around my insides and I was turning into a happy dumpling, fully prepared to pass the baton of my life into someone else's hands.

Gordon said, 'Are you sure it's mine?', which was fair enough though I felt injured.

'It's going to come out speaking German like a native and with a well-developed taste for Königslager Brauerie,' I said crisply. 'Of course I'm sure it's yours . . .'

'In that case,' he said, 'we must get married.'

Which we did.

Like so many people who are not and never will be creative, I admired the artist in Gordon—maybe revered would be truer—and during the years that followed I subjugated myself to it. I can't blame Gordon for that since I did it to myself. I would wait up for him, with something hot to eat, and see him safely into his chair with his video at one in the morning, before I went off to bed. And I would say to myself, 'There, there. He has had a busy night wrestling with his art, moving an audience to tears, and what have I done? What offerings have I got to put on the table of life?

Hoovering, ironing, shopping and the school gates.' Out loud I would say these matters were just as important and valuable as opera, but it was only a lip-service liberation. Inside I knew I was unworthy, yea, verily, unworthy even to kiss the hem of his robe. Which might have been all right, I suppose, if he had not also felt this and begun to show it—quite soon after Rachel was born really—which led to my not only thinking I was unworthy to kiss the hem of his robe, but also thinking that I didn't want to kiss him very much either.

CHAPTER THREE

As I sat in Mr Pownall's office with him looking so thoroughly normal—greying hair, cheerfully lined face, dark suit—and asking me 'Why?' I had to go back and dredge up some reasons. Not that I intended to describe the minutiae for him (it all came under the heading 'irretrievable breakdown'), but for myself. While Mr Pownall took a telephone call I stared at his clean hands, his starched white collar, his wholesomeness, and I thought that if I had married someone like him then I would probably have been all right. Even duller, of course, and given to wearing navy blue a lot, but stable. Absolutely stable. It had been just my luck to get caught up with an egocentric husband, one who could not only justify his egocentricity, but whose very performance depended upon it. Oh, Mr Pownall, I thought as I gazed at him, if only I had met you. His eyes met mine and looked away uncomfortably. Perhaps he could read my mind? I apologised mentally for the nefarious thought, and regrouped my marbles. He talked on, and I dug into my past.

*   *   *

There was one night when Rachel was about three weeks old. Gordon had been to a party for Pavarotti. He reeled in around midnight—something which I both expected and excused—sank into his chair and began flicking away with the remote control for the television. Funny how you remember absurd detail. I distinctly recall that the film that evening was Bergman's *Seventh Seal.*

The Health Visitor had called that day and being a nice, bright, liberated lady, and noticing my zombie state, she had suggested that I would be a healthier person and therefore a better mother if I got a good night's sleep now and then.

'Why not get Rachel's father to feed her in the night sometimes?' she suggested breezily

Suspending images of Gordon struggling to bring milk out of his own flat and ginger-haired nipple and realising the lady must mean something else, I remonstrated. My babycare bible by Penelope Leach had been very firm about breast-feeding and the untold harm of introducing even one bottle into the infant's routine. Apparently babies were to be treated like reformed alcoholics: they'd stay on the straight and narrow path of mother's own so long as they were not given even a whiff of Cow and Gate—once *that* was introduced you'd never get them off it again.

'But I'm *breast-feeding*! I don't want her to have that processed stuff . . .'

To which my liberated lady said gleefully, 'Quite *right*, Mrs Murray,' and began digging around in her huge black bag to produce a dangling tube and a bottle. 'You can siphon off with this'—she waggled the appliance triumphantly—'and have a good night's sleep while your partner feeds his daughter!' We faced each other like a pair of women in an advertisement for floor cleaner.

I do remember a profound sensation of bliss warming me. A sudden lightening of the load, a release of muscular tension, an easing of the pricking rawness in my eyes. Like all perfect solutions it was so simple. So I waited for Gordon to come home that night in quiet anticipation.

'And how are my lovely wife and my lovely daughter?' he said, with half an eye on the Bergman.

'We're both fine.' I perched on his chair arm

and told him about the Health Visitor's revelation. 'So, if I get everything ready, will you give Rachel her three a.m. feed?'

It was very stupid timing on my part. I should have waited until the next night when he was more in tune with home-life, less high on life-life.

He said, with remarkable astuteness, 'But you've got the tits. I haven't.'

'I know,' I said, 'but I can express it . . .'

He was amused. 'You can, my duck, and you do, very well. We all need expression. As I was only saying to old Pav tonight . . .' (Ironic this, I think, since he probably got nowhere near him. Gordon was no sycophant.)

'How was he?' I asked, stalling for time.

'Fat,' said Gordon with satisfaction. 'Fat, fat, fat.' He squeezed my thigh abstractedly which I took as a good omen. 'I don't see how I can feed our daughter.'

'You can, you can,' I said excitedly, 'because I've got this!'

I copied the Health Visitor's frenzied wagglings and explained. Gordon removed his hand from my thigh, put down his plate and the remote control, got up and went out into the kitchen. Whence he returned a minute or so later carrying a very large whisky.

'I'll drink that,' I said, half playfully, half anguished. 'If you have any more tonight you'll be too drunk to feed her.'

'I love my daughter,' he said, and took a

26

swig.

'Give me the glass,' I said, reaching for it but still playfully. 'Go on . . .'

'No.' he smiled. 'I'll get you one of your own.' Then he stopped at the doorway and turned and said, 'But you can't. You'll give little poopsie-woopsie a hangover.'

'Not if I express first and *then* have it.'

'What *is* all this "express" nonsense?'

So I told him all over again. 'And,' I concluded, 'she said that as I was so tired you could take over the occasional night feed—'

'But you are the mother. I am the breadwinner. What is the point of us both being tired out?'

'Not always, Gordon. Not every night. Just once in a while.'

And then he must have read my face because he said suddenly, 'Fine. I'll do it. Of course I'll do it.' And he left the room.

There are lots of peculiarly female pains. Those little toes cramped into the crackling new patent-leather shoe, the first plucking of eyebrows, a hundred different gynaecological possibilities, but alongside all of these must rank the breast pump. One's tactile tissue suffers enough under the onslaught of an infant's hungry mouth; using this contraption (which has no doubt been much improved by now) was like suffering under the onslaught of several. But buoyed by the thought of a full night's sleep I sat there on my own and did my

27

best. It was a slow, difficult process and how unrewardingly thin and bluish the fluid looked. Was this really the stuff of life? No wonder the processed variety had got such a hold for it looked rich and yummy by comparison. When I had achieved the right number of ounces on the bottle I got up and went out into the kitchen. Gordon was sitting on the draining board with his headphones on. These were connected to his cassette player in which he had a tape playing; I don't know what it was but I knew he had it turned up because I could hear that infuriatingly tinny noise. By his side was the whisky bottle, considerably emptier than it had been, and on his face was an expression of beatific contentment. He had his eyes closed in rapture and was swaying and beating his heels to whatever the rhythm was. I stood there for a moment just staring, and then I think I saw every colour known to woman—the last of which was a great engulfing sheet of red. I dashed the glass from his lips and grabbed the headphones, pulling at them for all I was worth. Yank, yank, yank, I went, with all the brassy force of a madwoman.

Was it my fault that I grabbed one of his ears at the same time? Retrospectively, even now, I am amazed that the ear remained attached to the head. I went at it with such force, thinking in an odd way that the left-hand earpiece seemed to be more pliant than its right-hand counterpart, but not really stopping to consider why. In my rage I just continued to pull at it, getting more and more furious that the earphones would not come away, while Gordon rocked and howled and tried to defend his shell-like against the attack. Eventually some kind of counter-offensive suggested itself and he punched me on the nose. I fell and the breast-pump bottle broke and shattered. All my baby's milk seeped on to the floor, delicately interspersed with the crimson droplets from my nose.

'Bitch!' he yelled.

'Brute!' I yelled back.

'Whore!' he countered (apropos, I assure you, of no good reason).

He held his tomato-coloured ear and looked down at me. I got up and made to smack his face.

'Fuck you, Patsy!' he roared and took another swing, which missed me but hit the glass of the kitchen door. It cracked but did not shatter. It was still like that ten years later when I showed the mild-eyed young couple, who eventually bought the place, around.

*   *   *

The beginning of the end. Why do we have children? Those with ideas of a golden loving future *à deux* should stick to them. Children take you from blissful selfishness to profound and inescapable responsibility. Once you see

29

that little fruit of your coupling lying snuggled up against you, you are sunk. Father and mother alike. No going back. Those who try, those who have a kink in their make-up and cannot love their offspring, become murderers, abusers, absconders. The rest of us, the majority, are yielded up. June in the Med, late-night cinema, long, long Sundays alternating newspapers and heavy petting and cold white wine—all gone. In their place unselfish acts, unbidden love, the power of the child. We tried, as others before and since, to reassert our old selves: a favourite restaurant whose charm lay as much in the slow, quiet pace of its service as in its Beef Wellington, suddenly became a nerve-racking torture house. Would the souffle d'abricot arrive in time to be eaten before the babysitter blew a fuse? No. Result? Gordon and I bickering all the way back in the car because he hadn't had time for the precious brandy and cigar, and I had indigestion from my sterling efforts to eat up *all* my souffle in three seconds flat. Burp, burp, I went, all the way home. Which hardly led us in romantic mood towards the marriage bed. No, no. We could not go back to carefree indulgence, its days were over. Sadly, it transpired, the days of our marriage were also numbered.

Gordon would not have swung out at me that night if it were not for Rachel. I would not have nearly pulled off his ear. Instead I would have gone to the Pavarotti party with him and—most likely—at the exact time we were playing prize fighters across a sea of shattered glass and breast pump, we would have been in bed, or halfway up the stairs, or still in the front garden and fucking wholeheartedly, well-protected, of course, by some piece of contraceptive wizardry. So, keep taking the pills, keep wearing the condoms, keep checking the calendar, I urge you, unless you too wish to be in the grip of a love that is so powerful, so inescapable that you would eat cooked worms for it. You cannot walk away from *that* love. It demands without speaking, it hurts without desire to. It is a wonder, the most beautiful thing, that precious bane that stays with us till death close our eyes. Right.

Therefore and given all that, one turned the other cheek and continued—glass door cracked—for years and years more. Rachel had a loving daddy, Rachel had a loving mummy. What she did not have, gradually, gradually, were loving parents who loved each other or, at the end, who even cared very much. But that was not her concern. She had what she needed and I thought that would be all right. You can get used to anything with time, particularly if you don't stop and think too hard about it. 'There must be more to life than this' is not a phrase to repeat too often. I said it once or twice to myself during the first few years and then forgot the words. It really was easier that way.

By the time Rachel was six I knew that she was the centre that held. Everything else about us, apart from her, was lived on the surface. We became a cipher of coupleness. And we lived within that framework easily enough. On the rare occasions that I thought about it at all, I thought vaguely. When she is a teenager, I would say to myself, maybe I shall move on, though the vagueness put no boundaries on which end—thirteen or nineteen? Would I be forty-three or forty-nine? It didn't seem to matter very much. It was all fudge anyway. Mothering completed I might leave Gordon, or he just as easily might leave me. Poor Gordon. There he was, railing against the slow demise of his sex-life and putting all his ardour into his work. We were no longer intimate with each other in any real sense though we still managed the odd bit of nooky, but it had become just a poor thing, a little weed, struggling for life on very stony ground. Which is perhaps why he sang better and better and better over the years while I maintained a cool, calm detachment from anything to do with him beyond the occasional crossness, damningly slight irritations that were no more than fleabites or the droning of a bluebottle on a summer's night. We stopped sex when Rachel was seven. I remember saying no to him on the night after her birthday party; the decibels of twelve children playing Pass the Parcel and

Kiss Chase around the house still resounded in my head and I thought as I felt his hand poking around on my inner thigh that I didn't want it, it was just another chore, I was too tired and anyway I had a right to sink into oblivion.

'I think you've gone frigid,' he said.

'Probably,' I answered, genuinely sleepily.

'Then you've got a problem.'

'We've both got a problem.'

'No, we haven't. *I* still desire you. *You* don't desire me. You've got the problem.'

'Yes,' I said, turned over and went to sleep.

I didn't mind having the problem. It was much easier to have the problem all to myself because it didn't feel particularly worrying. It was only worrying to pretend that I ought *not* to have it. Gordon decided that because he could get an erection as he lay beside me he was problem-free. I didn't really mind that, so long as I didn't have to perform any more.

There was a beautiful clarity after that, similar in intensity to when the Health Visitor gave me the breast pump all those years ago. Such a simple solution. Give up sex. There was almost no discussion. It just happened. And I was a much happier person during the next few years, at least in the sense that I felt that curiously hackneyed thing: True to myself. I hadn't realised until I gave it up how angry making love with Gordon used to make me. All that grunting and groaning and trying to sound and look sweaty and fulfilled when inside I was counting the minutes. After it ended I was much calmer about the house and, true to the male disposition, he never, after the first week or two, referred to it again, except when he got drunk in company and sent barbs down the table. To me he no longer made overtures. I was a frigid woman who would not help herself. He was a lusty man who had been foiled by the headache syndrome. It was another piece of *Angst* in his life and one, like all the rest, from which he could feed his art.

Once he said to me, more in puzzlement than in anger, 'You never come to hear me sing any more, Patsy. Why is that?' And I said something about not having time when really I should have said, 'Because it cuts me like a knife to think that I am no longer a loving part of you. Because I no longer love you I cannot hear or celebrate your beautiful gift.'

Enough, enough, enough of all that.

So the years passed. I think he began to hit what is generally misnamed the male menopause; anyway, he hit a patch of self-doubt and began what the Victorians liked to call 'making demands'. I couldn't reach out, couldn't step across that gulf we had created, couldn't soothe his sadness and his rages. He drank more heavily, sat more often dull-eyed in front of the television, put on weight and generally made such a miserable picture that I became racked with guilt. Yet we could not talk, could not rediscover that intimacy, that regard, those feelings that might lead us back towards each other again. I viewed his success with envy, with sourness at first. Then, slowly, I saw it as a relief. When he was working he was out. When he was out I was happier. When he was in, and I was in, we were tolerably polite or occasionally spitting bullets. We began to function pleasantly only in the company of others. Left to ourselves we were in separate worlds. We became an institution for our friends, warmly social, unchangingly entertaining as a public couple, but, oh dear me, when the door closed upon us and the night time fell we were aliens. Part of Gordon's mid-life crisis was the realisation that it would always be like this, and that he was unable to do anything about it; more, that he was frightened of any change for he knew what that change would be. But banish it from my mind as much as I tried I knew that we could no longer go on living like that. In its quiet unrelenting way it was destroying us.

*　　　*　　　*

I took Rachel away for the October half term. There was nothing particularly ominous or sinister in this. Most often it was just the two of us who went away. Gordon's schedules were always tight, and when he wasn't working he was usually either doing some recording or practising. Anyway, these trips apart were breathing space for us both. We usually got on much better for weeks afterwards.

We went to stay with Phillida, an old pal of mine from way back. We met when I worked for the estate agent and she came there one summer to do some temporary work during her vacation. She was a lousy typist but had tremendous cachet because she was studying psychology—no one quite dared to criticise her work since they all felt she would analyse them. She was studying at Queen's, Belfast, which, given those hairy times, made her all the more enigmatic. I invited her to the flat one evening for a meal and we were chatting in the kitchen, she sitting at the table, me on my feet making that good old standby macaroni cheese. One minute I was saying something amusing, and she was laughing, the next, as I poured the dried macaroni into the waterless pan, she went chalk white and dived under the table top.

Apparently it sounded like gunfire. As she emerged, shakily, from her cover and tried to light a cigarette, she said, 'You've seen the effect on one lone student, can you imagine what it's like for the children who live there all the time?'

As far as I can be sure, that was my first awakening to the real world: the smooth dispassionate BBC news made flesh. An inkling that there was more to life than

36

swaying to Lennon's 'Imagine' on stack heels.

Phillida and I kept in touch by writing and I was not at all surprised that after qualifying she stayed on in Belfast and became a children's psychologist. I visited her there once but hated the town. Not for itself but for that indelible first memory of arriving at the airport, a British airport, to find soldiers with guns held across their chests staring with bland, cold eyes as we struggled off the plane and waited for our luggage. Threat was in the air, aggression was on the streets, I was British and the only slogans I saw told me to go home, I was not wanted. It was Philly who calmed me down, explained things, rationalised my misplaced jingoism, made me see the picture as a whole, without ever telling me that what I was feeling was wrong.

Back at her flat she lit one of her ubiquitous cigarettes, pushed from her eyes the fringe which she said stopped people prying into her soul, and said, 'I'll probably last here for about three or four years. It gets to you, you know . . . And then I'll up sticks and come back to somewhere nice and safe and ordinary.'

Which is precisely what she did, though she lasted more than five years in Belfast before eventually settling down in Bristol. It was Bloody Sunday that finished her she said. By then I had Rachel. Philly didn't have to explain anything to me any more. I already understood from the news pictures. It could have been my bloodied daughter carried by that weeping priest.

So, Phillida and I were close. She neither married nor had children though she continued mainly as a psychologist to the latter. With remarkable perception she said that it did not matter one jot how much she knew on paper or how good she was at counselling, she was unlikely to be any better at her own personal life than any of her clients. She had the standard string of affairs and was in the middle of one when we went down that October.

'Robert's in Scotland,' she said when I rang to check we could come. 'But I've invited his children for the weekend. They'll be company for Rachel and it'll leave us free to talk. I've got some filthy grouse which are just about walking off the hooks and a case of Bulgarian chardonnay. You'd better bring breakfast cereal and a sleeping bag for Rachel. Apart from that we can pull up the drawbridge.'

I was still laughing when I put down the phone. Gordon asked what was so amusing, so I told him. And I suddenly wanted to reach out and touch him because he looked so angry and bereft at the same time. He needed intimacy, any kind of intimacy, and he knew that I was going down to Bristol for a bellyful of it, while he would stay in London with his work and his colleagues never allowing anyone to grope beneath his skin. Oh, you chaps! If you would only *talk* about your feelings sometimes. If anyone needed to talk about his feelings Gordon did. But he just stayed mute, or perhaps he did let a little out once the fourth or fifth brandy had hit the stomach lining, but by then it was not intimacy, it was self pity. He envied me my friends as much as I envied him his art. And he feared them. After that weekend he had good reason to.

*   *   *

Phillida's house in Clifton is large and only semi-furnished. It would have been fully furnished only the roof needed replacing after she bought it. There are several rooms on the top floor which are almost empty. The children—her lover's two daughters and Rachel—made a camp in one of these and apart from the occasional appearance for meals and statutory bathtime, we scarcely saw them. Out of duty we walked them all up to the Clifton Suspension Bridge on Saturday afternoon just so we could say they had had some fresh air, but what they really wanted to do was get back to their camp where they were planning some kind of exotic midnight feast. Rachel, dangling precariously near the edge of the bridge, looked entirely happy. One of the girls was two years older than her, the other a year younger, which put Rachel into a kind of heaven. Someone to look up to, admire, emulate and be led by on the one hand, someone to do the same to her on the other. I watched them giggling and oohing as they looked down at the drop and for some reason it made me melancholy, a kind of Gather Ye Rosebuds melancholy. I looked down at the drop too and was horrified to experience a momentary desire to fling myself off, to end it all. Of course it *was* a very fleeting sensation and it certainly had no basis in real desire, but all the same it shook me. Just for a wild moment the thought of not being alive any more was wonderful. I refocused on normality and looked up. First I looked guiltily over towards Rachel and then at Phillida, who was looking at me. She smiled and said, 'Last century a woman jumped off here and lived to tell the tale.'

'How did she manage that?'

'She was saved by her voluminous skirts. They acted like a parachute and she just floated down into the sludge. She never tried again and I believe she lived to be a grandmother.'

'Do you have a motive in telling me this?'

She pinched a bit of my jeans between her finger and thumb. 'We're in the post-suffragette era,' she said. 'These wouldn't save you . . . Come on, let's get back.'

We bought crisps and Coke and bags of awful sweets on the way. And then, having pushed shepherd's pie and two veg into the children, and feeling that our dietary duty towards them was done, we let them loose with our additive-soaked purchases on the top floor with the rider that they should not appear again until morning. The three girls' faces shone with delight. Clearly they thought we had gone mad. They raced off up the stairs cackling and whooping before we could change our minds. We waited for ten minutes to be sure all was silent before, like a pair of sneak thieves, we took out our indulgent repast. We had smoked salmon to start with, Phillida's amazing grouse, roasted with fried breadcrumbs, bread sauce and chips, and a blackcurrant sorbet, with quite a lot of her chardonnay to wash it down.

It was during the blackcurrant section that she said, 'It may be a cliché but it's perfectly true.'

'What is?'

'That life, my dear Patsy, is not a dress rehearsal. It's the real thing.'

'I know that,' I said.

'Well then?'

'Well then what?' I said defiantly. I had a premonition of what was coming.

'Well then. When do you intend to take the stage?'

'I don't understand the metaphor.'

'You understand it perfectly well. Nowadays you are like a woman in limbo. You've put all your emotional eggs in Rachel's basket and that isn't fair, not on you and not on her. If you go on like this then one day you will turn to her and say "I gave up everything for you . . ."'

'Rubbish!' I said. 'I'd never say anything of the sort. I wouldn't put that on my own daughter. Anyway, when she's old enough I shall very likely make a move.'

'There you are. Already you're leaning on her as an excuse.'

'Phillida, how dare you? How fucking well dare you talk to me like that? You've never been a mother, you've never risked that most unselfish act. You don't know what you're talking about.'

'Yes I do,' she said quietly.

'Go to hell . . .'

'Well,' she said gravely. 'At least you can get in touch with your feelings where I'm concerned. And by the way . . .'

'Yes?'

'You've put your elbow in the butter.'

While we were scrubbing at my sleeve with the Fairy Liquid, I said, 'It is getting worse and worse at home and you're right, I have locked things in, but only for survival. I shall leave Gordon but not until Rachel is old enough. Once she's in her teens and more independent—then.'

Phillida ran the tap on the foamy sponge and then suddenly she threw the sponge up in the air and walked away. It landed at my feet and I bent to pick it up.

'Leave it,' she said commandingly. 'You and your domestic drudge role. Just leave it and come and sit down.'

'Don't bully me,' I mumbled.

She ran her hand through her fringe and took a deep breath. 'Sorry,' she said. 'But really! You've got to think beyond your own little island. You've got to think seriously. You've got, my dear old friend, to think about *your* place in the real world.' She refilled our glasses. 'Do you seriously suppose it ever comes easy to a son or daughter when their parents split up? I can tell you from the countless poor souls I come into contact with that there is never, ever, ever a good time. But from my own experience I can definitely say that waiting until they reach puberty to tell them is just about the worst timing I know. I mean, think about it. Take Rachel. There she is, suddenly sprouting hairs in unlikely places, breasts about to pop out, boys beginning to be more than playmates—'

'She's only ten,' I wailed.

'She's ten-going-on-thirteen that one, they all are. It's no use looking back fondly at your own ten-year-old days—Enid Blyton and Uncle Mac on the radio—that kind of innocence is long since gone—'

'She still reads Enid Blyton,' I said defensively.

'And she also watches *Neighbours* which is breaking her in nicely for *Dallas* and *Dynasty*

43

later on. They're probably all up there in the attic now discussing Charlene and kissing and brassières. The God-awful ritual of adolescence is just around the corner for her and you're thinking of adding to all that with the sudden announcement that your marriage is over. What are you going to do? Wait until she gets her first period and then as you hand over the sanitary towels say, "Oh, by the way, your father and I are splitting up and I'm sure you'll understand . . ."?'

'Shut up! Shut up!' I yelled. You can hate your friends sometimes. '*You've* never had kids. *You've* never put yourself on the line emotionally like I have with her. Don't talk to *me* about my parental responsibility because you don't know what you're talking about.' I got up and paced about the kitchen, wine glass sloshing and dripping gouts of redness (we were drinking port by now) on to the floor. I kicked the soapy sponge wishing it was Gordon or Phillida or even—God help me—Rachel.

'I've given up so much for her,' I said.

'Sure,' said Phillida cruelly, 'and you'll no doubt be telling her that at some point—'

'I certainly will *not*!'

'You will, if you go on putting off the inevitable. She'll stay out all night after a rock concert, or she'll do a fourteen-year-old flip, and you will say to her "How can you treat me this way when I gave up everything for you?"

44

That'll really improve her adolescent security problems—'

'Phillida,' I said, 'you're being cruel on purpose.'

'Yes,' she said, 'I am. Because if you wait another two or three or five years then you will be able to convince yourself that you *have* "Given everything up". You'll be self-righteous. And both you and she will be on a loser for the rest of your lives.'

'That's too dramatic—'

'I see it all the time—'

'What should I do?'

'Make a decision that is right for you. Kids are notorious for being literal. Tell her the truth now, or when you are ready. But don't put it off in the mistaken belief there is a good time to tell her away in the dim and distant future. You've got to *take* your life and make yourself as happy as you can. Jesus!' She threw her hands up in the air in an uncharacteristically dramatic fashion. 'Who wants a mother who's miserable and who blames you for it?'

'I don't blame Rachel—'

'Why else are you still living in misery with Gordon then?'

'Because I'm a coward.'

'Decide, Pat. Decide for yourself. But don't use her as an excuse.'

'I'm protecting her.'

'You're protecting yourself.'

45

'So endeth the first lesson?'

'Clean up my floor,' she said tartly. 'You've made a right mess of it. Clearly you are a woman who cannot hold her drink.'

I burst into tears and we had a good old hug. Afterwards, while I mopped up the mess, Phillida put *La Bohème* on very loudly and when it got to 'Che gelida manina' she became Mimi and I was Rodolfo. It was one of the songs Gordon sang very beautifully—though he never, of course, did it professionally—and I realised that the connection between the music here in this Bristol kitchen and the man sitting at home in London meant nothing to me any more, except perhaps a little regretful sadness for what had once been. We did Mimi's reply, 'Si, mi chiamano Mimi', and then launched together into that wonderfully sloppy duet, 'O soave faniculla'. It was at this point that the three little girls appeared, crisp crumbs down their nighties, smears of unmentionable E-numbers around their chins and looking most put out.

'We can hear you all the way up the stairs,' *they* said crossly.

And Rachel said to me in a mixture of embarrassment and wonder, 'But you're *singing*.'

'Well, I *do* sometimes,' I said, giving her sticky cheek a kiss.

She rolled her eyes in the direction of the other two girls, quite eloquently expressing that she disowned the folly of her parent. 'Please don't,' she said. 'It sounds awful.'

'I think it's time we tucked them up in their beds and put out the lights, don't you, Philly?'

They were gone in a puff of wind, out of the kitchen, up the stairs, leaving only the slight swinging of the door to announce their departure.

And some time later, much later, another glass or two of port and the whole of Puccini's second act later, when we followed them up to bed and looked in, they were sprawled in happy sleep, surrounded by empty Coke tins, sweet wrappings, crisp packets and Rachel was clutching both her teddy and a picture of Michael Jackson close to her heart.

CHAPTER FOUR

During the next couple of months, as Christmas loomed, I seemed to view my life as if it were under a vast raking arc light. Nothing escaped the glare. If I stooped to pick up a tossed-aside sock, I noted the contemptuous carelessness of the sock-tosser; cleaning the bath *before* getting in it became a chore of extraordinary significance; when I put meals on the table I waited, breathless, to hear a please or thank you, but none came. What the arc light picked out was that I had become—in

Gordon's eyes at least (and beginning also in Rachel's no doubt) what Phillida had said—a domestic and drudge. My own fault entirely but it still hurt. Never mind, ducks, I would say to myself as, Cinderella-like, I sat among the cinders of my life, soon you are going to change all this. But if I gave myself that counsel quite often, I think I was also hoping that the arc light would pick out nice things, things that I had overlooked, things about which I would want to think twice before giving up. But there were none. Well, except the practical things I mentioned before, regular housekeeping, bills paid, the sheer comfort of security. But no emotional or sensual aspects, nothing that touched the woman in me, nothing at all. The mother, yes. The mother was touched by the dread of disrupting Rachel's smooth, contented life. The thought of telling *her* what was going through my mind was appalling. I didn't allow myself to dwell on it.

But the catalogue of the awfulness of what our marriage had become grew week by week inside me and it was only a matter of time before it began to burst out.

Christmas saw me quietly weeping into the screwed-up wrapping paper and the drying holly, trying hard not to think, This will be the last one with us all together. Resolve was gaining a terrible momentum and Phillida's card—the slyboots—said 'A happy and positive

New Year to you all', which didn't help. Then came the New Year.

New Year's Eve, 31 December. And of course it was much more poignantly hypocritical than the previous five or six. That bloody arc light put the whole thing on a stage and wouldn't have one softening shadow cast. We went to Joanna and Simon's party locally— we always spent our New Years locally except once when Gordon got very pig-headed about it and insisted that we went to a rather grand party in Highgate. Since it was either a taxi or the night bus back and since I refused point blank to come home in the wee small hours in a drunks-filled No. 27; and Gordon refused point blank to pay for a taxi, we drove. A small victory was mine when I said we should toss a coin for who stayed sober to drive. Gordon lost but did not remonstrate (I eased the situation by saying I would pay the babysitter out of my housekeeping; little things like that oiled our paths considerably—ridiculous looking back, but so it was . . .) and off we went. The party was at some cellist's house and was very ostentatious and noisy. Once or twice I caught up with Gordon to make sure he was drinking sensibly which he was. He assured me he would drink no more than three glasses of champagne and after a while I was convinced and relaxed enough to enjoy *my* few glasses of bubbly. Of course the silly thing was that I was probably quite all right to drive

49

home; a little merry perhaps, but since I had hacked my way through the mountains of delicious food and spent much more time with a plate in my hand than a glass, not seriously so. Gordon seemed fine when the time came to leave. A bit strident, but then I was a bit giggly. 'Sure you're OK?' I said.

'Sure,' he replied.

And off we went. Near Shepherd's Bush he swerved to avoid a cat, missed it, and rolled beautifully and majestically into a lamppost. Being Shepherd's Bush and about two in the celebratory morning it didn't take long for the police to amble over to us with their pleasantly enunciated 'Excuse me, sir. Have you been drinking?' And of course he had. Three glasses of champagne may have been the truth, but I should have investigated what size glasses. He was breathalysed positively there and then and taken off to do all the other things at the police station. I was not there because I went home to relieve the babysitter, limping back in our dented Peugeot, very ashamed and very angry. Supposing he had killed us both? Somehow he talked his way out of it and was not prosecuted. I think he was not too badly over the limit and apparently he gave them a bit of a sing-song which, being home-loving boys fed-up with night duty, they liked. So he came home.

'Don't lecture me,' he said, raising a warning finger.

I didn't.

But I never forgave him the crass stupidity of such behaviour. And ever after we went to local New Year's Eve parties, like Joanna and Simon's, instead.

Philly's words kept reverberating around my head. When I was smiling and laughing with the Evanses, or the Draycotts, or the Simpsons, or listening to one of Simon's eternal (but quite funny) stories about the lads in his sixth form, I was thinking all the time that this sham of a marriage could not go on. I was dreading more than ever that wretched moment when the clock pinged twelve and I would have to do what the others did and kiss *my* partner in life, and try to look as though the good wishes and greetings flowing all around were real and rich and full, and not the hollow pretence I knew they were. We steeled ourselves for the moment. Gordon kissed me full on the lips (I don't think he meant to, I think he just missed the more neutral territory of my cheek) and since our lips had not met for some years I was shocked at how horrid it was and how his beard tickled so unpleasantly. I moved away as rapidly as I could and we stared at each other, steely-eyed, frozen for a moment in the misery of its meaninglessness. And then someone kissed me, someone kissed Gordon, he was hauled away to the safety of the piano and began to play, and we were saved from any further public pretence.

Nineteen-eighty-eight had begun.

We walked home, hands in pockets against the frost, me silent, Gordon humming 'Silent Night' so sweetly, both of us knowing yet not speaking because it was too frightening to say. I felt a kind of relief—perhaps he did too—for we had skimmed the thin ice. It looked as though we had avoided confrontation again. I began to think that I could go on like this for ever.

But then, on 2 January, which had brought a day of sparkling sunlit frost and velvety blue night, and when I was down on my knees cleaning the oven, the dénouement came.

Rachel was in bed. I had got into the rhythm of such a distressingly thankless job. It had, after all, to be done, or the deep litter detritus of the preceding year would produce either burning or an explosion. I always cleaned the oven at the beginning of January. It was a kind of penance, my martyr's flail, and I felt wonderful when it was done. So wonderful that I would pour a gin and tonic, fetch a chair, and sit in front of the open oven door basking in its cleanliness while I sipped from the glass. I loved that bit. However, when the telephone rang I was nowhere near that stage and my plastic gloves were coated with grease, slime and detergent.

'Answer the phone,' I called to Gordon.

It went on ringing so I got up and stumbled towards the hall table.

Gordon was watching television in the front room. 'It's *Porgy and Bess,*' he said, as if that excused him phone duty.

I grabbed the receiver, thereby transferring a goodly amount of greasy muck and suds on to it. 'Yes,' I barked. Even Gordon looked around surprised. Good God, I found myself thinking furiously, a woman can't even skivvy without being interrupted . . . And then, even more furiously, I thought, Good God, here I am actually *cross* at being dragged away from oven duty. Something is distinctly wrong somewhere.

From the telephone issued the quavering tones of Gordon's Auntie Maggie trying to reach him for the third time that week. She and her spinster daughter, who lived together on the coast near St Andrews, were Gordon's last remaining family in Scotland. The aunt, elderly, and the cousin, devout, were always keen to keep in touch with him, their talented kinsman, of whom they were very proud. 'Pop up any time' was Auntie Maggie's favourite phrase—as if five hundred miles was a mere bagatelle—but Gordon didn't want to. I wouldn't have minded, it was an idyllic place for a child to holiday in and once or twice I suggested that Rachel and I could go on our own but nothing came of it. Gordon would say he might be able to manage it this year, next year, some time and never did. I knew why. It was quite simple: he would not spend money on fares to go somewhere that *he* did not wish to go. We went up there once, when Rachel was about two, and they didn't even have a television. He had to take us out in a boat and go for walks and—ye Gods—make *conversation.*

'Helloo,' said Auntie Maggie. 'Is he there, m' dear?'

I saw that the credits were rolling on the television screen, so I put my head round the door and mouthed at Gordon, 'It's your Auntie Maggie.'

He mouthed back, 'No, No,' and put up his hands in mock horror.

'He's just coming, Auntie,' I said, looking daggers at him.

She, meanwhile, began waxing lyrical about the beauties of the snow scene outside her window and how the wee chuckie Rachel would jus luv t'see it.

'Gordon,' I mouthed again. 'Please . . .'

Gunge was dropping from my plastic gloves all over the carpet.

'I don't want to speak to her,' he whispered.

'Well I don't either,' and then I said very firmly into the mouthpiece, 'He's right here. I'll hand you over.' And I held the telephone out to him. Unfortunately he was just saying an irate 'Fuck you' and I heard Auntie Maggie's puzzled voice 'Wha' wuz tha'?'

I pushed the receiver into his hand. He covered it with his free one and roared 'Fuck off,' again before commencing to speak. And, quite suddenly, I knew that I would. Fuck off, that is. There had been one too many of those invitations just recently. I went back to the oven feeling quite calm and quite determined. The moment had come.

It was no good his sauntering into the kitchen afterwards and saying that he was sorry, that he hadn't meant it, that he just didn't feel like engaging in conversation with anybody at that particular moment. No good at all.

'One fuck off too many,' I said, giving the inner rungs one final wipe. 'So now I am going to. I have had quite enough of your disdain. We must get a divorce.'

It came out so simply that I wondered why I had feared the words for so long. And curiously enough, with that innate sixth sense that must exist between couples of long standing, he knew at once that I meant it.

The first thing he said, as I stood up to survey the pristine cooker, was, 'You'll not get Rachel.'

'Oh yes I will,' I said, quite confidently. 'No one would separate a child from her mother.'

There is something wonderfully contemptuous in the snapping off of a pair of pink plastic housegloves. Snap, snap, they went as I pulled them off and tucked them behind the draining board.

'What about separating her from her father

then?' he asked spitefully.

'There are some sacrifices, Gordon, that must come to an end. In this case, mine.'

I got my chair and my drink and sat in front of the cooker. And though he railed at me from the sidelines and stomped about and punched at the wall with his fist, I observed him not. I kept my eyes on the gleaming enamel and sipped and sipped and sipped.

Eventually he said, 'You'll have to tell her. Think of that.'

And I did.

For the next month I thought of little else while Gordon transformed himself into the kind of father he had never hitherto been. He cancelled things so that during the rest of the Christmas holiday he could take her out and about. He read her stories at night. He bought her comics and sweets and sat her on his lap for long sessions of melancholy cuddles. All this made me want to puke, but I bided my time. Until I was absolutely sure, until I was quite clear in my own mind what I was going to do and what I was going to say to her, I would not be moved. And, strangely enough, that month was a heavenly freedom. I knew the goal, I was sorting out the route. My destiny was back in my own hands again. I was a free woman, about to embark.

CHAPTER FIVE

Rachel put back her head and howled. She was like a little animal, kneeling on the carpet of our bedroom upstairs, expressing her pain in a series of noises. I held her very tightly, as if she were having a fit, and stroked her hair and rocked her and cried with her. Cried and cried. I was a little afraid of her just at that moment. She, of the three of us, seemed most capable of getting to the core of her emotions and giving vent to them in this unselfconscious, gut way. Don't lose that ability, I remember thinking, hold on to it and keep it.

When her howling ceased she sat up straight, looked me in the eye and said, 'I never, ever thought it would happen to me. This will change my character.'

My heart, already heavy, sank to my boots. 'What do you mean?' I asked.

'From now on I will know what it is like to suffer so it will make me a kinder person to others.'

She was *ten*, for Christ's sake. Now you know why I could deny her nothing, not even a dog, if it compensated in some way for what I was doing to her.

Her arm stayed round my waist while she questioned me. I was so grateful for that. I knew of friends whose children had bitten, scratched and kicked them when they were first told of a looming divorce, and others who had just remained silent, withdrawn, with burning accusation in their eyes. But our Rachel, our lovely, kind, thoughtful child, kept her arm round my waist, her body pressed up to mine, and said, 'What stopped you loving Daddy?'

'I don't know. But at least we can still stay friends.'

'Then why don't you stay in the same house together?'

'It's more complicated than that.'

'You aren't going to get married again, are you?' She looked stricken. If ever I had remotely thought in a sugar-fluff kind of way that one day I might just possibly meet some tanned Adonis with beautiful body and brilliant brain it was at that point that the sugar-fluff melted. At least, with honour, I could deny *that*.

'Certainly not,' I said. 'You will always be the most important person in my life.'

'Oh I know *that*,' she said. 'And in Daddy's too.'

'Certainly,' I said, thankful for her big, beautiful ego.

Then she howled afresh and I let her go on for as long as she needed. She withdrew her arm eventually and very quietly said, 'I must go downstairs and see him now.'

I followed her.

She cuddled up into his lap and closed her eyes. Gordon stroked her head and, looking beyond it to me, standing in the doorway, he said very slowly and deliberately, 'Mummy will have to get a job now.'

Those were his first words to her and I could have killed him. Let no one speak to me about the sensitivity of the creative genius.

Rachel sat up and looked at him with genuine astonishment. 'But she's got one already,' she said. 'Looking after me.'

I tried to keep the triumph from my face. We're living in a liberated age, you bastard, I thought.

Gordon's brow darkened but he said no more on that subject. Not then, anyway. It was only afterwards that he spoke about it again. He'd contribute towards Rachel's maintenance, but as for me—as for me—I could bloody well whistle.

Hence my interview with Mr Pownall. There was really no point in pursuing ideas of financial help for myself. Right from the outset I knew it would be painful and useless. Money continued to be what Gordon had always made it—an issue of his strength over mine. I decided to let him keep that. It was, after all, a very small item in the sum of things.

*   *   *

There was a lot of collateral in our house. The

59

proceeds of the sale would provide enough money for a small house near Rachel's school for we two and decent accommodation for Gordon.

'Will Daddy live near us?' she asked.

'Oh yes,' I agreed. 'As close as he can.'

'In the same street?'

'Probably not quite *that* close.' Please God, no, not *that* close.

And then began his property hunt game-playing. Perhaps it was a blessing in disguise. Perhaps while it went on she was both protected by the abstraction of the situation and yet had time to prepare for the reality of living apart. She certainly seemed to take a pragmatic view of things and unless Gordon went into one of his soulful sessions with her managed to look on the bright side pretty well and tune in to the potential excitement of the coming situation. First the promise of a dog to replace Daddy. Then the interesting prospect of moving to somewhere new. Also she attained a kind of ascendancy among her peers at school. Those whose parents were already divorced gave her counsel—two sets of Christmas presents, two summer holidays, double pocket money—and those whose parents were not gave her kindness and special treatment. Gradually the initial misery subsided and she became quite stoical about the whole thing. She even walked about the garden with me during the early spring pointing out the shrubs and stone urns and bulb patch which she said we really must try to take with us. It took my breath away at first but I soon settled into this new child of mine's ways. As long as she would see Daddy regularly and as long as she could have her dog and a bigger bedroom, on the whole she would accept what was happening. Life must go on.

One day she said to me on the way back from school, 'Daddy keeps reading me stories when I go to bed at night.'

'Yes,' I said. 'Isn't that nice?' It was something he had never done much in the old days.

'Well, yes,' she said unenthusiastically. 'Except he's not very good at reading out loud and I'd much rather get on with my own books.' (Lest I make this child out to be a monster of high IQ let me quickly add that she was firmly entrenched in Enid Blyton at the time and having an all out love affair with the Famous Five.) 'So do you think you could try to tell him I like reading on my own?'

'Well,' I said dubiously, 'he might be a bit hurt.'

She pondered this. 'Mmm, yes I suppose so . . .' Her acceptance was a real gift. The thought of trying to tell Gordon that she didn't want him reading to her any more was ghastly in the extreme. But she dealt with it on her own.

A few nights later he came down the stairs

61

looking really pleased with himself. 'Rachel's teacher says she must do some reading without parental help, so I've left her to it. She's a good kid, you know. Honest. Most of them wouldn't tell you and would just let you go on reading to them without you ever knowing . . .'

I smiled. 'At least we appear to have got something right,' I said.

*   *   *

I saw Phillida briefly about a month after telling Rachel. She came up to London and we had a very hurried lunch together.

'I just cannot believe,' I said, 'that I haven't scarred her for life. She's covering up all sorts of feelings, I know she is, but she just doesn't let them out.'

'What kind of feelings?' said Philly. She was eating lasagne at a rate of knots and I could have crowned her for looking so normal, so relaxed about everything—and so bloody hungry. In out, in out, went her fork, and chomp, chomp, chomp, went her unexcitable mouth.

'God knows,' I said.

'Does she cry?'

'Sometimes.'

'Does she let you cuddle her? And Gordon? Does she let him?'

'Yes.'

'The most important thing is to make her

62

realise it is your and Gordon's decision—'

'Mine, you mean—'

'No, I don't. I mean both of you. At least, that the inability to live together is a direct result of both your and Gordon's behaviour, and nothing at all to do with Rachel's. Given the chance kids will take on all manner of guilt. If you can stop that then most of the battle is won. Honestly, it is.'

'My God,' I said. 'Rachel is the only reason we've stayed together this long. If anything it's her that's stopped the rot up to now.'

Phillida put down her fork which soothed me a bit. 'And don't go saying that to her either. Don't put anything on to her at all. Just make sure she knows that she's the good thing in all this. You two have made the mistake: apologise to her like you would over any mistake, but don't even hint that she has a role to play in all this beyond the passive one of just being there.'

'You mean tell her that she's our lovely, perfect daughter whatever happens?'

Phillida sighed and retrieved her fork. 'I don't mean that at all. If you say that to her she'll think for ever that she's got to *be* perfect. Just tell her that you and Gordon are unable to stay together, that you are sorry it's going to cause her sadness, but that you can't change what has happened.' Here she prodded the fork in my direction. 'Bloody well make sure she knows that there is absolutely nothing whatsoever she can do to change things. Don't even hint at it. "This is the way it is, Rachel," you say. "Sorry, my darling, we both love you, but this is the way from now on . . ." Then, suffer as she might—if you and Gordon can maintain some kind of reasonable relationship, it shouldn't be too bad—she will at least never feel she had anything to do with it.'

'It sounds extremely easy said like that over lettuce and lasagne.'

'You've done the hard bit, the telling. And you're managing to rub along in friendly fashion with him. Christ, Patsy. So far so good. Don't knock her for appearing to come to terms with it. She probably *is* coming to terms with it. Let her. What else can you do? Tell her it's all been a ghastly mistake and you're not going to separate after all? You can't go back. You've *got* to go forward.'

'Well,' I said. 'That's my pep talk done. I wish to God someone would give one to Gordon.'

She clinked her fork back into her empty dish and gave me a quite wicked look across her glass of Perrier.

'I'm meeting him tonight,' she said. 'Didn't he tell you?'

*   *   *

I don't know what she said to him, probably the same kind of thing she had been telling

64

me, but it must have worked because he became much better with Rachel after that. Far less the woeful ill-done-to and much more his old self. And I could see at once what Phillida had been talking about, for as soon as he began to lay off the poor-me stuff Rachel was much more relaxed. The high spot of this recovery was the evening they lost their tempers with each other during her piano practice. I heard her yell, 'Haydn is junk' and start boogie-ing away with a Scott Joplin rag and I heard Gordon thunder out, 'Are you thick or something? Stop playing that muck and listen to me!' And the boogie-ing went on, as did the shouting. I knew then that the false rosy light had at last given way to the much more acceptable and normal light of day. And after that, except in the matter of actually finding a new home, he was without fault and there were no more of his sighing asides to her and those eternal ah-me,-remember-whens.

God bless Philly, I thought to myself. And then again, when the mood darkened, I thought, Why God bless Philly? She started all this. I had to have someone outside myself to blame occasionally, you see. And it did no harm. Quite often it was a release to feel angry that she had done all the advising and then was nowhere near the scene when the shit hit the proverbial. I quite liked the mental picture of myself as the Trilby of New Wave Womanhood and her as the Svengali. At any rate, it got me through some of the gloomier days and never seriously damaged my affection for her, nor my gratitude underneath.

*   *   *

We put our house on the market in April. By then Gordon had seen about twenty places and rejected them, and I had not even begun to look. It was my neighbour Joyce who said, 'Get a buyer for yours and he'll *have* to make his mind up.' Joyce had been divorced, though without children, and had remarried Henry. They rowed constantly in blissful marital disharmony but since she was a buyer for a fabric firm and he was an engineer their paths seldom crossed. They had no children but a crotchety old aunt housekept for them and managed to stay with another relative when they were at home together. It seemed like an ideal situation. They even had separate bedrooms though this apparently enhanced their sex life. As Joyce said, you really had to be keen and prepared to make the other equally so when you had a bedroom floor and a landing to cross whenever you fancied it. And since she seemed to have got her act together in this respect, I took her advice about the house and rang a few local firms.

Like smiling hawks, along came all the local estate agents to view it and assess its value. Little plastic men they were, all in stripy suits, terribly polite and able to avert their eyes when it came to the leaking skylight on the landing or the damp patch on the ground-floor wall. 'No problem, Mrs Murray,' they said. 'No problem at all in selling such a lovely property.' In the end I decided that they were all charlatans and put it with the agent who valued it highest. Then we sat back and let the floods of potential buyers pour in. Which of course they did. But none made any offers until the mild-eyed young couple. They—newly married, selling their two separate flats, she pregnant—liked it at once. You could tell.

'I want a big family,' the woman said. 'So we have to get somewhere to expand into.' She fixed me with big, hungry eyes. 'It's a real family house,' she said. 'You can tell you've all been happy here.'

I had no heart for confidences. 'Oh yes,' I lied. 'It's perfect for kids: so near the school, such a quiet road . . . Of course it's a bit knocked about in places.' I stood in front of the damaged glass pane in the kitchen. 'But then, what can you expect in a family home?'

'Shirley's expecting twins,' said her husband.

It was on the tip of my tongue to say, And what are you expecting? But I held off. Just as well. They made a good offer and I accepted it there and then.

Gordon threw a corker of a wobbly. 'I have nowhere to go yet. I have seen *nothing* that remotely interests me as somewhere to live.

And you, *you* have the brass face to agree?'

'Calm down,' I said, inexcusably enjoying his crossness. 'You've got plenty of time. They don't want to move until September. I've told them we want to move before the new term starts, so that'll be the first week. Surely even you will find something by then?'

'Unlikely,' he said, 'I have special needs.'

And that was when the real agony regarding Gordon's new home commenced. He took to the *Angst* like a trooper. And, as I have said, he would come home full of good reasons for not choosing any of the places he went to see. And, indeed, he might have kept it up much longer had Michael not come to call one evening while Gordon was working. Michael had a very different tale to tell.

*   *   *

It was somewhere around the end of June. Rachel was tucked up with *Five Go on a Hike Together* and I was sitting in the garden feeling miserable and frustrated. Gordon was away doing something in Newcastle and the only high spot on my horizon was that he would be gone for a few days. The calm of the house without him was somewhat dampened by the knowledge that while he was out of London he was getting no nearer finding somewhere to live. I was aching, almost literally, to begin my own search but still did not dare for fear of finding and losing the perfect home. I gnawed my finger ends in the waning June sunlight and abandoned the attempt to make a cushion cover. The crumpled material lay on my lap as I chewed away at what had once been a set of decent nails. I had thought that some kind of stitchery would ease me, as in Victorian times, through psychological difficulties but the creased-up square of Liberty roll-end was merely a mockery. The birds in the trees were twittering away and the noise jarred my nerves. I could have happily wrung their necks. Even they had their nests somewhere. Damn you, I was thinking, both of Gordon and the cushion square. I just can't go on like this. I am going to explode. It is as if I have climbed Everest only to find Kilimanjaro waiting beyond. A vague contemplation of what would be the most painless way to commit suicide was punctuated by the ringing of our doorbell, so I hauled myself out of the sunlit blackness and answered it. There was Michael. Aptly named, though at the time I considered him only as an intrusion rather than the archangel he was to prove himself to be. He stood on the doorstep looking uneasy. I hadn't seen him for months since he was really Gordon's friend and I never knew him very well. He was long, thin, bearded in a dark wispy way and had soulful eyes. These looked nervously into mine as he said, 'Look, Patricia, I know this is a bad time to put this on you, but may I come in?'

Relieved to be excused more nail biting and cushion wrecking, and intrigued by the intensity of the plea, I invited him in at once.

'How is the medieval music going?' I asked as we walked through to the garden. 'I heard your talk on Radio Three last week. It was very good. I had no idea you were such an expert.'

He shuffled along behind me and his sandals made little plopping noises. He really was a character out of his time and should, by rights, have still been sitting in a field somewhere with flowers in his hair and a dreamy look in his eyes. He was certainly not the kind of companion I sought that night—not that I sought one—but his arrival made some kind of hiatus in my own messy state and I was quite pleased about that. I was about to offer him some nibbles when I remembered that we only had smoky bacon flavour left and he was vegetarian. I risked his not being teetotal too and got out the wine box. I was quite glad to have an excuse for a glass of wine. I tried not to drink when alone—a few weeks earlier in the spring I had taken to getting quite sloshed on my own at lunchtime (easier to drink than eat) and hated it because it solved no problems, apart from the immediate solace of numbness, and produced many more, such as feeling tired, crabby and looking a bit blotchy when the effect wore off.

He accepted a glass of vin rouge plonk and

said, 'It's going very well,' relating to the music, and 'Cheers' relating to the wine.

'I'm afraid Gordon's out of town for a few days,' I said.

'Yes,' he said unhappily. 'I know.'

I waited, intrigued, to hear why he had come. We sat down opposite each other under the apple tree and I said, 'Cheers,' and waited some more. He looked really uncomfortable and kept pulling at his beard. I took this to be because he knew Gordon and I were splitting up and I didn't know what to say to help. He was far too sensitive a soul for me to say what I would have said to anyone else which was, loosely, 'Don't shed any tears on my account I'm really looking forward to going it alone'. So I stayed silent, smiling encouragingly at him. Since he was quite uninterested in women and, as far as I knew, not very interested in men either, I was sure this was no prelude to anything excitingly amatory.

'What are you making?' he said eventually, looking at the crumpled cloth at my feet.

'A hash of something.' I laughed. 'As bloody usual.'

He leaned out of the deck chair a little and took a big gulp of his wine and said most earnestly, 'Look, Patricia. I know that just about the worse thing is having pressure put upon you while you try to work things out but if you could only see your way to making some kind of decision, *soon* . . . Well, *God*, I'd be so grateful . . .'

I was astonished. The earnestness of it, the lack of pause for breath, the penetrating pleading in his eyes—what did it mean?

I felt my way. 'Well, er . . . Michael, I have, er . . . um . . . made a decision, you know, and, er . . . um . . . well—' sip from glass '—there we are . . .'

He looked less of a lost soul at this. 'You *have*?' he said. 'That's wonderful. Where?'

'Pardon?'

'Where have you decided? I hope it's what you want. You know, somewhere nice for you both . . . Rachel and you—'

'Michael,' I said. 'What are we talking about?'

He went back to being concave-chested. 'About you finding somewhere to live, aren't we?'

It was beyond me. Why was Michael—more acquaintance to me than friend—so seriously concerned about my future domicile?

'Are we?'

'Please, Patricia. I know this is a terrible imposition but I simply have to know. I can't keep the Americans waiting indefinitely. And, really, you should think of Gordon too. It really isn't doing him any good. And what about Rachel, I mean—'

I interrupted him. 'Michael,' I said. 'I'm not quite sure what you are trying to say, and I certainly don't know why you are so concerned. Can we go back to that bit regarding where? Why does where I'm going to live interest you? I mean, I'd give my eye teeth to be able to say to you that I have found somewhere, that it will be fine for me and Rachel, but let me tell you there is no way I can begin to do that until Gordon makes his mind up about where he's going to fucking well park himself. Forgive me for being blunt—' His eyes had gone a bit poppy behind his glasses by now '—but, well, I really don't know what all this is about.'

'Are you serious?' he said quietly.

'Michael. Why did you come?'

He looked uneasy and puzzled and swirled the wine in his glass before drinking it. Then he said, without looking at me, 'I think perhaps Gordon is being something of a bastard to us both.'

'That,' I said with luscious venom, 'would not surprise me in the least.'

Oh, it was so *nice* to have someone think the same way as I did. I had played the role of well-mannered woman for so long I had forgotten the pleasure of letting real feeling surface. 'Now,' I said, leaning back, letting the warmth of the word 'bastard' from another's lips drift over me, 'please explain *why* you think that . . .'

*   *   *

73

By the time he had explained neither of us was left in any doubt that Gordon had, indeed, been unkind, in an Attila-the-Hun sort of a way, to us both. Five or six weeks earlier Michael had received a long-term offer from an American Research Foundation, a kind of dream come true. For five years he would be paid to do what he loved—play, buy, talk about and generally immerse himself in ancient music and its instruments. But before he could up sackbuts and depart these shores he needed to sell his flat. And this is where Gordon came in. Gordon was going to buy it. They had already agreed the price. All poor Michael was waiting for was confirmation of a moving date, and—since he was enough of this world to know some of its financial vagaries— a legal commitment. Gordon's story to Michael was that he could not do this until *I* had made up *my* mind about where I was going to live.

Well, I need hardly say more. Except that the old wine box sloshed about a bit between the two of us and not a few ripe epithets were strung round the absent Attila's neck, aye, and pulled exceeding tight too. As, indeed, was the shuffling, sandal-plopping form of Michael as it made its way off into the night about an hour later. 'Jee-suss,' he said, in valedictory stance at the front door. 'If that's what being married does for you I'm glad not to be interested. Give me solitude any time.' And away he went.

Next morning at breakfast Rachel was munching up her Wheatacrunch when she said, 'Mum, what's a bastard?'

I was not particularly alarmed, after all one's offspring should enquire all manner of things and at least we weren't sitting next to a nun on the top of a bus.

'A bastard is someone whose parents are not married.'

'I thought Granny and Grandpa Murray were married before they died.'

'Of course they were,' said I drinking my orange juice in an attempt to offload the effects of the wine box.

'Well, why did you and that man last night call Daddy one then?'

'Because we were cross with him. Rachel! Were you earwigging? That's a bad trait in a child, in anybody.' And I huffed and puffed for a bit.

'I wasn't trying to,' she said. 'Only it was so hot my window was open. What has he done now?'

I wanted to tell her—didn't I just—but it was hardly worth my passing moment of pleasurable spite. So I swallowed deep, a thing I had learned to do, and said, 'There's just been a muddle. That's all. But we've sorted it out now.' Then I kissed the top of her head as

75

lightly as if it *were* all a nonsense. 'But the good thing is that it means we can begin to look for a house for ourselves now. Daddy has found what he is looking for.'

'At last,' she said.

And amen to that, I silently replied.

CHAPTER SIX

Gordon rang from Gatwick at about nine to say that he was back and on his way. He had always done that and despite our changed relationship he continued to do so. I thought nothing of it until that post-Michael Sunday night but I was so raw about his deceit that every single thing connecting him with me was not only under the arc light but magnified as well. So when he said, 'Hi, Patsy. Just to say I'm back and on my way . . .' I realised that, rather like all those dog walkers who say 'walkies' and really mean 'shitties', what he was really saying was, 'You can start the supper, I'll be back in about an hour . . .' So I didn't. I just waited.

Rachel was staying overnight at her friend Katie's house. Normally I would not have agreed, since she hadn't seen her father for several days and he liked her to be there, but I saw no reason to promote his pleasures any more. And since it did not even occur to

Rachel to refuse the invitation on the grounds of her long-lost daddy, I let her go. Besides, I had a premonition that dealing with Gordon would be a lot easier if she were not asleep upstairs. I had an idea that there might be a noise level not conducive to slumbering infants remaining that way.

In he came, looking pleased. And he began to say what he'd done, how it had gone, etc, etc. We were face to face in the hallway. I just turned my back and walked into the sitting room leaving him standing alone out there. I don't think at this stage he thought much of it. He went upstairs. And came down again.

'Where's Rachel?' he said.

'At Katie's.'

'What, for the night?'

'Uh-huh.'

'Well, that's a bit much. I haven't seen her since Tuesday.'

'No,' I agreed.

It must have been a particularly successful few days because he didn't rise to this. If it had gone badly he would have been at the panting stage by now. He did look puzzled as he followed me into the room and saw me sit down and pick up a newspaper. He rubbed his hands, saying rather lamely as he did so, 'They gave a little drinks party before we left for the airport but I haven't eaten.' He crossed to the television in that automatic way of his, pressed the switch. 'Have you?'

'What?' I did not look up from the property page.

'Eaten?'

'Yes,' I said.

'Oh.' But his attention was taken by the lack of life in the set. He prodded the switches for a few seconds, then got down on his knees to check the socket.

'It doesn't work.' He sat back on his heels and stared at it in disbelief.

'Patsy,' (that was better, he was beginning to sound rattled) 'this set is on the blink. Have you had it on today?'

'No,' I said, still scrutinising the paper.

'Well, look.' He pointed, expostulating.

I did not look.

He fiddled some more. 'Have you called the engineer?'

'No.'

'When did it go wrong?'

I shrugged.

He began huffing and puffing and shuffled towards me on his knees. 'Patsy,' he said warningly. 'I'm talking to you.'

I put down the paper—we were eyeball to eyeball now—cupped my hand in my chin and gave him my best imitation of a pitying look.

'The television. It doesn't work. Why?' His voice rose at each word.

'I have no idea,' I said. This was a lie since I had taken the fuse out of the plug that morning.

'When did it go wrong?'

This was irresistible. I stood up, tucked the paper under my arm and exited, saying over my shoulder, 'Eleven years ago. On the day I said I do.'

'Oh, ha ha,' he said acidly. 'Where are you going?'

'To bed.' I looked at my watch. 'It's nearly eleven. I've got a busy day tomorrow'

'Oh yes?'

I began ascending the stairs.

'Yes?' he said more urgently. 'Doing what in particular?'

'I'm going to start househunting.'

Then came the Pavlovian response. His voice, half warning, half self-pitying, saying, 'Well, don't get too carried away by anything. Remember *I'm* not going anywhere until I find just the right place.'

'Goodnight,' I said, continuing upwards.

He was gripping the banisters now, like a monkey in a cage, an angry one. 'I'll not be rushed—I'll not—I'll not. Not by you, not by anyone.'

Then I turned. 'I think you will,' I said. 'In fact—' I made a wonderful play of checking my watch again '—it's still just about early enough for you to ring him.'

'Who?'

'Michael, of course. He's putting his flat on the market tomorrow, *if* he hasn't heard from you before then. He wants an exchange within the next two weeks, I think he said that, anyway. So you see—' oh what a smile I gave him '—I've got to buck up or it'll be my turn to slow things down.'

He began to jig up and down while still holding on to the banisters in such a way that if I had had a banana in my hand I might have chucked it at him.

'You make me sick,' I said suddenly, thrusting my head near the bars. 'All that supposed deep love you have for Rachel and you not only put *her* through all this misery in order to get back at me, but on top of all that you're buying somewhere that hasn't even got a separate room for her to sleep in. You can't even be bothered to make some space in your life for your only daughter!'

'There are two rooms,' he said defensively. 'Two huge rooms as you well know. I need all that space. And I can get a screen to close a bit off for her. Or she can sleep in my bed when she comes. I'll sleep on the floor in the music room.'

'Great,' I said. 'That'll make her feel wonderful. All these months of letting her hope for somewhere special and now you're going to shove her in a corner behind a screen. You're a selfish, egocentric—'

'My, my,' he said. 'Such long words from such an ill-educated termagant.'

'I tell you Gordon—' I began. He recognised the threatening tone and there was something approaching a light of triumph in his eyes. When I saw this I stopped. He had almost brought me to the brink he craved. I had almost, almost made Rachel into an object to be pulled and tugged between us—almost said to him that he would have to fight me for her now—and I saw as I looked into his eyes that that was precisely what he wanted. Just like the *Angst* necessary to his flat buying, so he needed conflict over his daughter. Well, he wasn't going to get it from me. Besides, give him any opportunity, any opportunity at all, and he was just as likely to call off the whole deal with Michael. If I continued like this he could suddenly pull out the switchblade and cut all the strings and leave me lifeless, immobilised again. No. I had freedom in my nostrils now and it was too sweet to risk. Rachel would just have to put up with her father's home being less than satisfactory. At least the flat had a small garden belonging to it. Already in my mind I was pointing out compensations to her. Conciliatory to the last in my starring role of motherhood. She could walk to the museums, walk to Holland Park, walk to Kensington Gardens and visit Harrods whenever she felt like it . . . Oh yes, I thought, things could be a lot worse. I looked through the bars at Gordon whose vestigial shame was almost eclipsed by defiance. The game was up but he had had a good run for his money. He had kept me on my toes, really made me pay—

never mind that he had put both his daughter and his friend through the mincer with me. Never again, I vowed—how many times have I said that before and since? Never again. He unto his unsuitable flat, me unto my search for the perfect house. And whatever I felt about Gordon and his behaviour, however he goaded me or played upon my sensitivities, I must not react. Blinkered and tin-plated against him I must stay. It was all I could think to do.

Men do not make good mothers on the whole, which is why, of course, they are fathers instead.

*   *   *

Number 10 Florizel Street was so perfect that I eschewed my usual dismissive attitude to the estate agent who showed me around it (having once worked for one, one is inclined to be even more cynical than the general public) and became all fluttery *eyes* and rapt attention. I wanted him on my side in the purchase of it. When he said absurd things like 'a little minor decoration required' to the maroon flock wallpaper in the small back bedroom, or 'the price includes all fittings' to the shower curtain with a life-size nude lady painted on it, I merely looked ecstatic. I wanted him to believe that *he* had sold it to me, so that he felt inextricably bound up in the successful outcome of the sale.

'My word, really?' I said when he told me that we were only five minutes from the tube station. Having lived in the locale for eleven years I knew perfectly well that he was talking Olympic-runner standards.

He warmed to the theme. 'And as gardens go in this area this is really a decent size,' he said as we practically tripped over each other in the twenty foot of overgrown grass.

'I'm sure you're right,' I said meekly. It didn't matter that I was giving up three times the space back at home. I nearly baulked when he got to the bit about 'another one down the road went for x thousand more last week' but held on to myself enough. 'Oh well then. That really *is* a bonus. I'd better offer the full amount right away to be sure of getting it. Hadn't I?'

He puffed up his little pin-striped chest. 'Mrs Murray,' he said, 'that is a very sensible attitude if I may say so.'

His name was Jason Wapshott. I took comfort from that. With a name so awful it mattered not that he took me for a right prat. Or maybe he didn't. Maybe he actually believed all the hype. Though surely, surely he could not have genuinely felt in his heart that the pair of concrete lions firmly fixed on either side of the mock Adam fireplace, three foot high, sitting on their haunches with one paw up in a pastiche of campdom, were really and truly a laudable feature. Jason Wapshott, I vowed privately, if you get me this house, you shall have them as my gift for your own little yuppie kingdom.

Why, given the flock wallpaper, the postage-stamp garden, the nude in the bathroom and the leonine accoutrements, was 10 Florizel Street so right? And the answer is that I don't really know. All I do know is that as I walked through the front door and saw the coloured light from its stained glass make patterns in the tiny square of the hallway, I was certain that this one was *it*. The space was right: a through room downstairs, a decently sized kitchen with double doors into the postage stamp, three bedrooms upstairs and an overall sense of having been kindly cared for underneath all the loud and strange décor. I was almost tempted to keep the royal and ice-blue marbling of the walls in the living room as a kind of conversation piece, only it was a bit like walking into the Arctic. Gradually I would change it all and make it mine—I had time, all the time in the world, to do that. Meanwhile Jason Wapshott had my offer under his belt and—true to my hopes and no doubt helped by all the eye-fluttering—the sale went through smoothly by September.

He never did get those lions, though. When I brought Rachel to see the house, once I was sure the offer had been accepted, they were the clinching factor for her. She gave a little shriek of delight when she first saw them and ran across the room to kneel at their stony sides, stroking them and instantly giving them names. 'This one,' she said, 'is Mrs Protheroe,' her favourite teacher at school, 'and this one is Julian.'

'Why Julian?' I asked, certain that it would be a classmate, half fearful (remembering Phillida's counsel) that it might indicate some burgeoning adolescent romance.

'Oh, Mum.' She rolled her eyes. 'From the Famous Five of course.'

She snickered over the nude lady in the bathroom.

'And what shall we call her?' I asked.

She put her hand over her mouth, gave me a half sly, half embarrassed look and shook her head.

'I think,' I said, perching on the lavatory, 'that we should call her Phillida.'

And Rachel gave such a raunchy guffaw that I was momentarily alarmed. Could my daughter have a wicked sense of humour under all that open-eyed innocence? Very probably. Now that I had inner happiness on my side again I could afford to spend some time observing and enjoying her. Sitting on that lavatory with the bulbous-bosomed Phillida staring down on us I felt so happy suddenly. So sure that out of all this anguish I had made the right decision, that I could deny her nothing. It was then, as we confronted each other in the bathroom, that she asked about having a dog. And it was then that I agreed. Since we had nearly two months before moving in, and since, as is the way of things, I had no thoughts about our neighbours, it was surely not my fault that Brian became a projected part of our household long before I knew that the family next door kept a rabbit?

*   *   *

Naturally enough, before we finally moved there were certain things to iron out. We did most of these: how the money for Rachel would be paid, who would have the car (stroke of genius here—I had it valued as a trade-in vehicle and then Gordon paid me half of that towards my buying a new one. Somewhere along the line I think I missed out in the deal but it was better than nothing), which one of us would be the forwarding address (me), etc, etc . . .

And then came the furniture. Gordon had always eschewed the trappings of the bourgeoisie. Being blessed with a creative talent he had every right to eschew them. 'You, my poor dear *hausfrau*, may consider stylish chairs, unlumpy beds and untattered curtains at the window to be relevant to a home, but for me—pah! What do I need such items for? They are merely the trappings of a mind bogged down by silly materialism.' I

86

paraphrase about ten years of Gordonesque pronouncement in that one sentence. Over the years I had, where possible, squeezed a little extra here, gone to auctions there, and used that most excellent emporium for the winter sale, Arding and Hobbs. It might not be Conran but at least it's solid.

But suddenly this changed. Now the very things that he had despised he cherished. The Edwardian *chaise-longue*—criticised as a hopeless piece of heavyweight discomfort— was perfect for his large, bare rooms. The bookshelves—those big black comfortably hideous monstrosities—were suddenly needed by him, though he had few books compared with my collection and never read novels. Music was his life, you see; he was caught up, absorbed, totally involved with it. Which is why, despite my fury, I also found it extremely funny that he should develop this passion for all the outward trappings.

I fought hard for the *chaise*, pointed out that the little sewing table *(sewing table?)* had been a wedding present from my deceased father and he ceded some of his other claims like the coffee grinder, the wing armchair and the desk. But when it came to the washing machine, I would not be moved. When I thought back to his bitter prognostications on the necessity of spending good money on this, well, it really was too much.

'I've got to do washing too, you know,' he

said.

'*You* can use a launderette.'

'You can use a launderette. I bought the damn thing.'

'Yes,' I said. 'And I used it. You don't even know how it works.'

'I can learn.'

'Bugger that! It's mine. I need it much more than you do.'

'That's an extremely unliberated attitude on your part, Patsy.' Which was rather like Dylan Thomas telling Bernard Shaw to take more water with it.

Naturally, I overreacted and we ended up having one of our most spectacular fighting rows over that innocent little Hotpoint. The finale was grotesque, with me draped across its dear little user-friendly control panel protecting it from Gordon's determined onslaughts with a saucepan.

'If I can't have it,' he yelled smacking away at the switches, 'then no one will!'

It says much for the quality of the item that he barely scratched it. The saucepan, however, was a different matter. Quite dented, it was. When I finalised the list of who should have what I included it on his side. A little memento of how absurd we had both become.

*　　　*　　　*

A few nights before we finally moved into our

separate domains we experienced a sudden reversal in all this anger and passion. There were no fights left to us in the current state of things. There might be more fights later, but, *pro tem*, we drew a truce.

Gordon rang me during the day and said, 'Can you get a babysitter for tonight?'

His voice was so ordinary and calm and everything it had not been for months—if not years—that instead of jumping down his throat and saying, 'What the bloody hell are you playing at giving me just a few hours' notice?' which is the kind of thing I would otherwise have launched into, I just said rather sweetly, 'Why yes, of course. From when to when?'

'Eight till eleven,' he said. 'I'm taking you out to dinner.'

'Where?' I said, most intrigued.

'Gigondas,' he said, with immense pride, as well he might. This was a newish local restaurant with about a million stars. Extremely chic, extremely expensive and the stuff that dreams are made of, as far as getting Gordon's wallet through the doors.

'You're kidding.'

'I am not,' he said, slightly huffily. 'I thought we should go out in style. Besides, we can walk there and it's completely neutral territory. I've never been and you've never been, so it won't hold any—' he hesitated showing, suddenly, a sensitivity that I scarcely knew he possessed, or maybe, through the years, our awfulness to each other had just buried all vestiges of it '—memories.'

'Right-ho,' I said. 'And thank you.'

'Don't mention it,' he said, and rang off.

The babysitter was no problem. Rachel was a slight problem because, naturally enough when I told her I was going out to dinner with Daddy, she got a slight gleam of hope in her eyes which I had to dash. But remembering Phillida's counsel, dash it I did.

'We're just going out together to prove we can still be friends,' I said. 'Just because we can't live together doesn't mean we have to fight all the time.' Rachel had been privy, from the top of the stairs, to the washing machine débâcle and to several other more minor affrays before and since, so I felt quite pleased with myself for being able to turn Gordon's dinner invitation to good psychological use. Since for most of her lifetime she had known us only as peaceful cohabitees this sudden domestic verity, with saucepans flying, had shocked her. To show friendliness now would make us all feel better.

'All right,' she said. 'But I wish we were moving *tomorrow.*'

'Poor thing.' I stroked her head. 'I know what you mean. But it's only a couple more days. It's all this endless uncertainty and wanting to get the horrible bit over, isn't it?'

She snuggled down under the duvet and yawned. 'Not really,' she said, with devastating honesty. 'It's because we can't collect Brian until we do.'

Patricia Murray, I thought as I dabbed on some scent, you may be able to iron a shirt in nine seconds flat, but as a child psychologist you are *terrible*.

But the real problem, in terms of 'Blessed are the Peacemakers', was that Gordon had been quite wrong about one thing. I *had* been to that restaurant before. And only last week, too. What is more, I had been there with a *man*. And what is more, more, more: I had left my umbrella there and still had not gone back to collect it. I hoped to God that no one there would recognise me or I really would be in the soup, right up to my neck in it. Gordon might want to be a little conciliatory but there was no way on earth—given the likely size of the bill at the end of the evening—that he was prepared to be that conciliatory. Worse too, it wasn't quite my umbrella I had left there. It was Gordon's. It had his name on it. I knew it had because, being a good wife, I had sewn it there, together with our phone number. He was always losing them, you see. It had seemed a good idea at the time.

*   *   *

Everyone should have at least one rich friend in their lives. The kind of friend through whom one can work out all one's decadent yearnings vicariously. The kind of friend who is so rich, and so delighted to be rich, that they are incredibly vulgar with it and bent on including the world (or, at least, their *coterie)* in their pleasure. Vanessa and Max were like that. He made his money in wine and was always gadding off here and there sampling the vintages, or whatever he had to do to keep sloshing lolly on to the huge pile he had already made. Sometimes Vanessa went with him but more often she stayed at home. *One* of their homes, that is. They had one in London, naturally, another very grand old rectory in Suffolk (which seemed, in my experience, to be the real home: Max wore jeans and kept his horses here and always sounded relaxed on the telephone, while Vanessa wore very chic tweeds and had her dogs and read novels). There was an apartment in Cannes, which I had never visited—partly because their boys were twelve and fourteen years older than Rachel and they had forgotten all about sticky fingers and slopped orange juice (if, indeed, given the nanny and the maid, they ever knew about it) and partly because Gordon, who might conceivably have paid the fare, would in no way have tolerated South of France prices.

Vanessa never cooked in London but she gave about six mammoth dinner parties a year using caterers and sometimes we were included. These were strange affairs in which one might find oneself sitting next to an archbishop or a pop star (she did an immense amount of charity work) and dining on things like tsetse fly wings in filo pastry, or salmon noses in aspic, or baby Andes bear with wild rice garni—well, not really that, but stuff that was so outrageously exotic that it might just as well have been. I had learned from those music parties in the old days that it was best not to admit to being a mother-at-home, so I became a very good listener instead and not a few indiscretions leaked into my ears during these occasions. To my bourgeois mind the most indiscreet and hung up of all public people are politicians, closely followed by ecclesiastics. All that having to appear so moral and righteous in public, I suppose. An archdeacon once told me most sorrowfully during the port and pink Tibetan goat's cheese stage that he had never felt a living woman's breast though he had stroked the odd statue in his time. It was on the tip of my tongue to offer him a quick go at one of mine but good sense prevailed.

They were odd dinners one way and another. Though very proper and top drawer and all that, in their way Max and Vanessa were splendidly eccentric. How sad, I used to feel, that of all the marriages I knew well the best two were undoubtedly theirs and Joyce and Henry's next door. The reason for this was quite damningly obvious: both couples spent very little time together.

93

They were very matter-of-fact when I told them about Gordon and me.

'Well,' Vanessa said, 'we've known you longer than Gordon so we'll blow him out and stick with you. Gordon won't mind.'

She was absolutely right but it took my breath away Why couldn't I be so straightforward? Confidence. That's what money and success breeds, if you're careful about it.

It was the combination of this eccentricity and confidence that brought me to Gigondas with a rather beautiful young man who was a complete stranger. Gordon was away and Vanessa and I were supposed to be dining out together. 'You choose the place,' she said when she rang, 'because you've got babysitters and things to think of.'

I decided on Gigondas because it was nearby and because I knew I'd never get inside it any other way and, I suppose, because I was a bit fed up with hearing how other people locally had gone there and loved it, and it would be nice— if the occasion arose—to say that I, too, had experienced its subtle atmosphere and rich cuisine. In short, I wanted to keep up with the foodie Joneses just for once. And since Vanessa paid for everything in life—including, so far as I knew, her tights and tampons—on a gold credit card, the bill was hardly to be considered.

Well, on the morning of the day we were

supposed to go there, Vanessa rang to say that she had been up all night with toothache which had proved to be an abscess.

'But we won't cancel the table,' she said. 'I'm sending you an escort instead. He's a very nice chap and I sometimes use him myself. He's quite reputable up until midnight and then after that it's up to you—'

'Vanessa!' I shrieked. 'You can't be serious!'

'Why ever not? He's an excellent conversationalist, looks pretty and his manners are impeccable. Besides, I've already paid him. The car will still pick you up at eight only it won't be me in it it'll be him instead. You may as well go, Patricia. Live a little. He really is quite, quite charming . . .'

'I can't let Rachel or the babysitter see me going off with a strange man. What on *earth* will Gordon say when he finds out?'

'You're divorcing Gordon. You're moving into your house next week. You are a free woman. You can do whatever you want. I thought that was the whole *point*.'

'Yes, but I haven't got to the stage where I can flaunt toy boys at him.'

'He's *not* a toy boy, Patricia,' she said very crisply. 'He's thirty and he's going to be a very successful actor one day. Heavens above. He's not going to make mad passionate love to you on the hall carpet. He's just going to take you out for a very pleasant meal and talk to you and listen to you and bring you back by

95

midnight. Or anything else you want . . .'

'You are joking about that last bit,' I said. 'Aren't you?'

'I don't know,' she said with her usual devastating honesty. 'If you're interested, try it and see. Anyway, he'll pick you up at eight. OK?'

I made a sort of long-drawn-out yowling down the phone which, loosely translated, said, 'I don't want to hurt Gordon, and Rachel would have a *fit*.'

'Oh, all right then. I'm not going to argue with you any more. My tooth is hurting too much. I'll arrange for him to wait for you in the restaurant. Can you get there under your own steam?' Vanessa had more or less forgotten that people drove themselves, or took buses and taxis, or even, God help them, walked.

'It's only ten minutes away. Of course I can.'

'Good. He'll be there waiting there from eight.' She sounded really irritated by now. 'And, Patricia?'

'Yes?'

'Don't, for God's sake, try to *pay* for anything.'

It was raining when I left, hence taking Gordon's umbrella with me. My heart was bumping away beneath my ribs as if I really were going out on a proper date. Even Rachel, as I kissed her good bye, said I looked giggly, which was a good interpretation of my nervousness. How *can* I have let myself be talked into this? I thought as I stumped along in the rain. When I got to the restaurant I nearly ran home, especially when I realised I didn't know what he looked like, didn't even know his name, and—what was more—I had forgotten my glasses. I couldn't put them on and peer at all the tables even if I had remembered them. 'Oh no, oh no,' I whispered as I was ushered through the door by a haughty-looking man in a braided cap.

'Mrs Murray? Ah yes,' said an even haughtier-looking woman at the desk, 'Aaron will show you to your table.'

Which Aaron, a short fat man with lots of hand movements, did, moving liquidly among all the tables until we fetched up at a small one in the corner. I was still clutching the dripping umbrella though my coat had been clawed away from me by the long red fingernails of Miss Hoity-Toity at the door.

Before me rose the most wonderful vision of smiling white teeth, brown silk-lashed eyes, graceful dinner-jacketed arm and a warm, dry handclasp, whose voice said, 'Paul. How nice to meet you. Won't you sit down?'

I crumpled into my chair, which thoughtfully in the right place thanks to Aaron, and slid the umbrella under the table.

'Patricia,' I said, and it came out in a series of staccato burps.

'I know.' He smiled. 'I am delighted to meet

you.' Pause for the brown eyes to do a little devouring—I nearly died. Only my napkin saved me from screeching out an 'ooh' as I twisted it, Victorian heroine-like, beneath the table.

'You look very beautiful tonight,' he said as he resumed his own seat. 'I hope you don't mind my saying that?'

And I could have killed him, and Vanessa, and then myself, for I blushed, and looked down and said, with the most horrendous simper, 'Oh, thank you *so* much.' And wished that I was twenty-five and single again or rich enough to pay for this sort of thing more often.

*   *   *

The point was that there was no point to it, which is what made it so enjoyable and silly and such pure delight. I wish I could turn this into a really saucy story and say that things did happen on the hall carpet afterwards—but they didn't.

Cinderella came home by midnight, still tittering at some of the funny things exchanged with the excessively handsome and—to Cinders's mind at least—quite unobtainable and just-as-well-really prince. She was left at the doorway with another warm handshake, went in, paid off the babysitter, and went to bed. All she had lost in the entire evening was Gordon's umbrella, which was easily reclaimed and not at all in the same league as a glass slipper, and some of her faintheartedness for the future, which was not . . . Successfully managing four hours of non-stop conversation with a strange man under such circumstances did quite a lot for the self-esteem. Vanessa the Fairy Godmother—what a quaint notion. All the same, as Cinders mounted the stairs, she found herself thinking, with uncharacteristic meanness, that she was glad Vanessa was blessed with a very sweet tooth.

But you can quite see why Gordon's umbrella being already at the restaurant, was a problem. Places like that remember faces and names—it is their pride and it contributes to their commercial success. Gordon's pleasure in showing off and taking me to such an exclusive setting would only be sustainable through and beyond the paying of the bill stage providing he continued to believe it was mutually virgin territory. Bad enough, God knows, if I had been there with Vanessa, but worse, infinitely worse, was the thought of him knowing I had been there with a man. Even if it was no more than a professional acquaintanceship. So I tucked up my hair on top of my head, wore the most different dress I could find and put on my glasses so that I looked as unlike the woman of last week as I could.

At least it wasn't raining when we set off, so I was spared the guilt of Gordon hunting for his umbrella. In fact, it was a beautiful golden September evening not dissimilar to that day, nearly twelve years before, when I broke the news of his impending fatherhood to Gordon. And in the same way as then, when I could think of nothing much beyond protecting my unborn baby and doing right by it, I now set off thinking that if I could keep Gordon sweet tonight then we might be friends for all the tomorrows, which would make things so very much easier between us and therefore nicer for Rachel. And, really, I couldn't think much beyond her and her needs. I was quite happy to subjugate myself entirely to those . . . For ever and always, despite Phillida's counsel. I would devote my life to being happy away from Gordon by being a good and perfect mother to Rachel. That was all there was and I was quite, and uncomplicatedly, prepared to do so.

Gordon looked at me a bit oddly as I shuffled in sideways to avoid the man in the braid cap but to my relief Miss Hoity-Toity on reception had been replaced. And we didn't get Aaron either as our table was on a different side from his patch, so all in all I could breathe a sigh of relief and let the evening go on as it would. It was quite easy not to say things like 'I had the omelette with truffles last time' and to remember to ask where the Ladies was rather than appear familiar. But when Gordon held my hand and squeezed it across the table and said, quite suddenly, 'You look very beautiful tonight—if I'm still allowed to say such things,' I found myself beginning to say that he wasn't the first to tell me such a thing in here and if I wasn't careful I'd have my head turned. I stopped myself though and I just said, 'I don't mind at all. Thank you.' I knew it wasn't really true just as I knew it wasn't really true when the pulchritudinous Paul said it—and at least with him I hadn't been bespectacled. Still, it set the tone for the evening. We were owed a bit of harmony after all the misery and I settled into it quite comfortably. We talked about the past, remembering happy times and, treading delicately so as not to apportion blame, times beyond when it all began to go wrong.

'If I'd been a bus conductor,' Gordon said, 'it would never have happened.'

'If you'd been a bus conductor we'd never have got married in the first place.'

'No?'

'Of course not. Bus conductors don't get all-expenses-paid trips to Germany'

He looked at me, genuinely puzzled. 'I don't get the connection,' he said.

'Rachel. She was conceived there. Remember?'

'Of course I remember, but what's that got to do with our getting married?'

I was going to say something harsh like 'Oh, come off it' or 'Don't be so vacuous' when I realised he meant it. 'Have you really forgotten that we got married because she was on the way?'

'We got married *sooner* certainly, but we didn't just do it because of her.' He looked up at me. 'Did we?' I didn't know what to say so I just gazed back at him. 'I mean, I *loved* you, Patsy. I loved you then, I loved you later, I love you now.'

There was a terrible lump in my throat. He wasn't drunk, he wasn't conniving, he was quite, quite genuinely telling me this thing. I took off my glasses to see him better. Those very blue eyes of his were sending a most serious message into mine. I began to feel all scrambled up inside with confused feelings of uncertainty and its oft-time twin, fear. This was a move that I had not, in any of my most percipient imaginings, considered. I suddenly realised what we were doing in that restaurant. Gordon was courting me all over again.

I said, 'Are you telling me that after everything we've done to each other—after all those things we've said and felt—after—'

He put a finger up to my lips. 'I know, I know,' he said. 'But maybe with time I can make it up to you. Maybe when I'm in one place and you're in another we can get a different perspective on things. Begin again. You are my life—you and Rachel. I don't know what I'm going to do without you, I really don't. All I'm asking you to do is to leave the door open an inch or two—a little chink. Don't close it completely, Patsy. Will you?'

What could I say? Could I say, 'You're about ten years too late'? Could I say, 'You've had an odd way of showing it'? Could I even say, 'I don't believe you. I don't feel anything for you'? I could not. He was looking so earnest, so positive, so little and crumpled in front of me that such rejoinders would have been cruel. So I said, 'I'm really sorry, for both of us—and Rachel—that it ended so badly. I really am. But I just don't see how we can bury all that history and start again—'

'Just don't close the door, that's all I ask. Don't close the door and put me out in the cold.'

There's a great deal of difference between an alcohol-induced Gordon—Gordon the plaintive, Gordon the mawkish—and what he was that night. He was fairly sober and absolutely sincere and I felt so guilty at not feeling the same way about the future. I could think of nothing better than closing the door, locking it and chucking away the key. On the other hand, I thought, that may be a temporary emotion. Perhaps, once I remove myself from him, perhaps we can start to reappraise what we have got, maybe build on it. I damped down the anger that had begun flickering at this unwonted assault on my almost-freedom and told myself not to be churlish about it, not to put on blinkers.

Gordon could very well be right. There was a big world out there and it might prove unfriendly. At least he was the devil I knew. So I smiled across at him. 'Why don't you have a brandy now, and a cigar? You deserve that at least.'

'Not at these prices, I don't,' he began, and then looked at me and stopped himself. 'You're right. I do deserve it. Just as you have deserved this kind of thing—' he gestured around the restaurant with his hand '—over the years and never got it. I see that now. It's only money after all. I should have given you more pleasures.'

Oh hell, I thought, for it was all so seductive.

The gesture had brought our waiter over and Gordon ordered his two little finales and a Cointreau for me. While we waited for them to arrive he beamed across the table at me looking happier and more relaxed than I'd seen him for years. 'I never meant to make you so unhappy,' he said. 'I suppose I just took centre stage all the time. A professional handicap. The gap between my intentions as a husband and father and the reality seems to have got out of hand.'

A sharp little needle of a thought pricked me, which was that the term 'out of hand' seemed a subdued way of referring to separation and divorce. But I didn't say that. 'Oh well,' I offered instead. 'The road to hell is paved with good intentions.'

'Hell?' he said lightly.

'Well, yes. Really it was a kind of hell all those years.'

'Oh, I don't know . . .' The waiter brought the drinks and the cigar. Gordon leaned back in his chair sipping and puffing with pleasurable relaxation. 'It wasn't really *hell*, Patsy, was it? I mean that's a bit of an exaggeration.'

'Perhaps,' I said, sipping my drink and thinking that it was. I changed the subject to him. 'How are the recordings going?' I asked. And he began to tell me.

For the next twenty minutes or so he talked, as he always could, about himself and his work. And I was relieved because anything, frankly, was better than talking about us and the future with its out-of-handness and its slightly open door. I had felt so positive before tonight. Now I just felt guilty about feeling so positive. It was as if I was unprepared to give either him, or Rachel, a chance. I will exchange the arc light for something softer and more kindly, I thought, and maybe—who knows?—maybe Gordon will be proved right. Maybe I am being too selfish, too certain. Maybe this is all going to be resolved one day and we'll get back together again. It would certainly make things much simpler. I hadn't realised until then how much fear there was in my situation. Fear of not breaking free. Fear of the freedom itself.

Oh, Gordon, I thought, looking across at him. If only you really could change. If only you really could court me and win me again. How much, *much* more satisfactory that would be. And I put out of my mind the thought that followed this one, which was that the term 'satisfactory' was a distinctly unexciting one.

When the bill came I watched my husband closely. His Adam's apple disappeared a few times and he began checking the piece of paper very thoroughly, which was exactly in keeping. But then, on realising that he was observed, he suddenly chucked it down on the plate, took out an amazing wad of ten-pound notes and said, with gay insouciance, 'So what? It's only money after all. A *lot* of money, it's true, but I think you're worth every penny.' He leaned over and squeezed my hand. 'Every penny, my darling Patsy.'

And I tried to make the smile I gave him stretch upwards from my mouth to reach my eyes.

As we got up from the table to go I felt that I had lost something. I came into the restaurant as a whole woman and it felt as if I was leaving in pieces. Gordon did things like hold my chair for me as I got up, putting his hand very gently on my arm to guide me to the lobby, and keeping up a constant cooing discourse about how much he had enjoyed tonight, how he hoped that I had too, how we should do more of this sort of thing and how—

106

given the chance—he would win me all over again as if I were a new woman in his life. I just nodded and smiled like a marionette as we made our way out and waited for our coats. There was nothing else for me to do. I couldn't argue with any of what he was saying and Florizel Street seemed suddenly to be very far away and unreal. Someone was helping me into my coat and I let them and then Gordon was holding open the door for me. We were about to step out into the night when a voice behind us said,

'Your umbrella.'

We turned and there was stocky little Aaron, looking so pleased with himself, holding the offending item out to me. Quite mechanically, I put out my hand to take it when Gordon said, 'No, no. Not ours.' And made to proceed out of the door.

'But yes,' said Aaron. 'Mrs Murray. It is yours, I think?' And puff, puff, went his rotund little chest.

'Well, er . . .' I said, not having a clue what to do and hoping that we would all be transfigured or something.

'No, we didn't bring one. You've made a mistake, I'm afraid.' This was Gordon's cheery certainty.

Aaron was clearly not going to accept the allegation. He moved nearer. The umbrella was now close to my outstretched hand.

'You left it here last week, Mrs Murray,'

said Aaron triumphantly. 'Didn't you?' And he gave Gordon a settling look.

'A case of mistaken identity, I think,' said Gordon, apparently quite tickled at being right.

'Not at all,' said Aaron, doing what I realised I had been praying he would not do and folding back the place where Gordon's name was sewn.

'Well, I'm buggered,' said my husband, going over and peering at it. 'It is mine.'

Aaron looked at me. Gordon looked at me. Even the replacement for Miss Hoity-Toity suspended looking detached and superior enough to look at me.

'Yes,' I said. 'It is.'

'I hope,' said Aaron with a little bow, 'that you enjoyed your meal tonight as much as you enjoyed your meal last week, Mrs Murray?'

Why, oh why, in the full flush of having had such a funny and foolish time with Paul the perfect last week, had I paused to say as much and so fulsomely to Aaron before I and my paid-for date left? I winced. Very fulsomely I had said it. Indeed, I had waxed lyrical about it. No wonder Aaron the professional had no doubt at all about who I was and whose umbrella it was. I had given him enough eulogies then to keep his little waiter's soul afloat for years.

Sanity surfaced sufficiently for me to look my husband directly in the eyes and say, 'Oh!

108

Ha ha. Didn't I tell you I came here with Vanessa last week? Ha ha.'

And sanity had only time to note the light of semi-belief in Gordon's eye and give me a fleeting sense of victory upheld, before the poxy little waiter said, 'Such a charming young man, your companion,' no doubt feeling he was returning the compliment for all those gastronomical eulogies I had so recklessly heaped upon him.

Gordon took the umbrella and held its neck very tightly as he stormed out into the gentle night air. He let the door swing back on me and I was rather relieved. This was, after all, more like it . . .

* * *

The next morning Rachel said, 'It didn't work, did it?'

'What?' I said.

'You and Daddy—being friends.'

'Well, I . . . er . . .'

'I heard you when you came back.'

I put my arm round her shoulders. 'We were friendly for some of the time,' I said. 'And then unfriendly for the rest. I think it will always be like that between us. You get like that with Katie sometimes, don't you?'

'Yes,' she said. 'But I never chase her into the garden with an umbrella and try to hit her.'

'Your father has a very quick temper,' I said.

'But it doesn't really mean anything. You saw that he was all right this morning.'

'When we move it will be better,' she said.

'It will,' I agreed.

'It's today we collect Brian,' she said anxiously. 'That's still going to happen, isn't it?'

'Of course. Four o'clock and he's ours.'

'And the removal men come tomorrow?'

I nodded.

'Mum?'

'Yes, my love?'

'When we *have* moved . . .'

'Mmm?' Anything, I was thinking, anything you like.

'Can Brian sleep on my bed?'

'Well, I don't know about—'

'Blimey,' she said to herself. 'You'd have thought there would be some compensations. It's not much to ask.'

And it wasn't, really, not considering everything else.

'All right,' I agreed. 'He can sleep on your bed for the first week. After that he's downstairs in the kitchen. OK?'

'OK.'

'Off to school now.'

'Right.' She got up and took her bowl out to the kitchen. When she came back there was the faintest hint of amusement and triumph about her.

'Rachel,' I said warningly. 'I really mean one

week. One week only.'

'Sure,' she said agreeably and began doing up her shoelaces. With her head bent, her face out of sight, came another question. 'Mum?'

'Mmm?'

'What's a fucking whore?'

'I'll tell you when you're older,' I said, pushing her towards the front door.

Brian slept on her bed. For one week. For two weeks. For a month. And then I forgot about it. There are some tactical points that it is not worth pursuing with children. Yes?

CHAPTER SEVEN

I saw myself as some gently ageing matriarch devoting myself singlehandedly to the upbringing of my treasured daughter. A task which would absorb my time dutifully and completely, absolving me from the need otherwise to exist. I was quite happy about that. What did I need with a social life of my own? Such a thing would be costly—clothes, tickets, babysitters—and could be threatening as well. Who knew if there was not another Gordon out there just aching to have his pristine groin attacked by flying crab claws? I had to be vigilant. If such an unlooked-for and unlikely incident had brought with it twelve years of misery, what might not other invitations and excursions bring forth? I was even nervous of taking Rachel to see the Thames Barrier in case I fell in and had to be fished out by somebody dishy.

No, no. Tea with other mothers from school, a short chat while I waited to collect her from Brownies, the odd evening out at Jo's or Lydia's. Not much more than that presented itself during the first few weeks of life singular. It is not mere mythology that a divorced woman is less desirable and less easily accommodated socially than a divorced man. I had only to think back to some of the meals I had invited friends to: somehow the men fitted in beautifully even if the numbers were uneven, while, to my shame, I had always found a spare woman worrying. I made myself very chirpy around and about, and told people that I had a hundred things to do because of the move and on the whole most peripheral friendships withered away. Presumably they were only able to deal with us as a couple. I had some sympathy with this, perhaps because it suited me—the very thought of having to work twice as hard socially now that I was alone was abhorrent. Rachel gave me my pass through life. She was, anyway, the only reason I was in this situation. If I had fouled up on everything else I could at least acquit myself honourably there. Losing those peripheral friendships was not particularly upsetting. There was nothing overtly snubbing, I mean, no one actually spat in my eye or crossed over to the other side of the street when they saw me coming, but they just ceased to stop for a chat. Our exchanges became the greetings of almost strangers: Hello, How are you, Nice day, See you, etc, etc.

This withdrawal began well before I moved to Florizel Street and, again, you could hardly blame them: it was extremely difficult while Gordon and I continued to live under the same roof. Supposing someone wanted to invite me to dinner and rang up only to find it was Gordon who answered? Or if they called round and he was there—which he quite often was—what should we talk about? The weather? That would be like having tea in a parlour containing a filled coffin and pretending it wasn't there. Also, I didn't have anything very terrible to say to explain our separation. I could hardly don sackcloth and ashes and beat myself with flails. If I had discovered him having an affair, or leading a double life, or that he was a brute, then it would have been straightforward, but I had nothing like that to offer in explanation. People didn't quite know where to hang their hat—my peg or his—and nobody likes being confused. I expect it was as a direct result of this that among some of my friends there was a definite feeling of disapproval. I had nothing to complain of that they could see and Gordon was a highly respected piece of neighbourhood cultivation while I was merely a rather dull woman-at-home. It was as if I had got a bit too big for my boots in chucking away such a glittering marital prize. Most people had rather enjoyed having an opera singer sitting at their table, but what did they want with his unremarkable wife?

And if it wasn't *that* bit of no man's land dwindling down the numbers of my pals, it was that other unforeseen emotion, perhaps the greatest killer of friendships ever: envy. A subtle piece of snubbery this, a kind of 'Why couldn't she stay down among the women like we do?' No one would have acknowledged this. Indeed, they would have been mad to unless they planned to do something about it themselves, but it was there all the same. A definitely pervasive sense of being the wilful pariah, making myself out to be a cut above the rest with my bid for—how dare she?— freedom. And freedom it was. But I had to be quite ruthless about it from the start. Right from the word go the battle lines were drawn, within hours of setting foot in that little stained-glass hallway.

After the removal men had gone and I was left alone with my cornucopia of hidden delights—to wit, tea chests I had forgotten to label, and assorted furniture looking surreal and uncomfortable in its new surroundings, and Rachel and Brian sitting in the garden looking like a poor man's trailer for *Lassie*

Come Home—I felt one of those blessed moments of sheer joy creep through me, right to my finger and toe ends. I stroked walls, looked out from each window, turned on a tap, slowly and methodically working my way around the house so that my presence had covered every part of it and made it mine. I looked down from Rachel's bedroom window and waved at her. She, still a bit pink-eyed from her earlier tears and wearing her Walkman, waved back with a smile that was cheerful enough to tell me that her little heart had been bruised today but not severely broken. And then she picked up Brian's boneless paw and made him wave it too. He put his chin on her lap and his tongue hung out on one side and there was no sense of achievement in his eyes.

'Dog,' I muttered to him through the window pane, 'if you don't spark up I'll put you on speed.' For I could foresee a time quite soon when Rachel would realise that she didn't, actually, have a father substitute *or* a dog—only a Brian who was in every particular, apart from the functions of his most westerly and most easterly tips, deceased. It was while I was thinking these thoughts and gazing contentedly from the upstairs window that Gordon arrived with a large bunch of roses and a bottle of champagne.

I couldn't believe it when I opened the front door. I mean, only hours earlier his van had taken the high road and mine had taken the low road—we'd put Rachel through the grinder of real separation—and now here he was: Back, and, what was more, back as if he had every *right* to be. And clutching in his hands the kind of tributes he'd have swallowed shattered glass before providing in the old days.

'I thought I would just pop over,' he said with the kind of beaming smile I had not been privileged to see for years, if ever. 'And see you both in properly.'

'Gordon,' I said, not letting him pass. 'This is not the right thing to do. This is my house, my *home*. I've got to spend some time in it first before I invite anyone else in.' Only extreme diplomacy kept me from clouting him over the head with the champagne bottle and shoving those monstrous hot-house roses up his nose.

'It also,' he said, still smiling but not so cheerily, 'represents the home of my daughter.'

'Yes, I know. But it won't do her *any* good to have another emotional upheaval tonight.'

'But what about me?' he said, not unfairly. 'I miss her already. Have you any idea what it's like knowing she's not around any more?'

Dear old guilt, familiar friend, shook me warmly by the heart. I wavered. What right had I to keep him from his daughter? It was only the less familiar friend, common sense, who nudged between guilt and me and advised me to stick to my guns: if not for my sake, then for Rachel's and the future status quo.

'I know this is hard,' I said, 'and I know that it would help you to see her now, but it honestly wouldn't help her. She's just about getting over the removal vans this morning.'

'But I haven't,' he said.

'I know. Neither have I, but we're adults and we can rationalise.'

'You can,' he said. 'You can rationalise, deprogramme feelings, because basically you haven't got any.'

Getting angry was not going to help, though I did vow as I counted up to ten that if he said that I had no feelings once more I would impose penalties. After all, if he thought I was the archetypal unfeeling bitch, then I might just as well have the pleasure of acting like it.

As gently as I could, I said, 'Give her a few days. After all, she's coming to you for the whole of next weekend. Don't let's get her confused already by changing arrangements. We agreed stability was important . . .'

'*You* agreed stability was important. I didn't.'

I nearly laughed out loud. Poor Gordon. He was always doing that. In an effort to be as contumacious as possible he ended up in impossibly perverse corners from which there was almost never an honourable way out. In the old days I would have pounced but there was no point now. What I needed—what we all

117

needed—was a bit of calm.

'Leave it till the weekend, will you? Pick her up on Friday as arranged and bring her back after tea on Sunday. It'll be much better for her to stick to that arrangement.'

'Ah!' he said, looking slightly shifty.

'Gordon,' I said, warningly. I knew what was coming.

'Well—'

'Well, *nothing.* If you let her down at the first hurdle I'll kill you.'

I think I meant it.

'The thing is I've just been asked to do something on the Saturday night so I thought that I could bring her back a bit early—'

'Like a whole twenty-four hours early.'

'You said I ought to get my social life sorted out.'

'I know I said that. But I didn't say you should dump your daughter in order to do it.'

'Can't I come in?' he said. My voice had risen and we were still on the doorstep.

'No,' I said. 'You can't.'

'Look. I'm not dumping her. I'll have her on Friday as arranged, and all day Saturday, and then bring her back at about six. That's all right, isn't it?'

'Bring her back where?'

'Well, here, of course.'

'There's no point in doing that.'

'Why?'

'Because I won't be here.'

His jaw fell open. He looked at me angrily. 'And just where are you going?' he said.

'I don't have to tell you that.'

'*More* paid-for men?'

'Certainly not! Though I wouldn't mind, if I could afford them. No. I just won't be in, that's all. So you can't possibly bring her back here.' I was beginning to get a little weary of all this drama so I added, quite reasonably, 'Why don't you do what we used to sometimes and take her with you? You could bed her down. You know that she's no trouble if you give her a book to read and a few treats.'

'I can't bloody well bed her down for God's sake. I'm going on a riverboat party.'

Oh dear. I had to grab the roses very quickly and press my face into them. The very idea of Gordon at a riverboat party was so funny, though I'm not sure why. 'That's unusual,' I managed from behind the floral tribute.

'Some of Michael's students from the College of Music are giving him a farewell do—'

'And he's asked you? After what you did to him over the flat?'

'I told him the balance of my mind was disturbed at the time, which it was.'

'Still is,' I said, too late to think not to.

'Patsy,' he said. 'You have no right to keep me out here and away from my daughter. Let me in at once.'

'I have every right. And, anyway, your

daughter is not in the house.' That was perfectly true.

'Where is she?'

'She's out with Brian.'

'Who?'

'The dog.'

Your substitute, actually, I wanted to say.

Very much in character Gordon took back the roses and, still grasping the bottle, marched off down the path. He paused at the gate with his chest heaving slightly. 'And you are absolutely adamant about Saturday night?'

I nodded. 'Bitch and whore,' he said simply.

'Arsehole,' I said gamely, and felt instantly better.

When he reached the pavement, and because of the instant betterment, I was moved to be kind. 'You can try Mrs Pomfret,' I called. 'She may be free to babysit and she drives herself home afterwards.'

'What's her number?'

'It's in your Filofax. You'll find I've put all the things you're likely to need in there for you. Including my new telephone number.' I began closing the door. 'And I'd be obliged if you would use it before visiting in future.'

The heaving chest metamorphosed into his usual fulsome panting, not surprisingly, and I just had to add, before the door closed completely, 'Mind you, she doesn't come cheap, but, then, you've got to learn how to stump up in future, haven't you?'

Through the crack in the door I saw him weigh up the pros and cons of chucking the champagne at me and come to the decision that, at fifteen quid a bottle, it would be foolish. Instead he chucked the roses but at least after that he went. It took some minutes before I got the shaking under control and then I strolled out into the garden.

'Hungry?' I said to Rachel.

'Starving,' she said.

We tucked Brian up on a blanket in the corner of the kitchen where he gave a pretty good impression of a dying Landseer stag, and trotted off to the pizza place. And if appetite is considered an indicator of emotional stability, Rachel was to be congratulated on her rock-solid balance.

*   *   *

That first weekend alone was the harbinger. I saw Rachel off into Gordon's arms and from then on I played house, unpacking the tea chests and discovering my possessions all over again. When I told Gordon that I would be out on Saturday night I was perfectly truthful, except that I was going nowhere that I could not have taken Rachel if I had wanted. Jo, Lydia and I were taking advantage of the absence of Lydia's husband Dutta to converge at Lydia's house for wine and a kebab takeaway. This may not sound like desirable high living but it was exactly what I wanted to do. And therefore, given that I would not be setting foot out of my new front door until that night, it seemed silly to bother to wash or dress or even brush my hair before then. Slobbery is a temporary giving up of social mores and, providing it remains temporary, there is no better way to unwind. By the time six o'clock chimed from inside one of the tea chests upstairs, I had got jam in my hair, dripped tea down my front and my hands were filthy from digging about in the boxes. My pyjamas had taken on a certain streaked and crusty quality over their lemon-coloured cotton and the fronts of my bare feet were grey from kneeling on newsprint. I describe this detail for reference, for when the knock on the back door came I had no thought at all of how I looked. I was as happy as a pig in muck and *quite* at home being so.

CHAPTER EIGHT

It did not occur to me as I picked my way through the assorted flotsam cluttering the route from dining room to kitchen that there was something odd about a knock at the back door. It was only when I passed the corpselike Brian (with some irritation at his complete lack of interest in the approach of strangers) that it occurred to me what was wrong. There was no back entrance to Florizel Street. There were however two shadows on the frosted glass of the back door. Curiouser and curiouser, I thought, as I opened it. I felt pretty safe since it was September, early evening and, anyway, one of the shadows was thin and female and the other was squat and child-sized.

The woman was a little younger than me and looked exactly as I imagined I would have come to look if I had married Mr Pownall. She was slim and upright with that kind of well-bred straight fair hair swept off the forehead and held in an alice band. Her eyes were bright, her cheeks a healthy pink, and she wore no make-up. On her face was stamped the unmistakable smile of one at her duty. She wore a navy-blue frock, of course, with cap sleeves, buttons down the front, and a skirt that neither clung nor swirled. Her toe nails were clean and unpainted in her neat leather sandals.

Next to her was what I can only describe as a pudding of a child. Female, though not dramatically so, about two years older than Rachel and about two stones heavier. She had one of those smug, unchildlike expressions on her face. My instant thought was: spoilt; borne out as I took in the tubby body encased in a Disney World T-shirt and the tubby legs in their Bermudas. She had on her feet a particular brand of trainer that was flavour of the month with the kids around about, which cost the earth and which I had had to tell Rachel that she could not have. The child was holding two Mars bars, one of which had already been attacked. Finding the whole rather obscene I returned my gaze to the woman.

'Penelope Webb,' she said, holding out her hand. I was about to shake it when I realised it held a fruit cake. 'We thought we'd just pop through and say welcome. You don't mind?'

She kept her expression quite solidly bright though I could see her eyes flickering up and down my person. I realised, suddenly, what a state I was in. I moved the Rowlandson print up a bit to hide most of the tea and whatnot that decorated my chest.

'Putting up your pictures, I see,' she said cheerfully, which tailed off somewhat as she took in the kind of image before her. Her jaw sagged momentarily but righted itself.

'Couldn't find a hammer,' I said quickly, shaking the axe.

She stepped back a little way, understandably, and the child, who was also staring at it, Mars bar in her mouth, goggle-eyed, stuck out one pudgy finger and traced the edge of its head.

'Alison,' said the woman nervously, 'don't touch, dear. Say hello to our new neighbour.'

Alison gave me a bold and silent look and then shoved past me and went on into the kitchen.

'I'm sorry,' she continued. 'I don't know your name?'

I was desperately torn between removing the lurid picture from her gaze and keeping it there to hide the state of my pyjamas beneath. Both options had their shock value. I looked at her quite blankly.

'Oh, er . . . it's um . . .' What the hell was my name? 'Patricia. Patricia Murray. Come in, won't you? I'm afraid I . . . er . . .' I gestured down my body with the axe, noting with horror how its filthy yellow robery culminated in a set of filthy toes. 'I'm in a bit of a pickle as you can see, unpacking and whatnot.'

She gave me another bright smile—she was very good at them—and offered me the cake again. This time, managing to hold both picture and tool in one grip, I took the gift. 'How nice,' I said. I was still puzzled about how they had got here and looked past her shoulder to see if a back gate had suddenly materialised.

'Hope you don't mind,' said Penelope Webb, 'but we came through the fence. The Gibsons never minded. They kept it like that so that Bulstrode could roam free.'

'Bulstrode?' I said, imagining some fabulous creature with horns and swinging tail, why, I don't know.

'Our rabbit,' said the lady. 'Well, Alison's really.' And she stepped through the door.

The child was running a chocolaty finger over my refrigerator as if, it occurred to me, she would like to get inside and plunder its contents.

Penelope said, 'Don't do that, Alison,' in a mechanical sort of a way, to which the child did not respond.

And then suddenly the lady gave a little shriek and stood back, both hands up as if someone held a gun to her. 'My God!' she said. 'You've got a *dog*!'

'That's torn it,' said the child, ceasing her disgusting finger painting.

'Oh,' I said carelessly, looking down on the unmoving pile that was Brian. 'Don't worry about him. He's sort of dead.'

Children, as we all know, have a deep interest in death and Alison was no exception. She went straight over to Brian and pushed him with her toe while her mother looked on aghast. Brian, clearly thinking that this kind of treatment was more like it, opened his eyes and whimpered, while she-who-had-been-aghast let out another little shriek, clutched her navy bosom and backed into the garden.

The child said, 'No he's not,' rather disappointedly.

'It was just a figure of speech,' I said damping down a desire to do the same thing to her with my filthy toes. To the mother, cowering by the kitchen door, I said, 'It's just a joke,' and shrugged, which had the unfortunate result of my dropping the cake. It broke into three crumbly pieces and Penelope Webb added a veneer of huffiness to her dog-fearing gaze. It was at this point that Brian decided to show his maximum effort to date. He sort of belly-slid out of his box and began nosing at the cake. He didn't actually eat it or anything sensible, just pushed it about a bit.

'Oh God,' I said. 'I *am* sorry.'

'I can't stand dogs,' wailed the woman, moving even further away. Behind her I noticed a large white thing on my flower bed, very fluffy, nibbling at the weeds.

'Oh,' I said, thankful for a change in direction. 'Is that Bulstrode? He's lovely . . .'

Then all hell really did break loose.

The child, taking its lead from its mother, gave a great yell and raced past me to scoop up the surprised-looking bunny rabbit. It sat in her arms looking about as daft as any living thing could, with a little trail of greenery floating around its twitching nose.

'Quick, quick, Alison,' called her mother. 'Take him home. *Quickly* now, before the dog gets him . . .'

'You really don't have to worry about Brian,' I said. 'He's got absolutely no instincts of any kind, certainly not—ho ho—hunting ones—'

It was just as I said this that Brian raised his head from its cake-snuffling activities, gave a fair interpretation of the Bisto kids, and charged past me, past Penelope Webb, and jumped with the grace of a Russian pole vaulter right up to Alison's shoulder, pushing at Bulstrode with his paws as he went down. Down fell the child, and I saw the rabbit, which she gamely clung on to, squeezed almost flat beneath her. Its face looked in danger of exploding and its eyes were popping wildly. Brian, eyes aglow with the thrill, stood hopefully nearby wagging his tail and pawing at the ground pleadingly.

'You'll *kill* it if you squash it any more,' I said, throwing down the axe and the Rowlandson and running to Bulstrode's rescue. It was only as I leapt on to the path that I realised I was shoeless and the gravel was sharp.

'Shit!' I yelled, feeling something gouge its way into the soft underside of my toe. 'Shit! Oh, *shit!*'

Penelope Webb's healthy complexion was considerably ruddier by now.

'Alison,' she said icily. 'Take Bulstrode next door. This minute.' Even the child could tell that her mother meant this one, and she obeyed, limping off through the two-plank opening in the fence, arm grazed, T-shirt muddied, trainers scuffed. The rabbit bobbed over her shoulder as she wobbled off.

Brian followed her a little way and then perhaps a kind of embarrassment overcame him because he suddenly turned round, resumed his head-down, slumped defeatism, and returned to his bier in the kitchen. Penelope Webb and I watched him warily as he made a path straight through the lumps of cake and resettled himself.

My foot was hurting so much that it was impossible to be more than peremptory. 'No harm done,' I said through gritted teeth. 'I'm sorry it shocked you. It certainly shocked me— he's never done anything remotely like that before, never.'

She relaxed very slightly . . . 'How long have you had him?'

'A week,' I said.

. . . And tensed up again. She began to move sideways towards the hole in the fence speaking as she went. 'I hope you will keep him on your side because if he gets through to us . . .' she shuddered. 'Well, I hope you will make sure that he does *not*.'

My foot, plus a certain sense of unfairness, caused me to answer this in a less than placatory fashion. 'Well, if you'd keep your rabbit to yourselves we wouldn't have the problem.'

'Our rabbit,' she said, half in half out of the open planking, 'is no trouble. There was nothing remotely like this in the whole time the Gibsons lived here. People shouldn't have dogs in London.'

'Well, what about bloody rabbits then?' I yelled, limping towards the gap through which, like Alice, she had just departed. 'It's hardly nature in the raw round here. At least dogs act as deterrents, there's a place in the city for a guard dog. All rabbits want to do is breed.' The planks were slid across the gap.

Penelope Webb's voice rang out quite firmly now she was safe. 'If there is any more trouble—if your dog does any more attacking—I shall tell the police and he will be put down!'

'And if your Bulstrode so much as nibbles one blade of grass over here I'll, I'll . . .' I looked for guidance, saw the Rowlandson, saw the tool next to it and managed, 'I'll chop his head off.'

The noise of a door banging indicated that she was now beyond my range. I went and sat on the kitchen step and lifted my heel to inspect the wound which was horrible to look at: dirty, bleeding and lumpy with grit, and it throbbed. Tears spilled down my cheeks and I just sat there, clutching my foot and sort of poking at it tenderly and feeling totally wretched. I sat there for quite a while doing this with great, heaving, chunky sobs, the kind that you can't control. I was probably crying for everything and I decided not to fight it.

In *Lassie Come Home*, the dog would have sidled up to its owner and put a friendly paw on her arm, whined in sympathy, and probably licked the wound. The owner would have stroked his silken ears, said something like,

'Oh, Lassie, you are my only comfort,' and brushed away her tears with a brave hand, ready to do battle with life once more, thanks to her canine pal.

Brian simply farted in his semi-comatose state, reached round to lick his anus, and went back to being a breathing piece of Co-op gingersnap. So much for the canine myth. On balance I suppose I was lucky. God knows what he would have transferred to me via his tongue if he had lived up to the legend. The thought made me smile through the tears—and then laugh. How on earth could I have ended up shouting through the palings at someone in defence of dogs? Especially that gutless halfwit? A place in the city indeed. Did I really say that? A guard dog? Brian? I could just see him as a night prowler crept through the house. 'Come on in,' he would say. 'But be quiet. I've got a lot of slumping to get on with before morning . . . The mistress is upstairs asleep; if you're going to rape her keep the noise down. Oh, and by the way, her one good piece of jewellery is kept in the blue jar on the mantelpiece . . . Snore, snore, snore . . .'

*   *   *

Still, it gave us a laugh that night as we sat together on Lydia's carpet.

'It's a shame,' said the pragmatic Jo, 'that you've wrong-footed your neighbours. They

131

can be useful if you're on your own.'

'I think I'd rather keep my distance from people like that.'

'All the same,' Lydia said, 'there might have been times when they could have helped you out. Taking in parcels, having Rachel in an emergency, that kind of thing.'

'I know,' I said. 'But honestly, she's not my type . . .'

Jo gave a great hoot of laughter. 'We weren't suggesting you went to bed with her.'

'Just let her have Rachel while you went to bed with somebody else.' Lydia joined in the mirth. (We'd had a couple of glasses by then.)

Somewhat prissily I said, 'I can assure you, under no circumstances do I plan anything like that—'

'Get away with you,' said Jo.

'I mean it. I mean it *ab-so-lutely*. I'm just going to concentrate on living my life solo and bringing up Rachel as best I can. If I can achieve harmony within these tenets I shall be more than content.'

'Smuggins,' said Jo. 'Just you wait. Someone will come along sometime and *pow!*'

'Rubbish,' I said, sipping daintily and looking at her severely. 'After Gordon I've had quite enough. Rachel and the house will take up most of my time. And anyway, I've got a job.'

That shut them up. I leaned back, still prissily sipping, while they made suitably strangled noises.

'What?'

'How?'

'Where?'

'When?'

'And more to the point, how much?'

After half a second I gave up the pleasures of looking mysterious and superior. 'I'm an Assistant Credit Controller.'

'Ooh,' they gasped satisfactorily.

'I just went to an agency in the High Road.'

'Clever you.'

'It's local. At a small company that sells computers.'

'Boring. But solid.'

'Quite.'

'Money?'

'Four hours a day, five days a week, nine thousand pounds a year.'

'Real money.'

'*Real* money.'

'And you might meet someone there. A man, I mean,' this from Lydia.

'No chance. Assistant Credit Controller really means bookkeeper. And I share an office with a past-retirement Mr Harris, who's got a hairy nose and—as he told me during the interview—angina.'

'Oh God,' said Jo. 'She's going to end up with a computer salesman.' She put her hand out and patted my shoulder. 'Never mind. We'll still welcome you.'

'I am *not* looking for a man. And I am *not* going to end up with what you said. I am just going to earn enough to live on and live—*sans* Gordon, with Rachel—in my own little house. That is all it's about. OK?'

I looked at them defiantly. They looked at me solemnly.

'Understood,' Jo said.

'No men whatsoever,' said Lydia.

I nodded. 'Well,' I added, 'not unless someone like Paul comes my way again. Which, by my *computing* . . .'

'Already in the parlance, please note,' said Jo.

'Is about four million to one.'

'So you don't need Penelope Webb.'

'Exactly'

'And *anyway*—' Jo burst out laughing '—you can always leave Rachel with me instead when the time comes.'

Fortunately for her, my glass, which had contained cheap Soave up to that point, was now empty. So my gesture of chucking it over her head did little physical damage.

When I got home I walked about the house for a bit, revelling in its freedom and the pleasure of having had a nice, uncomplicated, totally enjoyable evening out with my female friends.

'Who needs more?' I asked Brian.

He opened one eye and yawned. A very appropriate gesture.

CHAPTER NINE

I was quite happy being single and sexless. I really felt that after all those years of emotional bruising—the extent of which was only apparent once I had moved away from it—I couldn't risk my happiness, and Rachel's, by getting even slightly involved with anyone else. Gordon, on the other hand, got himself involved with someone straight away. Which was a great relief from my point of view. Gordon the virile pursuer of Woman was infinitely preferable to Gordon the dejected outcast.

When he delivered Rachel home on that first Sunday—a couple of hours earlier than arranged—I knew something was up. He came in looking like the proverbial cat and made no deprecating remarks as I showed him round the house. If not for the former, then for the latter, I should have guessed that something had occurred to make him very happy indeed.

We had a cup of tea in the kitchen and while Rachel was in the other room doing her piano practice, out it all came.

'You're early,' I said in a slightly accusatory voice. On the one hand I did not want to create any further bad odour between us, on the other I didn't want him to think he could trim the time whenever he felt like it.

'Yes,' he said. 'Sorry.' But there was no contrition there at all. Only more preen and cream.

I could see he was dying to tell me something. 'How was Rachel?' I asked.

'Fine,' he said. 'She seems remarkably stoical about everything. Takes after me there.'

That was too much. 'She has had lunch I suppose?'

'Oh, yes. I took her to a hamburger place.' He held up his hand as I was about to speak. 'And don't start saying that I'm feeding her crap. I'm not exactly brainless you know. She *is* my daughter too. A half-pounder plus salad and chips strikes me as a well-balanced meal.'

I couldn't deny the argument.

He looked at me wickedly. 'Mind you,' he said, 'I'm not so sure about the strawberry milkshake and the chocolate nut sundae, but as I said to her, anything for my little girl.' There was a deal too much truth behind the teasing. Here it is, I thought, the father as Santa Claus syndrome. It irritated me and I had to suppress a very strong desire to say so. I looked up. Gordon was watching me very closely. I cleared my brow and smiled at him. I knew that look, it was the hopeful terrier waiting for the fight to begin. So I said, 'Did you use Mrs Pomfret last night?' by way of an alternative.

I knew immediately what he was going to say. I knew by the light in his eyes, the set of his jaw, the drawing in of his stomach muscles. Someone had sparked off the Tarzan in him. 'Yes,' he said. 'Thank you. And just as well—' pause for tea cup, in the background Rachel was tinkling away most beautifully at an Air by Bach '—because it really took me out of myself. It's very beautiful moving up river on a September night. First the sunset, the dying golden light then gradually, the moon . . .'

Could this be my husband? Or had Shelley insinuated himself round my table while my back was turned? 'The dying golden light?' 'Gradually the moon?'

'What's her name?' I said.

'Miranda,' he said looking maliciously pleased. 'Does it bother you?'

'Well, I'm not going to chase you round the garden with an umbrella saying you're a fucking whore, if that's what you mean.'

'Sorry about that,' he had the grace to say.

'No, it doesn't bother me,' I said truthfully.

His look got more wicked. 'She's a student, in her final year. Twenty-one. Not bad, eh?' He leaned back giving his impression of the Cheshire Cat Rampant.

'I don't know,' I said resisting punching him on the nose by a hair's breadth. 'She might have greasy hair and acne.'

'I can assure she hasn't. She's gorgeous.'

I believed him.

'Anyway,' he went on, 'I think I deserve some pleasure.' If he had left it at that I might have had some sympathy. But he went on to add, 'After what you've done.' And he made a disgusting stab at humour by saying, 'Life in the old dog yet? eh?'

I conjured up the image of Brian with Gordon's face superimposed, which made me feel a whole lot better. And I suddenly remembered something. I got up smiling. 'Gordon,' I said, 'would you like some cake?'

He looked very surprised, as indeed he might.

'Well, yes, please—'

I went over to the bench and found the bag containing the swept-up bits of Penelope Webb's fruit extravaganza (my rubbish bin was too full to receive it *pro tem*). I took out the largest piece and, with my back to Gordon, sort of moulded it back into shape a bit and pulled out any recognisable detritus like dog hairs and garden dirt. Sitting on a plate it looked quite acceptable so I turned round and presented it to him. The pleasure I felt as I watched him devour it, remembering Brian's nose scuffling about amongst its ruins, was sweet. If I hadn't needed to maintain some kind of harmony for Rachel's sake I would have told him, once he had finished it, what I had done. Not quite as good as Titus' offering of stewed offspring to Tamora, but not bad in the circumstances.

'Very nice,' he said. 'I must be off now. Got a date.' And he winked.

I had good cause to be grateful to the non-acned Miranda because that first doorstep scene between Rachel and Gordon was far less emotional than it might otherwise have been. They kissed and hugged easily and naturally and Gordon went off with a whistle and a wave.

Rachel said as we came in, 'You do both seem happier than you used to. I just wish it didn't have to be because we all live in different places.'

'I know,' I said, 'but it can't be any other way now.'

'Mrs Pomfret said that I was better off than all the starving children in India whose parents *were* still living together.'

'She's probably right,' I said.

'She said the same thing ages ago when I sprained my ankle roller-skating.'

'It's just her way of being sympathetic.'

'Anyway, she let me stay up and watch the telly with her.'

'You see,' I said. 'There *are* compensations.'

'And this is the best one,' she said, kneeling down in front of Brian. 'I don't know what I'd do if this one went as well.'

A shiver ran down my spine. There was a profound quality in the way she said it that told me to take it very seriously. *I* might find that soggy scrap repulsive, but to Rachel he was succour indeed. Mending the fence went to the top of my list of priorities. Penelope

Webb's scrubbed skin and innocent hair-band belied the iron in her soul—I knew the type. The thought of Brian being dragged off and exterminated with Rachel breaking her heart in the background was genuinely frightening. She had, as far as I could see, accepted the situation of our lifechange as inevitable and something that had to be got on with, and while things remained on an even keel she would continue to do so. God knows what that half-baked dimwit from Battersea had brought to her—a release for some of the love she had for Gordon and could not give him while they were apart perhaps? An object to be pitied, something much worse off than her? Like Mrs Pomfret's starving children in India? Whatever it was, it was good, and it needed preserving.

*   *   *

Later that night when Rachel was in the bath I told her what had happened with the Webbs next door.

'Does she go to your school?' I asked. 'I haven't seen her before.'

'No. She goes to boarding school. It's not fair. I'm already back and she's still got a week of holiday left.'

'That's the difference between state and private. You pay more to go private and you get less time at school.'

'Can I go private?' she said yearningly.

'You certainly can *not*,' I said. 'Anyway, how do you know so much about her?'

'We talked through the fence. She's got a rabbit.'

'Yes,' I said. 'I know.'

'She said they hate dogs.'

'What did you say?'

She laughed and gave me quite an evil look. 'I said we *ate* rabbits. Get it?'

I like to think my daughter's wit and sense of humour stem directly from me.

'She said if our dog ever went into their garden they'd shoot it. But they couldn't, could they?'

'Of course not.'

'But they do shoot dogs if they bite people, or sheep, don't they?'

'Yes,' I said. 'But not if they bite rabbits.'

'We'd better get the fence done right away,' she said.

'I'm going to.'

'And *promise* me when I'm not here you'll make sure Brian doesn't get into trouble.' I assured her I would.

Why, oh why, I thought, couldn't she have selected a canary as a father substitute? Surely that would have been more appropriate given his calling.

I received a telephone call from La Webb the following evening, in which she basically said that she had registered a complaint with

141

the police about Brian attacking her daughter and that, frankly, the best thing would be for us to get rid of him altogether. *She*, for one, would not be happy until we had done so. I called up all my dignity, which is not much, and said I was sorry her daughter had been startled but that it had only been fun, and that, so far as I was concerned, providing Bulstrode stayed in his own patch, harmony would be restored. She, with equal dignity and a certain threatening undertone, agreed. Soon after that they made a wire run for their beloved Bulstrode and he could be seen from our back bedroom window either hunched like the archetypal Easter bunny or hopping around idiotically within it. I breathed a sigh of relief. With their protective measures, and our fence now mended, I could at least relax about *that* item of responsibility. I had plenty of others to take on board. Some, like the new job, of my own making; others, like friendly attempts to pair me off with people, not of my making at all. But at least Brian and Bulstrode were out of my hair. And Gordon was sort of tidied up. All I had to do for the next bit of my lifetime was keep on a level. And that didn't seem to be too onerous a task.

CHAPTER TEN

Mr Harris was a sort of human version of Brian, really. He didn't move around much and had very watery brown eyes which, as far as I ever saw, were devoid of thinking light except when the challenge of sums was upon him. He enjoyed having angina very much and talked about it quite often in between the heady moments of real office activity. I gave him my full concentration when he began on this topic since it held a fascinating piece of by-play which I loved to watch: the moment a heart-valve thought came to him he would begin to twist the hairs from his right nostril with his left finger and thumb and keep this going for as long as angina moved him. I suppose it was a kind of comfort zone.

I wore very sensible clothes to work, skirts and jumpers and flat shoes, with just the tiniest hint of femininity like a pair of ear-rings or a scarf to break the monotony. This instinctual approach proved to be correct for, as he later told me, my predecessor had been considerably my junior, blonde, highly scented and annoyingly familiar with him. She also, it seemed, had little sensitivity where his health was concerned and used to flirt with the sales reps very loudly.

'What happened to her?' I asked.

'She married our sales director,' he said, rather mournfully. 'And left the books in a shocking state when she went.'

'Tut, tut,' I said.

'Indeed,' he replied. And then, fixing me with his wet eyes, he said, 'It was really for that reason I chose a mature woman for this post. One who could just keep her head down and not be sidetracked by, er, that kind of thing. Office romances are quite debilitating, don't you think?' Up went the hand to the nostril. 'For me especially it is important to have calmness all around me. Let the others out there—' removal of hand fractionally to indicate the door which led to the ordinary mortals who thraped for the company '—indulge in horseplay if they must, but in here I do need and like peace.'

'I am here to do a job, Mr Harris,' I said, covering the strange feeling of I don't know quite what that came over me at the description of being a mature woman devoid of horseplay, and I bent my head back to the accounts thinking, Money. That is all I am here for. Money. I can stand anything—even being a lackthreat—if I can continue to earn a crust.

Of course there were the occasional linkups between the world of Jarndyce and Jarndyce and the world of Hi-Tech Computerised Office Systems. Attempts to use some of our coffee when they had run out (certainly not, Miss Brettle), or the occasional cheery, bearded face (why do all computer salesmen wear grey suits and have beards?) saying 'Have you heard the one about' (No, Mr Harding, and I do *not* think we would wish to . . .). But, best of all, the thing that penetrated the soft inner flesh of our private heart like no other was the expenses claims. Bearded, grey-suited men would appear in endless rows, summoned by the hairy-nostrilled one to be cut down to size, reduced to little piles of ashes, by his mighty logic. Then he would lean back in his chair, twiddling away, and look so satisfied and happy that I thought, really, it would be churlish of they-of-the-beards-and-grey-suits *not* to fiddle their expenses.

On the whole, I quite liked working there and, despite Jo's and Lydia's predictions, there was never the remotest possibility of my being hijacked by any of these champions of software. Mr Harris now—well, the thought did cross my mind, as we sat opposite each other morning after morning, that it might be fun to suddenly launch myself on him and declare uncontainable passion, just to see what he might do about it. But really this was merely my version of making paper planes to pass the time. And with his heart I might be needing Mr Pownall to represent me on a charge of manslaughter. All the same, I was glad, as with the solicitor, that he could not read my mind. Mature and without horseplay indeed. It just so happened that he was right.

*　　　*　　　*

Rachel returned to school. We did quite a bit of crying together around her bedtime—she for her loss of the family as she both knew and wanted it, me for my guilt (there is no logic to this disease) for having made the wound. Quite often she rang Gordon just before bedtime and quite often he was out. The non-poxed Miranda was leading him a lively dance and we were all the better for it. On the occasions Rachel did manage to speak to him she came away quite distraught, sobbing for herself and sobbing for her father—Gordon laid it on pretty thick on these occasions—but I could not very well accuse or deprecate him. He was coping in his own way too and all I could do was soothe her from the shadows. Phillida just said Time, time, time, and I knew with a rock-hard sense of certainty that she was right. Brian, for his sins, drew out a lot of the feelings that Rachel might otherwise have kept to herself: he represented the new, the weak, the one who needed to be cared for (though not in his own opinion) and gave her an anchor point for her separateness from her father. As the weeks went on the bedtime tears diminished, and the routine of weekend visits and ordinary daily life became an established and easy pattern.

Rachel drew a lot of kudos from having a mother who went out to work and who turned up at the school gates looking smart and dull (on the whole children are a conservative lot where their parents are concerned—fashionable short skirts and silly hairstyles might make mothers feel pacey and in the swim but it makes their offspring very embarrassed indeed). I was much applauded for below-knee pleated skirts and sensibly tied-back hair, but the spin-off from this was that I got very freaky at the weekends. If there was any residual hope that a rapport might be established with the Webbs next door, this was absolutely vanquished by my polka-dot jump suit and assorted goes at the hair gel. My weekends alone were wonderful and I accepted any invitations that came my way with a pleasurable lack of desperation. If Jo and I went to see a film, that was good. If I was asked out to dinner I went—and enjoyed it—but I was not at all lonely emotionally and was never tempted to pick up on the odd spare man who might be floating about.

Vanessa and Max invited me to one of their absurd dinner parties and she sent me over a dress to wear for the occasion. 'I can't be seen too often in the same thing,' she said when she telephoned. 'And it's much more your colour than mine. If you don't like it, you don't need to wear it. But I think you will.'

It arrived in a Daimler (a *Daimler!*) and was handed to me by a man in a grey uniform who called me madam. Things like that make an amazing impression on me still. I took it out of its tissue paper and I knew that it had never been worn. Vanessa would never have bought such a thing for herself—if not for the style, which was a velvet bodice with an extremely silly yellow taffeta frou-frou skirt, then for the colour. I wore yellow well, she never could, nor would try. No. She had bought it for me. You see what I mean about having the occasional rich friend? Just wonderful.

I rang her to thank her and she couldn't *quite* keep the delight out of her voice that the dress pleased me. I didn't embarrass her by saying I recognised brand-newness when I saw it. Instead I asked her—wickedly, but without genuine intent—if she had also arranged the beautiful Paul as well as the beautiful frock. There was a pause and then she said, 'I could arrange that, if that's what you'd like. Or have you got a man you would like to bring?'

'Good God, no,' I said. 'And I was only joking about Paul too. Please don't hire him again. I might get carried away this time.'

'Oh, Patsy,' she said. 'Why on earth *don't* you? I mean, what is the point of not? I wouldn't have thought that Paul was really your type but you could have a go—'

'Vanessa!' I shrieked, both amused and shocked. 'I was *joking.*'

'I thought you probably were,' she said crisply. 'We'll send the car for seven-thirty.'

'Great,' I said. 'And one small question?'

'Yup?'

I could tell she was already doing something else in her head. 'What is this thing I'm coming to?'

'It's a dinner and dance.' She laughed. 'Think of it as that, my plebeian friend.'

'It's a bloody ball, isn't it?' My knees turned to jelly.

'We call them balls in the trade.' She laughed again. 'But I don't want to frighten you. I can tell you're not ready for balls yet . . .'

Vanessa can be quite raunchy when she chooses.

'Oh, blimey. I've never been to one.'

'Well, just think of it as the office do.'

'Where is it?'

'Why don't you just get in the car and think of it as a mystery tour?'

'Vanessa . . .' I said warningly, trying to stop the wobbling in my joints.

'Oh, very well, it's at the Dorchester but don't let that worry you. It's quite a homely venue really. They're not a bit stuck up or anything.'

My voice had become a squeak. 'Eee, eee,' I went.

'By the way,' she said. 'Have you got *shoes?*'

That brought down the octaves. 'No, but I can get some.'

'Sure?'

'Quite sure,' I said with dignity.

'Well, make sure they're roomy. You're expected to dance, you know.'

I spent about three days' wages on some black suede pumps and felt much better at having contributed my own persona to the proceedings. Up to a point one can be taken over by one's friends' largesse, but after that you have to assert yourself or you just become a cipher. Lydia lent me a black evening bag and a glittery black shawl which was a bit poncy but would have to do. Mrs Pomfret thought I Looked a Treat, and Rachel thought I showed too much knee, but there we are—you can't please them all—and off I went.

*　　　*　　　*

I knew at once what Vanessa and Max were up to. After all the shenanigan about being photographed, and after Vanessa had whipped the poncy shawl away sharpish and handed it, as if it were verminous, to one of the staff, I was introduced to a tall thin man with black hair that did that horrible curling up at the back of his neck. The sort you see being interviewed on television about economic crises, who invariably looks smug about Toryism and condemns the workers for holding the country to ransom. He had very pale skin and dark, rather intense eyes, as if his mind was on much higher things than all this social nonsense. Christ, I thought, we're going to have a whale of a time, for, as I suspected, he was seated next to me at the round table of about a dozen or so.

'Randolph needs cheering up,' Max whispered to me. 'His wife left him a few months ago and he's not been very good at playing the bachelor.'

Vanessa frowned at Max, one of her looks that said 'Shut Up', which Max then did. I knew what she meant. Unsubtle Max had unconsciously been telling me that this man to my right was *available*—with a capital A, too.

Right-ho, I thought, I'll cheer him up all right. And I jolly well did. So much so that during the sorbet he actually laughed at one of my jokes, put his hand on mine for a moment, removed it very swiftly, apologised (what kind of person has to apologise for touching something as harmless as a hand?), and said, 'I must say you are quite a tonic, Patricia.'

'Oh thank you, Rudolph,' I simpered. It was only then, having got his name so wrong, that I realised I had probably drunk too much to stop being Quite a Tonic.

I apologised but he was very amused—I reckoned he had probably imbibed a little more than was wise for a hair-curling economist—and he went on to tell everybody at the table about the misnomer, to gales of appreciative (and no doubt slightly alcoholic) laughter. I saw Vanessa and Max exchange told-you-so looks and felt, suddenly, truculent. The dress was one thing, the car was one thing, but being so highly organised into an affair was quite another. Oh no you don't, I said silently as I raised my glass to the scheming pair, Oh no you don't, at *all.*

Oh well. We danced, naturally, and I managed to damp down a certain sense of desire that *would* well up when he put his warm hand on the lower portion of my back—I knew perfectly certainly that this was merely biological and would pass. He told me all about himself, most of which I forget but it had a lot to do with the EEC and Brussels and 1992. He had a boy (afterwards known as the Boy) at Eton, a wife who had run off with one of the young rips from his office and who would not get a penny out of him, Patricia, not a penny, a Porsche, which he adored despite its being vandalised quite often by the great unwashed (those who voted your party into power, I yearned to say, but stopped myself), a house in Belgravia (yawn, yawn) and a neat little lodge with a few acres in Scotland.

'Ever been to Scotland, Patricia?'

'Yes,' I said. 'But I didn't like it very much.'

'Why not?' he whirled me around dangerously.

'Because all the men were wearing skirts.'

'Ha ha ha. Hee hee hee. Quite a tonic. Oh, quite a tonic.'

When I danced with Max he said, 'You are absolutely scintillating tonight.'

'Max,' I said. 'I am simply playing along. Nothing more than that.'

'But you *are* enjoying yourself?' He looked genuinely anxious.

'Of *course* I'm enjoying myself.'

'Good,' he said, humming 'In The Mood' to the band. 'Why don't you come down and stay in a couple of weekends' time? Bring Rachel.'

'I'd love to. Thank you. I could do with getting out of London and . . .' Suddenly I twigged. I stopped dancing and looked into Max's eyes. He is not very good at covering up.

'Max,' I said. 'Who else had you thought of inviting?'

We got 'In The Mood' for a few more bars before he said, 'Well, the Barnetts, you remember them? That nice literary couple with the daughter. Rachel could ride with her.'

'And . . . ?'

We both slid our eyes in the direction of the table, which was vacant save only for Rudolph/Randolph. He was leaning back in his chair looking at us very intensely, smoking a cigar, with a silly smile on his face and drumming his fingers on the table to the music.

'No, Max,' I said. 'No.'

And I excused myself and went to the ladies' powder room.

Vanessa came hot on my heels. 'Max,' she

153

said, sitting next to me at the mirror, 'is about as subtle as Rambo.'

I licked my little finger and de-smudged my eyes a bit. 'Vanessa,' I said, 'just about the last thing I want is to be pushed into an affair. In fact, just about the last thing I want is a man— any man. I really mean it. If you had any idea, *any idea at all,* how lovely it is not to be remotely involved with someone of the male gender—' She had the grace to snort mirthfully at this. '—then you'd celebrate it with me, not introduce me to people like Randolph—'

'Rudolph,' she said and burst into giggles. Even Vanessa can get tiddly sometimes.

'He's not my type anyway.'

'You don't know that. And you don't have to invite him into your life, not even your bed for that matter, but—' and here she went raunchy again '—he could certainly show you a good time.'

At which point we both collapsed into giggles, much to the disapproval of the very proper attendant who fixed us with a Lady Bracknell look of total disdain. Vanessa, noticing this, switched personality instantly. 'Fetch me a towel,' she said imperiously to the disdainful one. 'Would you?'

And bloody hell, she *did.*

Well, I somehow got out of it but he followed me out of the dancing, into the foyer and hung around me while the poncy shawl was fetched, offering to take me home. I was saved from rudeness on this point since his chauffeur was not booked to come for another half-hour or so, and thankfully, exultantly even, I slipped into a taxi and was hurtled back to safety without so much as a backward glance. Mrs Pomfret was asleep when I arrived. She looked so cosy and settled on the settee, so old and comfortable, that I knew I had done the right thing. I wanted to be like that once my child was up and grown and away from the hearth. Daffodil-yellow taffeta had its charms but my feet hurt chronically. A nice cup of tea, a quick look in on my sleeping daughter, and to bed alone. And back to sensible shoes and he of the hairy nostril on Monday. Balls, of whichever variety, were certainly not for *me*.

CHAPTER ELEVEN

Life became pleasantly (is there a duller word?) settled and normal, and much as I had predicted it would be in my erstwhile happy imaginings. Rachel was neither happier nor unhappier from what I could see. She seemed to settle down remarkably well into the new order and as time passed the sporadic tears and fears gradually diminished. She took a child's pleasure in milking the situation *vis-à-vis* Miranda in a thoroughly normal way and it seemed to me quite often when she came home and reported where Gordon had taken the two of them that it was getting progressively more as if he had two daughters to entertain instead of one. He looked well on it though, if a little tired around the edges sometimes, but since that had its fount largely in an activity which is not designed to elicit sympathy, or so I assumed, I could only be happy for him. And extremely grateful to her. He learned fairly early on not to get too cat-and-creamish with me about it so that when we did meet at handover times we were polite and relaxed, which helped Rachel's transition enormously.

Rudolph/Randolph rang a couple of times but I could deal with that, and when the weekend with Vanessa and Max came up I did not go. I was quite categoric with them about it. I said I did not want to be invaded by any choice of theirs, no matter how suitable on paper, and that if and when the time came—which was pretty remote—I would do my own selecting. Frocks perhaps, lovers definitely no . . .

In the meantime, I was perfectly happy buzzing about like a free bee: doing my job (with the bonus of fantasy asides regarding Mr Harris *in flagrante*), servicing Rachel and her life, seeing friends, decorating here and there and generally pottering on. I was certainly busy and, to my mind, life was full and rich. It was only my friends who seemed to think it wasn't—which I took as a bit of a cheek, quite frankly. Every time I said I was happy they seemed to get a covert, knowing look—even on the phone I could tell that Philly wore it—and Wanda just roared with libertine laughter and strengthening that remarkable Mauritian inflexion of hers just said, 'Honey, you just come down here to old Wanda's place. We got some real big men in the fens.' So that for a moment it felt like I was taking part in a saga from the Deep South.

I gave up trying to say that I felt very whole and complete because it always sounded so prissy. I would come out with pearls like 'We're very happy together, the three of us . . .' and then realise I had included bloody *Brian* in the statement just to pad it out a bit. I sort of thought that 'three of us' sounded less pathetic than 'two of us'. Not that saying the two of us sounded at all pathetic to me, but it acted like a red rag to a bull with everybody else. They all thought I was going to develop some inextricable and burdensome relationship with my daughter whereby she would either have to stay locked to my bosom for ever, or become a dangerous rebel (drugs, prostitution, the Conservative Party) in order to escape.

'Honestly,' I said to Lydia. 'I'm Patricia, remember? I'm not a maternal version of Miss Havisham. This is just me: Patricia Murray. A mother, that most automated appliance in the household. Right?'

But she received this with less amusement than I thought it warranted. All she said was, 'Do you know how many times you've mentioned Rachel in the last half-hour?'

I refuse to answer that kind of question at the best of times. The interrogator always knows the correct response, the interrogated never does. It also makes you feel very inhibited. Along with this it also made me feel I wanted to put her head in a bucket but I stood my ground. Silently.

She was serving her version of spaghetti bolognaise at the time, which was a curried version and a quite delicious marriage of Italian and Indian. She often did things like that, tributes to her husband's continent-mingling with the western palate.

'Do *you* know?' I said deciding to risk it, 'how many times in the last three months you have served me this particular dish?'

She looked up stricken (go for the throat with friends when they get too uppish, it's the only way) and then, slowly, the penny dropped. 'All right,' she said. '*Touché*. But all the same . . .'

'All the same *nothing*, Lydia. I'm happy and I don't intend to live entirely through or for my daughter. But just at the moment I enjoy her company and concentrating on her a bit. What's wrong with that?'

'Nothing, I suppose. It's just that you *are* only forty. It seems such a waste—'

'You mean if I was older—sixty, say—you'd abandon me quite cheerfully to a manless life? I mean, just when is it allowable for a woman to say she doesn't need a man and be believed? Fifty? Sixty? Seventy?'

'You're very defensive about it, you know.'

'I need to be. Good grief, Lyd. It's like being on an assault course out there. Everyone is gunning to get me hitched again. Why does nobody believe I'm all right like this?'

She put up her hands. 'All right, all right. Topic over. I suppose it's just that the rest of us are trying very hard to keep our heads above water and still be pacey and exciting and a little unconventional despite our domestic trappings, and you seem to be doing the reverse.'

'I'm fed up with being told things like I'm devoid of horseplay and dully domestic. I'm just *living*, that's all.'

'Quite,' she said, far too evenly.

'Anyway, the Webbs don't think I'm dull. Our Penelope turns her head when she catches sight of me.'

'I'm not surprised,' said Lydia. 'You look rather, well, wild sometimes. I mean, not many people go to Sainsbury's on a Saturday morning wearing large blue chiffon bows in their hair, spangled trainers and a sweat shirt announcing they eat dinosaurs—'

'There you are then. I'm not dull at all.'

'I think it's all symptomatic of your suppressed need for fun.'

'I have fun with you. And Jo. And I enjoy the other things I do. I even play Rod Stewart very loudly when Rachel's not there and bop about the house.'

'Well,' she said, raising those bucket-inducing eyebrows. 'What more can I say? There can't be anything more to life than that.'

'If it weren't for the fact that I want to ask a favour of you I'd exit huffily now. Can you have Rachel for me for a Saturday night next month?'

'Depends,' she said. 'If it's a sewing bee at the Town Hall then I will. If it's anything more torrid, count me out.'

'It's not torrid at all,' I said, laughing despite the gibe. 'It's Gertrude giving a party and it's a weekend that doesn't coincide with Gordon. I could take Rachel with me and bed her there but that means waking her up and dragging her back in a taxi at some late hour and she's been looking a bit peaky these last few days. It's reading late, I think. Did I tell you she's actually moved on from the Famous Five at last? I bought her a Judy Blume and she loves it. I'll try her on Paula Danziger next and then—' I looked up.

Lydia was regarding me quite kindly but with a certain amusement. 'Five,' she said.

'Five what?'

'Five. That's the fifth mention of Rachel's progress in the last three-quarters of an hour.'

'So?' I stuck out my chin.

'So nothing. Eat.'

'I had this same sort of conversation with Phillida ages ago. Just what is so wrong in being an interested and attentive mother?'

'Absolutely nothing.'

'And at least I'm going to go to the wretched party.'

'True.'

'I mean, I don't sit around in a heap at home being mother-to-my-daughter and nothing else, do I?'

'Certainly not,' she said, a little too drily.

'I've been to dinner here, I went to the theatre with Jo last Wednesday. It's a full rich life, you know.'

'It certainly is,' she said in such a manner that visions of buckets continued to present themselves.

'I went to Verity Smith's party last week and *danced* for Christ's sake. You saw me.'

'I did. You danced with everybody's husband.'

'So?'

'You *didn't* dance with that poor cousin of hers in his red jumper and winsome loneliness.'

'I talked to him.'

'You did. You talked to him about Rachel's toys—educational value of—and whether to get her a computer or not.'

'Well?'

'No comment.'

'He was a marketing manager for some toy and software people. Why shouldn't I talk to him about that?'

'But, Pat—'

'Yes?'

'You made his eyes glaze over.'

'I can't help it if I bored him.'

'But you do it all the time with any man who might vaguely be interested in you. One minute you're being your usual jolly self with the rest of us and the next you're telling some masculine stranger about *nits.* It's a self-induced barrier of boredom. You do it subconsciously all the time.'

'I do not. I was scintillating when I went to the Dorchester.'

'And you backed off quickly enough *there.*'

'Lydia, it is not my intended crusade in life to replace Gordon with a full-scale replica or a step-daddy for my child. Look at Jo. You don't go on at her about humping everything in sight.'

'I am *not* talking about humping. I am merely talking about remembering your womanliness in amongst all this maternalism.'

'Womanliness is not necessarily quantified by being connected with a man, Lydia.'

'I'm not suggesting that it is. But until you stop being plain frightened of venturing you're just living in an unreal state. I mean, there are friendships, like you've got with me, and Jo and all the others, and there are other kinds of friendships that touch other parts of you.'

'You mean sex?' I said, knowing that she didn't. 'I can assure you that it doesn't bother me in the slightest.'

'No, I don't just mean sex. I mean all the other bits that go to make up the whole of you, the bits me or Phillida or the other women you know can't bring out, those bits that lurk somewhere inside you and of which you are simply afraid.'

'I am not afraid,' I said, putting out of my head the thought of 'methinks-the-lady-doth-protest-too-much'. 'I'm just living the way I want to and not the way everyone thinks I should. Look at Jacqueline. She was desperately lonely, tried computer dating, tried someone else's husband, and now look at her—back down the pit with a new husband, whom we can't stand, and a baby on the way. Do you seriously suggest that would be better than being the way I am?'

'I just think you should stop pre-ordaining yourself, that's all. You should go into things blindly but with your eyes open. When was the last time you let yourself think about the feel of skin on skin, hmm? When?'

You can do without friends like Lydia and Phillida and Gertrude and all the bloody rest. Skin on skin, indeed. It was a sudden and acutely erotic thought there in Lydia's kitchen across half cold Ital-Ind food. My skin on skin, as I had to remind myself, was when Rachel crept under the duvet with me in the mornings. I could hold her to me with absolute purity of sensation and know that her need matched mine without fear of question. I was jiggered if I was going to erode that with any creeping thoughts about deeper lurking things. Rudolph/Randolph's hot hand had been a small reminder that they *were* there but good sense had prevailed enough to remind me of their utterly biological origins. Brian was a constant reminder of where being opened up and then rejected could get you. He was my *memento mori* for an untrammelled life. That he was also a pain in the arse and adored by my daughter despite his denials seemed an inappropriate thought to dwell on. So I didn't.

'Oh, go to Gertrude's party and discuss ear wax. I'll have Rachel for you, of course I will. It will be a pleasure as always.'

Suddenly I found I was gripping Lydia's hand in among all the dishes and condiments and saying fervently, 'At least I've got that bit right, haven't I?'

And there was a suitably warm squeeze back as she told me, 'Of course . . .'

*   *   *

Part of the servicing of Rachel was dealing

with Brian's bodily functions. Rather like potty-training children you need both luck and an amenable defecator. Fortunately, Brian was not anal retentive, which meant that with one or two honourable mistakes he could be taught the when and the how.

I took immense pride in walking him past those notices posted up on lamp posts which announced that 'People who let dogs foul the pavement are dirty, irresponsible, bad mannered and probably carriers of AIDS.' I was none of those things. Hah!

The local borough, in its wisdom, had created no-go areas for dogs in most of its open spaces. But there was one vast tract of common land where the little turdies were still privileged to crap uncontrolled, though naturally it was not a Designated Dog Shit Area in name. The pretence for those nefarious owners of canines was that it was a place to walk the fouling things, but the reality was always the same. One vast morning shit party—every day.

My routine with Brian was to take Rachel to school and then walk him on to this mound of bacteria where the grass grew in sparse and choking clumps, among the piles of whatsit that were forever deposited. But we had a pooper-scooper and, after a few times of using it, I learned to overcome the nausea attendant on cleaning up Brian's droppings. Rather curiously, as in the past I had found Rachel's nappies dealable-with, it became an automatically necessary, though unpleasant, part of life. Indeed, I took sort of exultant pleasure in going among the morning crowd upon Crap Green and using the equipment right under their noses. Of course, this banned me from their exclusive club. Owners, deep in conversation with each other while their little or large best friends nosed each other's nethers and fouled together joyously, would look upon me askance, as an alien, while I dealt with Brian's unspeakable. Even Brian was castigated. It seemed to me that in the dog world it was considered palpably un-macho to have some human clear up what you had a right to bestow upon the world. Fortunately, Brian maintained his death-wish throughout and made no move to go among his own kind. He was quite happy sniffing himself if he needed any kind of buzz and would crouch mournfully until the deed was done without so much as a backward glance at his achievement.

All I fervently hoped was that, unlike the rest of the paid-up members on that vast canine lavatory, I would not grow to look like my animal. For it is undeniably true: dogs look like their owners, and their owners look like them. The man in the brown trilby with a bristling moustache was an exact human twin for his Jack Russell. I could hear him sounding off about the heedless parking that was committed along the perimeter of the park,

'So you have to walk round the cars to get through' (I longed to say that it was infinitely preferable to stepping round what his dog had just done). And the woman with the fake-fur hat, large shoulders and matching coat could easily be her husky's sister. Of the two, the dog had the more appealing smile and winsome way with its lolling tongue. When her tongue came out, which was quite often during intense conversation, it was much more obscene. I knew she was called Hilary because I had heard the tiny blonde girl (the sort who wears jeans and anoraks and has rings under her eyes from living alternatively) call her that while her own little blond piece of nonsense nose dived the husky's well-furred privates. 'Oh, Hilary,' she said. 'How I wish people could be as friendly as dogs. Just look at Melchior *(Melchior?)* making friends with Bruce.'

I found an awful fascination in all this and was quite often so riveted that I forgot the time, and on realising it I had to run home, Brian slipping and sliding rubberily behind me on his lead (so that the RSPCA might have felt that they had a case), hurl him in through the front door and run like hell to get to Mr Harris on time. Unpunctuality was a disease, according to him, spreading out from the initial perpetrator and infecting everyone in sight. I had been foolish enough to agree emphatically when he made this pronouncement, which made time-keeping a high-tension business. I would arrive flushed and breathless and try to turn the expression on my face from bronchial collapse to eager-for-workness. Not easy . . .

Dog owners have no social boundaries. There was a very sinister young man with sunglasses *(in November)*, a black leather jacket and chip-pan hair who dropped his cool when he and attendant Alsatian met up with the likes of the trilby, Hilary and the blonde. He would saunter up looking like a vision from hell and then nod amiably while his slinky side-kick (called Tarquin, though—and let's be really snobbish here—I doubt he of the leather jacket was *au fait* with that Roman line. Or perhaps he just knew about Sextus's rape of Lucrece and liked the idea. Myself, I doubt if either dog or owner was capable of such an act, they seemed far too bound up in their own image to ruffle it by anything genuinely aggressive) made obeisance to the wormy ground. His conversation, comprising fairly short words, was mainly about dog food and where to get it cheaply and wholesomely Target was apparently a good brand name and I made a mental note to strive against subliminal advertising whenever I was roaming Sainsbury's shelves. Quite often I found my hand reaching for a can or two of Target, only to remember just in time and go for the cheap house-brand variety. It is so difficult being an uncommitted dog owner out shopping. I

168

just could never bring myself to pile loads and loads of tins into the trolley like the other uninhibited dog-food buyers—there is something quite nauseating about thinking of all those minced-up animals being fed to other animals. Someone once said that if all the stray dogs were rounded up and turned into dog food for their domesticated counterparts, then the world need never kill another whale or kangaroo for canning ever again. Eminently sensible, if too philosophically advanced for our civilised society's comfort. I'm sure it could be done quite, quite painlessly . . . but I digress . . .

I felt very sorry for the tennis players nearby. Beyond this denizen of shit lay a group of local-authority-owned courts which were much used in the summer and still patronised during the winter months by keen tennis players and women who perhaps thought they could tone up a muscle or two before returning to their domestic perches. In particular, quite regularly, there was a pair of lady players who were not very good but who seemed to enjoy themselves enormously. I used to see them picking their tennis-shoed way across the excreta, with understandable crossness when one or the other got sullied, and then they would get into the court, knock up and play, giggling quite a lot and trying hard to do right by their game. I envied them. I would much rather have been in that court than outside it with Brian, but we stood apart, like pariahs, from their healthy non-pollutant activity.

All around me, as I watched on those mornings, were the noises of dogs and owners. Both barking in their own ways and sometimes the red-haired female of the pair on court would glare outwards, through the wire, and shake her fist at the ghastliness that rent the air. I once saw her enter a savage verbal exchange with Hilary after Bruce had shat mercilessly in the lee of a plane tree. I am not sure who won but it certainly added vim to the redhead's game. She served a few times as if the ball were Hilary's head and left her partner standing open-mouthed.

These days were good days on the whole. Very peaceful, despite having to entertain the kind of conversation that Lydia and the rest of my women friends seemed bent on realising, and I was, as I had always imagined, extremely happy in a calm sort of a way. Days rolled on, Christmas loomed, with Gertrude's party somewhere in between, and when Rachel ran up to me at the school gates, with a heedless and childlike glow about her, I felt quite cheerfully fulfilled. I wanted to say to those others surrounding me, 'Look. See. Here we are, the two of us (well, and Brian as well, I suppose, though he hardly made waves of being) quite happy. Quite content, and so it will remain.' Unity. I liked that. Absolute unity. My life compartmented and planned on a perfect, unassailable grid.

CHAPTER TWELVE

Gertrude had given up sex years ago and said that she felt much better for it, so I felt pretty certain that I was safe from any matchmaking or humpmaking ploys with her. Her husband had been a vicar with a predilection for small boys. The Church, in its wisdom, had turned a blind ear to whisperings and had seen fit to sacrifice the odd childish anus to the greater glory of the Institution. This went on for several years before Gertrude herself finally blew the whistle on him. Even then he was offered some kind of mission posting in what was still Malaya. Gertrude refused to go with him and remained in England with their sons. In a neat bit of Justice Divine, as Milton would have it, within twenty-four hours of arriving in Kuala Lumpur her husband was mistaken for some visiting politician, shot at point-blank range by what were then terrorists and later became the esteemed government, and died instantly.

'Which means without suffering,' she would add in the telling. 'Unlike my life while I was married to him . . .' It was the only time I ever heard her speak bitterly about anything.

Unsurprising, really, that she abandoned sex after all that.

She lived—or rather held court—in a splendidly rambling and Bohemian home in Clapham, one which estate agents would be unable to resist describing as 'retaining all period features', though they might drop the bit about 'in need of complete modernisation and refurbishment'. Here she cooked and laughed and read and welcomed assorted children, grandchildren and friends with zesty pleasure. It was into her cookery that Gertrude had put all her energy and sensuality. She both created it and ate it. 'Over sixty in years and about the same on the hips,' she would say, pushing the inevitable wisps of sandy-grey hair back into her ever-loosening bun. She wore tent-like opulent creations of her own devising and an array of old hats—she collected them—quite often indoors. She had once given Gordon a chummy punch which had winded him for several minutes and for which he never forgave her. In consequence she remained much more my friend than ours and when I told her we were to separate she just said, 'Good for you.' She made her money from writing cookery books which said things like 'Slap in more butter at this point if you like' or 'Add some brandy and then add some more'—which made her books very popular. Her cook's maxim was Good Quality. Less of the best rather than more of the inferior. It was really a summation of her approach to life.

Her parties were never large-scale despite the size of the house. Since eating was a predominant part of the proceedings it was important that her guests should have plenty of space. There was no standing, elbows squashed at sides, with a plate and glass balanced precariously. Instead, there were comfortable squashy chairs and sofas, cushions on the floor, quiet chamber music (eat and talk . . . if you want to dance go to a nightclub) and excellent wine. She never paid for the booze, suppliers sent it—and if an ancient recipe required Chateau-Margaux, in it went. One should never leave a party of Gertrude's and attempt to drive home. By rights the Federation of Taxi Drivers should have given her a medal for aid to their industry.

So, I rather looked forward to going there and having a relaxing, unpressured time. Lydia was right in one respect, which was that whenever I was anywhere involving more than just my intimate friends it was impossible to relax. I was on my guard. Partly to do with being a divorced woman with its attendant old-fashioned notion (which I could not quite shake from my psyche) that such a one must, *de rigueur*, be liberally daubed in scarlet, and partly, despite my brave words and imaginings, because there is a world of difference between desiring to separate and *being* separate. You go out into the social world feeling as if you have lost a limb for a while (albeit a diseased limb) and you do feel quite shockingly vulnerable sometimes. It took me ages to decide what to wear, for example, to that party of Verity Smith's. If I went for the more foolish knee-revealing items in my wardrobe (of which there were few, to be honest) everyone might think I was attempting the miracle of mutton to lamb. If I wore something really dreary and conventional they would all pity me. (I tried this once, and they did—I actually heard Susan Shaw say to her husband, 'David, do go and talk to Patricia. She's looking so miz'—where usually women are supposed to protect their spouses from feral divorcées like myself. I couldn't really win, which I found very chastening. I mean, I didn't want to be Mae West, but I didn't want to be Shirley Temple either.) In the end, for Gertrude's party, I settled for that most useful and potentially boring standby, the little black dress, which, shortened to a good couple of inches above the knee and with the benefit of an outlandishly glittering brooch, which could have done well on a Knight of the Garter, made me feel both comfortable and a bit partyfied at the same time. It also—and let's be honest here—hid the few pounds I had put on since leaving Gordon. I put this down to contentment but my carping women friends said it was much more likely due to having such a sedentary job and not doing much else.

I didn't argue. Let them think I was not contented if they wished. I had learned not to waste my breath in denials.

*   *   *

I walked Rachel to Lydia's so that she could have tea there, taking Brian for a drag at the same time, and on the way back saw the Webbs: Penelope in a nice navy-blue overcoat with epaulettes and a belt, somewhat reminiscent of school raincoats, and Mr—whose name I did not know—in a City-smoothie grey coat with velvet collar. They were clearly going out. He was stowing a holdall into the boot of their Rover so they were not only going out but going away as well. They both managed not to look at me as I passed by which was fine. I heard Penelope say, 'Did you pack Alison's present?' so I guessed they were off to indulge their only child with a parental visit. This was a bonus since it meant I could play music as loud as I wished and have a good old whoop and holler about the house without bringing down their wrath. The couple on the other side of me were almost never there, and anyway when they were, and being young, thrusting and, from the looks of them, very dynamic, they quite often did the same. On went Rod Stewart then and off came my shoes and while I bopped about the house a bit Brian made a mournful exit from life in the guise of a much needed and often perpetrated dogaleptic fit.

'Bulstrode!' I yelled at him. 'Bulstrode, Bulstrode, Bulstrode.' But he was apparently beyond all influence.

It turned into a very wild night, atmospherically speaking. Wind got up, rain pelted down and as I got ready to go out I could hear the last whipped-up rustling of the trees as their few remaining leaves were ripped off and scattered in the squalls. It didn't matter to me. I just turned the music up louder: my daughter was safely ensconced with friends, I knew what I was going to wear and my taxi was due at eight. What more could I ask, really? Except, perhaps (and then only fleetingly) when the time came, a friendly hand to do up my zip. Of which there was none, so I just struggled alone with it instead. Once when I thought I had nearly got it done (the zip bit was all right but then there is always that infuriating little hook and eye which generally ends up gouging a hole in the material and missing the loop entirely) I was startled to hear someone knocking on the back door. Oh God, I thought, it's the ghost of Penelope Past, but it wasn't. It was only Brian's dogflap racketing away in the wind. I peered out into the darkness. It certainly was demented out there. I found it oddly exciting. There is an abandonment about that sort of stormy turmoil that is quite disturbing. Even

Brian was looking a hundredth part alert—translated, that means his nose was moving and half of one eye was only semi-comatose—but it was uncharacteristically acute activity for him.

Back upstairs the zip, hook and eye were fastened at last, the lady was ready and—exactly on time—so was the taxi. And off I sped towards Clapham through the roughly weathered streets.

I suppose it must seem that my life was no more than a series of unconnected parties. Do I hear other single parents out there snarling and saying, 'Huh! It's all right *for her* but what about reality? What about being stuck in night after night waiting for the telephone to ring or a single human voice—adult—to come calling at the door? Huh. And what about that most often encountered twin-to-single parenthood, lack of money?'

Well, in the case of the former there were, indeed, long stretches of being on my own. And I should say that the State has a duty to furnish any single parent without question or favour with a free television set, because without it mere mortals in such a situation could go crazy. And a video machine, too, while we are on the subject, *and* free membership to video clubs. But I was lucky. I was living in a nice middle-class area, with nice middle-class socially ept people. And funnily enough *that* has a bearing on the latter difficulty of money. Because going out to dinner with friends who live locally, or hopping on the tube for a quick burst of cheap seatage in a theatre somewhere, doesn't cost very much. (Especially when you have only one house-trained child who can be bedded with your accompanying friend's mob while her husband dozes over work he has brought home.) Neither does sitting around a kitchen table in the early evening and sharing a bottle of Sainsbury's plonk leave you penniless, yet its benefits of release from loneliness are priceless. I was just very lucky. Though perhaps not entirely (sing your own praises where possible for maximising that most necessary commodity, self esteem) lucky. You need friends. You need to work at friendships. Making friends is easy. Keeping them is the devil of a job. Never forget, even in the pits of the blues, that they need something from you too. Keep the bargain balanced and to every twentieth part of miserable moaningness add one part of twinkle in the eye, and generally they will stick around. Mine did and I am ever and eternally grateful to them for it (despite their apparently thinking that the only true saviour of Patsy's psyche should be a computer games expert from Slough or a nice, clean-about-the-house bespoke-tailored professional . . .). If of course you are living, as the majority of depressed single parents are, outside that kind of cared-for cultivated neighbourhood, with perhaps three children under five, the paucity of supplementary benefit and neighbours who live barricaded lives, then snarl you might. Even supposing your neighbours are not barricaded against you, they may well be in the same financial pit. Sainsbury's plonk metamorphosed into a packet of crisps and a Guinness across a plywood table in some high rise doesn't have the same uplifting quality. And even if the spirit soars enough to persuade you to venture out, the cost involved in getting a babysitter for the night, let alone sacrificing a pair of needed children's shoes for a frock in which you *feel* like facing the world, with the price of a couple of drinks at the local (even supposing you can run the gamut of beady male eyes sizing up your randiness) it becomes prohibitive. Sometimes I shivered at my good fortune. Wherever I turned there seemed to be kindness and concern. I was viewed as a social animal and not an outcast. Which was just as well. It would have been very easy to lie, like Brian, and give up the ghost until metamorphosed into the sleepy calm of being Mrs Pomfret, but life-external seemed bent on not leaving me alone. I couldn't, honestly, say that I wanted it to. You can have quite enough of pizza for two and ten-year-old's prattle. I quite often did. Parties happened, and I went to them. Though with my guard up, naturally enough. But I wouldn't confess that to anyone except you.

And rather like the requirement for a gripping novel being the struggle to overcome rather than the blandness of setting down unchallenged happiness (even the most escapist literature requires the ingredient of difficulties overcome; who on earth wants to read about a life of ease?)—and just as there would be no story to *Romeo and Juliet* if they had had parental blessing, no interest in D'Arcy and Elizabeth if she had suffered no prejudice, no nail-biting over Ahab and his ivory leg if Moby Dick had just lain down and died—so in a smaller, ungrand way, I give you the parties. In between them, to be sure, were quiet times—television times, sewing school name-tags on times, supermarket shopping and a few snatched words in the street times—but these were quiet, unmemorable, and moved my story on not one jot so far as the heart of it is concerned. So, the parties, the fun, the tickling up of Patricia Murray from her calm, unflustered existence to the 'great big world outside' where, with one skin fewer than she had before parting from her Gordon days, she looped the loop. Upside down it is quite hard to hold on to your guard. As I, rather unwillingly, discovered.

*　　　*　　　*

I had not seen Gertrude for nearly a year. Not

since I went over there to tell her that Gordon and I were separating. We had spoken on the telephone a couple of times but she had been travelling, collecting material for a new book and then I had cancelled a Sunday lunch with her because Rachel had a stomach bug, and anyway, with some friendships it just goes like that. We always picked up where we left off, which was fine. I ran up the path that night, buffeted by the wind, and it was Gertrude who opened the door. She looked and sounded exactly the same.

'So eastern Europe didn't change you at all,' I said, kissing her.

'I'm wearing cossack boots,' she said, lifting an enormous leg from beneath her purple batik tent and displaying beautiful red leather ones. 'And I've taken to their *hats* rather.' She reached out to the tumbled table in the hall, fished up a curly white astrakhan number which she plonked on her head and instantly looked Slavic.

'It suits you,' I said.

'I know,' she said, grinning. And then her expression changed to one of appraisal as I removed my coat and flung it down. The appraisal did not seem altogether pleased. 'You look very *severe*, Patricia,' she said. 'Are you well?'

I laughed. 'Of course I'm well. A bit windswept but very well indeed. And it's not severe, this brooch is bright . . .'

'Mmm,' she said looking at it critically. 'It's that sort of thing the Royal Family wears but I wouldn't have said it was you. Would you like to borrow a shawl or something? I've got *the* most lovely one that I found in Tashkent . . .' She dug into the pile again and produced a startling piece of material, old gold, faded pink with long black fringes.

'No, thanks,' I said, not at all offended. 'I'm no good with shawls or umbrellas. They're too complicating. I'll just stick to what I've got.'

I gave her another kiss and prepared to walk past her, when she put up her hand.

'Are you *quite* sure?'

Now I did begin to feel a little surprised. 'Why? What's so important about the way I look all of a sudden?'

'Nothing, nothing,' she said cheerfully, and began to push me along the wide hallway. 'You'll do.'

'Do for what?'

'Nothing, nothing,' she said again.

I knew that inflexion underneath the cheerfulness.

I stopped being ushered and turned to face her. Eyes a little too bright perhaps? Smile a little too stamped there? More than the usual amount of fluster in the way she pushed back the escaping bun hair from beneath that funny hat while shoving me so eagerly along the hall? I smelled conspiracy.

'Gertrude,' I said, sighing with certainty.

'Not you as well.'

'What do you mean, dear?'

'I mean, have you got plans to matchmake tonight?'

'Matchmake? Heaven forbid.'

'Sexmake, then?'

'You must know me better than that.' She gave me a little push, but I held my ground.

'I thought I did.'

'You do, dear. Now come along in. I've got some really good burgundies lined up for you to try.'

'There's somebody in there who knows I'm available, isn't there?'

'That is a very crude way of saying it, Pat.'

'All the same . . .'

Gertrude touched my cheek. Her eyes lost some of their false brightness and became just old Gertrude's again. 'Sorry,' she said. 'Interfering old woman. Forget all about it. Just go on and enjoy yourself. I won't introduce you to anyone so you needn't feel manipulated. Anyway, you know half the people here. It was only a thought . . .'

So much for being pretty certain of Gertrude.

I opened the door to the room—the party had not yet begun to spill over into the rest of the house—and I went in with a definite sense of foreboding. Somewhat, I suppose, as Caesar might have felt on the Ides of March.

Parties are very dreadful things. You just

never know who you are going to meet. Trepidatiously, looping the loop, I went in with Gertrude pulsatingly hot on my up-ended heels.

CHAPTER THIRTEEN

Gertrude had two main living areas downstairs. Her huge basement kitchen in which she spent most of her time and which housed comfortably, among her cook's paraphernalia, a somewhat battered Edwardian three-piece suite, just to give you an idea of its size. And above that a space created by making the two largish rooms at the back of the house into one. Into this she ushered me.

It had french windows leading out into a rather over-grown garden mostly devoted to herbs and edible things, though being early December and such a wild night these, naturally enough, were closed. But the curtains were not, and as I walked across the room towards them and the drinks table (neither looking to left nor right and trying to exude a careless aura of friendly indifference which, let me tell you retrospectively, is impossible) I could see streaks of lightning brighten the rain on the window glass and the tops of trees bowing dangerously. It seemed to me there was a definite sense of electricity in the air, though the people around me all seemed quite unaffected by it. Maybe there was just a sense of electricity in me. All that bobbing to Rod Stewart when I should have been listening to Elgar or something.

I managed to get to the drinks table like a blinkered horse, making no contact with anybody, and very thankfully poured myself a glass of wine. Such a thing in one's hand at a time like that produces a calming effect. I did feel much calmer. I held the stem of the glass with one hand and the bowl with the other and got my breathing a bit under control (how could Gertrude of *all* people? was a refrain that needed expunging from my mind before I faced the gathering). Looking out into the night was not helping much, it only seemed to reflect my own disorder. I had a premonition about all this. I didn't give a hoot for all the other attempts at pairing me off—Verity's party, Vanessa and Max, various dinners here and there—but Gertrude was a different kettle of kidney. *She* could be relied on to choose well, in the same way that as she had an instinct for the melding of flavours and textures in her food so she had the same kind of instinct for putting people together. At least, so it had always proved in a broader social sense with her parties, dinners and lunches. She had also been absolutely right about her son David's marriage to an on-paper bad risk: Steffie had gone from being a heavy-drinking waster to a talented hatmaker and wise mother within a year of their marriage, to just about everyone's surprise, including mine and excepting Gertrude's (though I have no doubt that Steffie's millinery skills added to her certainty). So all in all I knew I had good reason to be trepidatious tonight. Whoever Gertrude had decided (so uncharacteristically) to team me up with (unforgivable defector) was unlikely to be a toy manufacturer from Slough.

There were about twenty people in the room already and more arriving all the time. I turned from the window, glass in hand, deep breath taken, and looked out at this *mêlée* in which I must participate. And straight away, as in some perfectly wrought romance, I looked into a stranger's eyes and knew that it was him. Right, I thought to myself, I've got you placed, I've got your number. I looked away, saw Carrie and Joe, Gertrude's other son and daughter-in-law, at the other side of the room, and walked very purposefully across to them (still with what I fondly thought to be a gait of friendly indifference).

Carrie was pregnant again. That was good. I could make endless yardage out of that, probably talk about it all night if I had to. Carrie was very earth-motherish and had popped out four already. Having children was her forte in life, she enjoyed it unabashedly, and she was very good at it. Joe always had the amused air of a willing stud about him and seemed to enjoy his extending family well enough. Like his father before him he was a priest and I always found it darkly fascinating to try and imagine how a purveyor of God's pure love got on in bed. Do they think dirty like the rest of personkind and what happens if they feel horny right in the middle of evensong? I knew Joe quite well but not well enough to ask him things like that. And I hoped such a question wouldn't bubble up tonight. My heightened state could easily remove circumspection and despite his being a very liberal, no dog-collar sort of a priest, I didn't think it would make a very welcome enquiry.

I passed by the part of the room in which those eyes stood with, as I still fondly imagined, my mien of friendly indifference, and arrived in front of Carrie's bump. She had her hands clasped round it and one of those beatific smiles on her face.

'I'm being kicked to death,' she said happily as we leaned around it to kiss. The last stages of pregnancy are amazing in terms of engineering excellence. Just how does something so large and protuberant stay up? I used to look down at my own final-phase bump in simple wonder that it didn't just drop off. I put my hand where hers were and sure enough I could feel the vibrations of it thump,

thump, thumping.

'Another boy?' I said. 'Or a liberated girl-baby?'

'It might be both,' she said. 'It's twins.'

I looked at Joe. 'Bloody hell,' I said unable to stop myself.

He laughed. 'Bloody heaven,' he corrected.

'We thought you might like to be a godmother this time,' said Carrie all dreamily.

'Why I'd love to,' I said. 'But you know I'm not at all religious.'

'That's all right,' said Joe. 'We've got enough good Christianity surrounding us to allow for that. Anyway, we might convert you, you never know. You're looking very nun-like tonight. That's a start.'

'*Don't*,' I said. 'Gertrude's already told me I look severe. I thought I looked rather dignified, sort of halfway between grief for a marriage done with and optimism for a future alone. Well, not quite alone, I've got Rachel. But you know what I mean. Alone in the married sense. I can't tell you how good it feels to be free of all that . . .' I realised that I had begun to burble, more out of an effort to convince myself than to convince them, and on I went. 'I know it goes against all the tenets of the Church, Joe, but I honestly find being divorced a wonderful liberation. Being on my own—*entirely* in control of all I do—well, it's just *wonderful*, wonderful, that's all.' They were both smiling at me as I rattled on. 'Sorry,'

188

I said. 'It's hardly the sort of thing you two want to hear.'

'You carry on,' said Joe. 'It's good to hear something so positive for a change.'

'Ooh,' said Carrie. 'There they go again.'

And we talked for a little while about the pregnancy, the other children, and easy, general things. Including our hostess.

'Gertrude has flipped,' I announced.

'Nothing about my mother would surprise me. In what particular respect has she flipped this time?'

'Well, for some extraordinary reason she's done a complete *volte face* regarding the joys of being single, which, as you well know, has been one of her mainstays of belief, and she's gone and invited a potential man here for *me* tonight.'

Joe was almost laughing. He has a very big, mobile mouth that is most often on the borders of humour anyway. 'You mean he hasn't quite become a man yet?'

Carrie giggled.

'What?'

'If he's only a potential man, I mean. That implies he isn't quite there yet.'

'Oh, ha ha! You know what I mean. Somewhere in this room lurks a snare, set by the only person I thought I could rely on *not* to set one . . .'

I moved my head around to peek in the direction of the eyes but fortunately they were turned away, talking to a group of people, and I only caught the back of the neck, which was nice enough if you like that sort of thing. Neat brown hair just over the collar, non-sticky-out ears, broadish shoulders, hands in pockets— amazing what you can notice even when you are *quite* uninterested.

'I'm pretty sure I know who it is,' I said, turning back to them. 'He's over there by the fireplace, with his back to us.' I followed Joe's gaze. 'The one with his hands in his pockets.'

'There are three men with their backs to us,' Joe said, still bordering on a guffaw. 'And two of them have their hands in their pockets.'

'Well, anyway, I just know, that's all,' I said darkly.

'So do I,' said Joe, rocking on his heels and finally giving in to a hoot or two. 'Because *I'm* the one primed by Gertrude to introduce you to him later—subtle-like of course.'

'Don't you *dare*,' I said. 'I shall walk away if you do. I just can't think what's got into your mother. I mean this is just not like her, is it?'

'I can tell you what's happened,' said Carrie, coming out of her little reverie in which, no doubt, she was successfully breast-feeding two babies at the same time while doing a jigsaw for the others with her toes.

'What?'

'Gertrude is in love.'

There are moments when only silence will express emotion. So I stood there, absolutely silent. Silent in shock and silent, I realised, in betrayal. Until that moment I had not understood how important Gertrude was as a role model. She and Mrs Pomfret represented the acceptable, manifestly successful result of family life singular. Good grief! It only needed Mrs Pomfret to turn up at the next babysit sporting a toy boy and I might as well shoot myself.

'It is a bit of a shock, isn't it?' said Joe, a darned sight too cheerfully. 'But just look at her. You can see how happy she is.'

I looked. Gertrude was standing just inside the doorway with a tray of edibles and there was a very short man with a shock of white hair and a little goatee beard standing at her side. He had his arm circling, as best he could, her grand waist and she was—there is no other word for it—*simpering.*

'They met on a dusty road just outside Karachi while she was doing all that travelling for the new book. He's writing about temples and ritual but he's quite a gutsy character—or so she tells us. He certainly eats.'

'He'd have to,' I said without thinking. And then still without thinking I said to Joe 'Are they *lovers*?'

'Tut, tut,' he said. 'Such a question to put to a man of the cloth.'

'But are they?'

'Well, put it this way,' he said, 'sometimes, I gather, he doesn't go home at night.'

A degree of sense returned to me. 'Oh God,' I said. 'I'm so sorry, I shouldn't have asked, especially you—her son. Please—'

'Why on earth should I mind? I hope they are. I mean—' he managed to imbue his voice with a tone that had nothing to do with the pure Christian spirit '—it is one of the nicest things between two people. Isn't it?'

And he gave Carrie's shoulder a little squeeze.

'I wouldn't know about that,' I said crisply. 'My glass is empty. I wonder if you'd mind very much . . . ?'

He took it. I looked across at Gertrude who was now coming towards Carrie and me with her temple-ritual writer in tow.

'You looked a little miffed,' she said, offering me the tray. 'Has my son been trying to convert you?'

'In a manner of speaking,' I said, smiling as best I could and taking some little morsel which was probably delicious but which I did not taste at all. 'In a manner of speaking, I rather think he has.'

*   *   *

Alec was all right really and, despite trying to dislike him, it was impossible. He and Gertrude did seem to delight in each other's company and when, at one point, she leaned towards me and whispered, 'If only I'd known it could be like this *years* ago,' my sense of betrayal became mingled with a hint of gladness for her—and an awful lot of sorrow for myself. I suddenly felt dreadfully alone in that room. I mean, there were the Darby and Joan love's young dreamers confronting me, and there were Carrie and Joe all smiley together, and there—all around me—were other people all at one (or at two) with each other. And me. All alone. And the storm outside didn't help. The electricity was still buzzing both in and out of the room. It needed something loud and raucous to drown it out but there was only the softness of Mozart whispering in our ears.

Somehow I managed to relax a bit and talk to a few people over the next hour or so, and I was able to help myself to wine and food without going anywhere near that stranger's eyes when, suddenly, in the teeming kitchen, down at the pudding end of the table, just as I had my hand in a basket of florentines, I looked up and there he was. Helping himself to some ripely yielding dolcelatte.

'This stuff,' he said, just managing to get it on to his plate without dropping it, 'is the next best thing to sex, you know.'

'Don't *you* start,' I said. 'I've had *quite* enough of that for one night!'

He looked at me with highly amused surprise.

'Really?' he said. 'That's quite a confession

193

to make to a stranger.'

And I, not usually backward in coming forward with the verbals, could think of absolutely nothing to say. Not even to explain coldly that he had misunderstood. *Why* did I have to say something so waspishly stupid?

Why?

And then Joe came up.

'Victor!' he said. 'And Pat. How nice.'

Victor? Euggh!

Joe stood between us and helped himself to some food. 'So you two have got acquainted. Good. You were on my list for introductions.' He winked at me over his toasted goat cheese, which I felt a sudden irrational desire to shove up his nose.

'Yes,' I said sweetly. 'We have . . .' And I glared back.

'What this party needs,' he said, 'is livening up a little. I've got all my old records upstairs somewhere.'

'Oh,' groaned Victor. 'You're not going to trot out the Beatles? All that remember-the-sixties stuff is so self-indulgent.'

From Joe's face it was clear that he was going to do just that. 'Well, what then?' He stuck out his chin.

Victor shrugged. 'I don't know. What about Cream? Or Dylan?'

'You can't dance to *Dylan.*'

'Rod Stewart?' I said. 'I'm always dancing to him.'

194

They both looked at me with what I hoped was admiration but which I fear was unbelieving wonder. And while I was trying to live that down I was suddenly being frog-marched over towards the Edwardian three-piece suite and a group of people standing around it. One minute Joe had been frog-marching me, the next he had gone and I was left with Victor.

Polite conversation was called for, that dreadful commodity.

'Are you also a priest?' I said, dealing with the breathing as best I could. I found I had three Florentines in my hand, two of which were melting horribly as I attempted mastication of the third.

'No,' he said, dealing with his cheese a lot better than I was managing the biscuit. 'I'm a barrister.'

'How do you know Gertrude?' I could keep these pleasantries up all night and still not sound more than asinine. And I intended to do just that.

'She went to school with my mother.'

'Who is?'

'Dead.'

I could have spat in the eye of his maternal defeatist. Now I had to unbend a little. 'I'm so sorry,' I said.

'Not at all. It was when I was very small.'

'Ah. Um.' *Now* what could I say? 'It's odd we've not met before. I've known Gertrude for years and—'

'Not really,' he said. 'I've only just come back to London in the last year or so. I used to live in Lerwick.'

'Do they need barristers up there?'

'I'll say. A very criminal lot the Shetlanders.'

In my current state I would have believed him if he said they made their porridge out of goat dung. 'Really?' I said with interest.

He laughed. Which was hardly surprising. 'That's a joke, by the way. No, I had a place on Lerwick but I worked on the mainland. Scottish law is fascinating. Much more sensible than here.'

'Really?' I said again (such a useful word), feeling back on even ground. I was totally uninterested in either statement. 'How interesting. Do tell me more.'

'God, no,' he said laughing. 'The last thing I want to do is talk shop. Let me introduce you to this lot instead. Do you know anybody?'

I gave the group of about six or so a quick shufti. I had met one or two of them before and to these I nodded, but the rest were strangers, all more or less my age. They had that comfortable, fresh middle-classness about them which meant they were probably architects or teachers or something on the fringes of creativity. They were certainly not City men and women. You can always tell stockbrokers and finance people, even in their casual gear they stick out like a sore thumb, they have hungry, darting eyes and get a bit twitchy if they stand still for too long. This group looked quite at ease with itself and was probably quietly fulfilled. Channel 4 watchers and long-term members of the Greens, I reckoned. They were certainly not toy manufacturers and I doubted if any of them had ever even been near Slough.

'I don't know everyone,' I said.

He touched my arm very lightly as he went round the group and I was concentrating so hard on examining my response to the intimacy of the gesture that I missed most of the introductions. It seemed that the woman standing next to him with a pretty, flower-like face and a mass of blonde curls was called Ruth and was wife to the man standing at her side. We interrupted a laughing exchange between them as Victor said, 'And this is Roland,' a name of which I have always been very fond, what with the 'Song of' and all that. I managed to mutter something to this effect for which he thanked me, smiling very cheerily as he did so. He had a nice smile and nice light-blue eyes and I thought he was really very charming. He and his wife made a pretty couple, I almost said so but forbore. And then I lost track again but there was a John and a Juliet and a couple of something elses. We all chatted for a while, as the newly introduced do, before the group broke quite naturally into two, the one lot continuing a conversation about post-modernist architecture while our lot, Victor *(Victor!)*, Ruth, Roland and me talking about the boringness yet necessity of computers, which was—despite how it sounds—a very amusing conversation and one, thanks to Mr Harris and co, in which I could join. I began to regain my confidence and dropped the whole thing about being abrasive and keeping the barriers up. I had forgotten that meeting new people could be enjoyable, forgotten that very particular pleasure of presenting myself as a blank page while also filling in the blank pages of others, and, so far as I remember, I didn't *once* make reference to Rachel. Not *once*. I think Lydia's words had hit home, though I wasn't going to tell *her* that—ever.

Victor proved to be a bit of a wit and was enjoyable to be with but—oh, how relieved I was—I didn't feel a *frisson* about him at all. Not a fickle nor a spark of anything but the most social of interest raised itself. Gertrude, I thought to myself, you have got this particular one very wrong indeed.

It was quite clear that Ruth and Roland knew Victor very well and vice versa; you can tell these things, there were certain private jokes between them and they touched each other occasionally with that unselfconscious friendliness that only the passage of time will allow. Ruth did things with flowers and at one point she was recounting how she had had to take a series of bouquets to some Irish politicians at the House of Commons and how, by the time the security men had been through them, her careful arrangements looked, as she so succinctly put it, buggered. Victor gave her a great smacking kiss on the lips and told her not to swear so much and I looked at Roland to see how he was taking such a gesture, but he didn't seem at all concerned. In fact he was smiling. And Ruth didn't look at all bothered. So I decided to venture the fact again that I liked the name Roland, and why, and he said, very charmingly, that he rather liked the 'Song of' too, and quoted a little bit in which the hero shows his loyalty, courage and laudable honesty. I have always admired people who can quote things—a skill I lack—and on this occasion, strangely, it also produced a sensation of something-or-other down near my belly button which was not, altogether, proper.

To counter this I said, quite untruthfully, how well the names Ruth and Roland went together.

'Hmm,' he said. 'They do rather. Something about the rolling of the Rs. We've been known as Rolls and Royce for years.' He gave his wife an affectionate look.

'How nice,' I said, a little too positively. Such an affectionate glance between such a pretty couple should have been heart-warming. And it wasn't. I sent a note of command down to my belly button to please

199

stop twanging, and I changed the subject.

'Are you connected with the law too?' I asked. But I never got a reply because, quite suddenly, something absolutely extraordinary happened. There in Gertrude's kitchen, thonking away from the living room, pulsing through the kitchen, came the sound of—oh no, spare me, I thought—Rod Stewart! Fleetingly I decided I had probably gone mad. I mean, Mozart was usual, a little Chopin perhaps and once, on a summer's day at a lunch party, there had been some Club Quintet Jazz, but *this!* This was impossible.

'Well, well,' said Victor. 'Sounds like we might be dancing after all.'

And then Joe appeared, looking very wicked. 'When your mother is in love,' he said, 'you can get away with murder. I think you should all get going before she comes out of her rosy cloud and realises what I've put on. Ruth?' He held out his hand to her. 'Shall we? Carrie has quite rightly decided that she'll sit this one out.'

And off they went.

I sort of gaped in their direction just because the whole thing was so surreal and became conscious, eventually, of Victor's hand extended in similar wise, and his saying, 'Shall *we . . .?'*

Whereupon, unable to think of a good reason why not, I did. With him kind enough not to react to the chocolate which I had transferred so stickily to his grasp, we followed on Joe's and Ruth's heels.

I turned once, at the kitchen door, I don't know why, and saw Roland watching us all go and twang went the belly button again. Fiddle-dee-dee, I thought, and off I went.

Victor was a good dancer. At one point he said, 'That dress doesn't go with your enthusiasm for this sort of thing.'

'Doesn't it?' I said, puffing a little and trying to pull the skirt down a bit for it had risen higher than was seemly given the athletic nature of what we were doing. Even Gertrude and Alec were wobbling about together. It really was most extraordinary. 'I told you, I do this at home quite a lot,' I said, in between more puffs.

'Where's home?' he asked.

I told him.

'Ah yes,' he said, as if suddenly enlightened. 'Gertrude told me about you. You've just got divorced, and you've got a little girl?'

'That's right,' I said, thinking, You know darned well I have. And the dress is an indicator that I am in mourning for all that wasted effort.

Puff, puff, puff.

'Nasty business, divorce,' he said. 'I wouldn't want to be in that position.'

'Well, don't put yourself in a situation where it might happen,' I said curtly. 'I certainly never will again.'

'Trouble is you never know, do you?' he said.

'You just have to keep on your guard, that's all.' And I rolled my eyes and puffed a bit more to give the general impression of imperviousness, and on we went.

Gertrude was waving at us over Alec's by now much-disturbed white thatch. I waved back. Betrayer, I thought. Well planned, well executed, but no, not this one. This one is very nice but you can keep him.

Ruth and Joe were doing some quite wild things over by the fireplace. She was small enough for him to lift up and throw around which, in remarkably un-priestlike fashion, he was doing. And Carrie was holding her bump in the shadows by the drinks table and smiling milkily. Beyond her the wind and the rain were still making their presence felt and I turned my back on the sight, throwing myself even more feverishly into the music. I can dance quite well once selfconsciousness goes, and since I felt absolutely secure in my uninterest, and since it might be even better if I *did* make a complete fool of myself, I went at it with abandon.

We danced about two and a half numbers, which I knew so well that I was perfectly able to choreograph, and at the same time manage to fence any slight attempt on Victor's part to strike up further and deeper acquaintance by gasping a lot and answering in monosyllables.

So that all in all I was enjoying myself when Ruth suddenly appeared saying, 'I wish someone would dance with Roland. He's all by himself over by the door.'

'You dance with him then,' said Victor. 'I'm having much too good a time with Patricia. Go on, bugger off.' He laughed delightedly and grabbed my arm pulling me close.

'All right, I will,' she said, laughing back. 'I just thought you and I could have a go, that's all.' And she began to move away. 'Ro and I don't dance very well together. He always steps on my feet . . .'

Something snapped inside me. I just thought it was so disloyal of her. And anyway, Victor and I had been together for quite long enough. I didn't want him getting any ideas.

'I'll go and ask him,' I said. 'If that's all right?'

'Fine,' she said, putting her little hand on Victor's shoulder and already turning away. 'Come on, Gorilla. How about a bit of action?'

Really, I thought, what a *creepy* thing to say. I looked over at the doorway. You foolish, foolish wife . . . For I knew which one I preferred. So did my pinging navel. Well, on your own head be it, I very nearly said. Victor gave a wonderfully theatrical gesture of regretting letting me go before Ruth and he moved off together. So, over to Roland and the doorway I went.

'Will you dance?' I said, thinking, What the

hell, I might as well have a good flirt. I hadn't had one for years. It was another thing I used to be quite good at.

'All right,' he said cheerfully (he was a very smiley sort of a person), and he put down his glass. My hand, now devoid of chocolate, went into his, and we began.

Gertrude waved again, even more gaily, and I waved back with equal enthusiasm. Her hips were going like a galleon rocked within the safe haven of Alec's steadying hands. Oh, Gertrude, I thought, what fools it makes of us all.

By the time Roland and I actually got to a space where we could move around a bit, the tempo had changed completely and we were standing opposite each other in a don't-know-what-to-do-with-our-arms kind of a way, for the next track was a really slow and slobby one which begins 'First cut is the deepest', and is all about someone getting over one love affair and trying to start another. Which was *quite* wrong for the mood I was in.

'We could sit this one out,' I said, 'and wait for something a bit livelier.'

He shrugged. 'Why?' he said.

There was no answer to that.

It is a most peculiar situation, to go from the reserve of being strangers to holding each other in what can only be described, even if you keep a modicum of distance in your dancers' clinch, as an intimate embrace. No wonder the Victorians banned the waltz. Oh, well, I thought, for we couldn't go on shuffling in front of each other and looking like a pair of circling bantams, so I sort of dived in. It is an aspect of the party ritual, I reminded myself, and quite in order. I stopped shuffling and he stopped shuffling and we had to do *something*.

There is not much you can do in slow numbers like that if you are dancing with a member of the opposite sex. You can either dance with your hands lightly connecting with the other's body, a gap between the two of you, which means you have to engage each other's eyes or go squinty trying not to. Or you can hold on really close and then you have the problem of your face (if you are the female and—as is usual given the evolution of gender—shorter) pressing warmly into his chest or shoulder, while he, if you are lucky (or unlucky if you dislike him, which, I have to confess, was not the emotion uppermost in my mind at the time), has his face somewhere in your hair and near your ear. We came about halfway in this latter category, a kind of decent compromise which still left room for the odd snippet of conversation (nice those Florentines, what a dreadful storm, etc, etc) and I decided that, since I was no marriage breaker and was certainly *not* looking for anything romantic or sexual beyond this album track, I might as well enjoy the moment guiltlessly. After all, I had his wife's blessing.

So I did. And what Rudolph/Randolph had started, with that hand on my small-of-back, grew alarmingly. I found myself going quite sort of liquid in the muscles department. It is *perfectly all right*, Patricia, I told myself as I closed my eyes, and just concentrated on the pleasurable experience. *Perfectly all right* to be (only momentarily, for heaven's sake) held in somebody attractive's arms and smelling the smell that skin through shirt can sometimes bring. Next to hot buttered toast it has to be one of life's best nasal experiences.

And then—oh, thief of time—the music suddenly ground to a horrible stop and the lights went out. We stood absolutely still for half a second before Roland gave my waist the faintest squeeze, released me, and said in executive fashion, 'Stay there.'

Since I could see nothing, I obeyed, while confusion and babble grew all around. And there is no doubt that as I stood there, blind as a bat and being bumped and jostled a bit, I felt, well, very sorry it had had to end that way. *Very* sorry indeed . . .

CHAPTER FOURTEEN

Gertrude lit a candle and held it aloft so that we were all transfixed like rabbits in torchlight, caught in odd postures left over from the music of a minute or two ago. I could see Alec with his arm protectively round Carrie, and Ruth was, rather like me, standing in the middle of the room where, presumably, her partner had also left her. She smiled at me and I re-realised, crossly, that she was *very* pretty as well as very small and daintily made. I looked away.

Somebody called out, 'Is this part of the celebrations, Gertrude?' in a slightly edgy way.

'Not at all,' she said. 'The lights have fused or something. It might be the storm. Joe's checking the meters . . . I'll get some more candles. As a matter of fact,' she said happily, 'I should have thought to do a party by candlelight before. We all look so lovely in it, don't we?'

I looked back at Ruth again. 'Yes, we fucking well do,' I found myself muttering.

'Pardon,' said some polite individual standing just behind me.

I shook my head. What on earth was happening to me? Standing in a crowded room talking, nay, *swearing* to myself? Snap out of it, girl, I told myself.

'Pardon?' said the individual again.

'Oh nothing, nothing,' I said cheerily. 'Just praying, that's all.'

Ruth came over to me.

'Shame,' she said wickedly. 'I was enjoying that smooch.'

I was just about to say, with unseemly

fervour, that so was I, when I remembered it was her husband I had been smooching with. And anyway, what was she up to enjoying one with Victor like that? I found myself quite disliking her which was an oddly satisfactory emotion.

Our respective partners reappeared.

'All the street lights are out,' said Victor. 'And I don't know if it belongs to anyone here but there's a tree down right across a BMW out there.'

A blood-curdling cry, not unlike an animal in pain, rent the air and someone went rushing past me out into the night.

Roland said, 'Does anyone want another drink?'

'I'll just have a juice,' said Ruth.

'Me too,' he said. 'I'm driving.'

I thought—without wanting to—that he was absolutely the opposite of Gordon: not only *much* prettier but responsible about drinking and good things like that. And why, oh why, was I making *comparisons*? Wretched man. I turned away and looked at Victor and wished I could summon up a bubble or two for him, it would have been very nice to get close to someone in an animal sort of a way, but no bubble. I couldn't even invent one.

Victor rubbed his hands and looked back at me gleefully. 'Well *I'm* not driving,' he said. 'And I *will* have a drink. Beer, I think . . .'

That was a relief. It had crossed my mind

that later on he might offer me a lift home. At least that possibility was out of the way. Really, the way a woman's mind works in situations like that. It's so *arrogant* assuming things, but it's fifty-fifty likely so you just *have* to. I relaxed with him after that.

'And you?' he continued. 'Are you driving?'

'No, I came by taxi and I shall depart by taxi,' I said, very firmly. 'In fact—' I squinted at my watch in the flickering light '—I should really think about wending my way now.'

'Oh, don't go for a minute,' said Ruth. 'Or do you have to get back to your daughter?'

'Well, no. She's with friends.'

'There you are then,' said Roland kindly. 'You can stay. And drink. Those burgundies are amazing.'

'Well, why don't you go and get her one,' said Victor, 'instead of just standing around.'

'Right,' he said. 'Stay where you are.' And he pointed a finger at me. I felt like biting it off.

'Well,' I said to Ruth, assuming a bright motherly look. 'Do you have children? I've only got one. She's ten.' I waited for my usual fluency about Rachel to follow but it didn't.

'Er, no—' said Ruth.

'My, my,' said Victor to me. 'You must have been *very* young when you had her—'

'It's the candlelight,' I snapped. 'Smoothes the wrinkles—'

'Oh, bugger off, Vic,' said Ruth, so that I

209

began to like her a bit more again.

'All right,' he said. 'I'll go and see what's happening outside.'

'Do,' she said positively.

He did.

When he had gone she said, 'If she's ten you've probably forgotten all about the baby stage and everything.'

'Oh, no,' I said. 'You never quite forget all that.'

She cast her pretty eyes downwards and my heart sank. It seemed to follow her gaze to the floor and remain there, long after she had looked up at me again. I knew what was coming and I really did not want to hear it.

'Actually,' she smiled selfconsciously, 'I'm just pregnant and, I mean, I'm very happy about it, only it wasn't exactly planned.' She gave a rueful laugh. 'Is it difficult to manage a career and everything? Most of our friends haven't got children and I was talking to Carrie earlier . . .' She looked ceilingwards. 'That didn't help at *all*.'

'It wouldn't,' I said. 'But basically the answer is to—' my own horror story crowded back into my mind '—keep both your marriage and your baby alive. If you do that then you can do almost anything. I made the mistake of *not* doing that, which is why I'm divorced.'

'He's a good husband,' she said feelingly. 'And I love him very much. Only he does seem to think it will all happen naturally. He's such an optimist.'

'Really?' I said with as much lightly toned interest as I could muster. 'Well, it's not him who's having the baby, is it?'

'*Exactly*,' she said. 'That's just what I tell him . . .'

And we carried on the conversation (me rather lamely) until Roland reappeared, bright-eyed and bearing the drinks.

Ruth dismissed him. 'Take Vic's out to him, will you, Ro?' And like the well-trained husband he clearly was, he did so.

Lydia would have been proud of me. I found that just about the last thing I wanted to go on doing was discuss this erstwhile favoured subject of mine.

Still, knowing the form, I carried on. 'Do you get morning sickness?' I asked.

'Oh, no,' she said wide-eyed. 'I just feel wonderful. All the time.'

'You look it,' I said, through gritted teeth. Somewhere in the back of my sinuses was the smell of her husband's chest through his shirt.

She lowered her eyes and almost whispered, 'And the other thing—'

'Yes?'

'Well, I just feel so sexy all the time.'

'Really?' I said stiffly. 'How nice for you.' I took out a tissue and blew my nose very hard to remove what lingered. Then I knocked back my drink and said, 'I must go and find Gertrude and ring for a taxi.'

211

'Where do you live?'

I told her.

'Well, why don't you let Roland drive you home? He wouldn't mind.'

I put my hand on top of her shapely little arm, and thought, You naive thing. 'I think I'd prefer a taxi . . . But thanks for the offer.'

And I scooted off, cheeks afire with guilt, desire and drink, bumped unseeing into Roland and Victor in the candlelit hallway, didn't stop as Victor said, 'Hey! Steady' and held my elbow for a moment, and whizzed on to the kitchen telephone.

Gertrude and Alec were down there, eating again. With a few other doughty souls. I couldn't have eaten a thing. I just wanted to get away as quickly as possible.

'Have a brandy snap,' she called. 'If I say so myself they are very good.'

'No, thanks,' I called. 'Can I ring for a taxi?'

'Must you go? It's only midnight. I thought it was all getting warmed up again with the candles and everything. Alec says we should play Murder in the Dark.' She giggled like a schoolgirl and I distinctly saw Alec give her ear a lick. Disgusting, geriatric nonsense, I felt like saying.

'Babysitters,' I muttered. I don't like telling lies very much. I tried my own cab number.

'Sorry,' said the answering voice, not sounding sorry at all. 'Nothing.'

'What?'

'It's the gale—everyone's panicking. No cabs available.' He sounded joyous.

I put the phone down. 'Gertrude. Do you have a cab number anywhere?'

She unstuck herself from Alec's side and floated grandly across to me. As she bent down to get her Thomson's directory from the cupboard nearby she said, 'Why go? You seemed to like him well enough.' And she straightened up, handed me the book and smiled like a siren. 'From what I saw anyway.'

I took the book. 'I'm surprised you noticed anything at all in your state.'

'Hoity-toity!' She laughed. 'What a baby you are.'

'And you,' I said, riffling through the directory. And then remorse welled up. 'I don't mean that. I'm glad you're so happy'

'Not half,' she said, relaunching her bulk in the direction of her happiness and winking most annoyingly. 'And what is more—' she put her finger to her lips and lowered her voice '—*we* don't have to worry about condoms! There's a lot to be said for late blessings . . .'

Hah! I thought. And hah! again.

*   *   *

There were no taxis. Simply none to be had anywhere. I decided to swallow my pride and ask Joe and Carrie if they would make what would be a monumental detour and take me

213

home. So back up to the party room I went. A lot of people had gone already. Joe was there but Carrie wasn't.

I took a deep breath—I *hate* asking favours—and said, 'Joe, you couldn't possibly see your way to driving me home could you? I can't get a taxi for love or money and—'

'We haven't got the car here,' he said with genuine concern. 'The kids are at a friend's for the night and Carrie and I are staying—otherwise of course I would. Alec brought us over and he's taking us back tomorrow. As usual, the old grey horse is in dry dock.'

I remembered that he and Carrie lived permanently at war with their huge Peugeot. 'Ah,' I said. 'Yes, well, I understand, and thanks. Perhaps if I ask Alec he might take me . . .'

'Weeell,' said Joe. 'He's probably drunk too much for a start, and for another thing—'

'Yes?'

'Well, he'll be staying here tonight too.'

'Oh, *shit*,' I said and I stamped my foot.

'You could stay,' he said mildly.

'No, I couldn't.' The thought of getting up in the morning with all those happy, sexually fulfilled souls noshing around the breakfast table was a bitter one. 'I have to get back for—for—' I couldn't lie to a man of the cloth and say for Rachel '—for Brian.'

'Brian?' asked Joe.

'Brian,' I said.

'Brian?' repeated a voice. I looked at Joe. So far as I could see his lips did not move.

'Who's Brian?'

I turned round and there was Roland, rocking on his heels, hands in pockets.

'Brian?'

'My dog,' I said.

'God,' he said. 'I hate dogs.'

'Well, *I* love them.'

How could I *say* that?

'Despite that,' he said, smiling, 'may I offer you a lift home? Gertrude said you needed one and I can go in your direction.'

'Where's Ruth?' I said.

'Over there.' He nodded in the direction of the french windows. She and Victor were looking out and pointing at things.

'Well, if you're sure, I suppose it's all right,' I said, as ungraciously as I could muster. 'Thank you.' And I dived out to the hall to fetch my coat before anything else could be said.

I put on my coat and buttoned it so savagely that one of them came off in my hand. I thought, I am not even going to say good-bye to anyone. I am going to keep this anger I feel so that I can build a wall with it. In the mirror in front of me was myself, looking dark as thunder. What the mirror did not show was that my heart was beating loudly and mercilessly under the best quality Liberty wool. Why did he have to go and smell so nice? Why did he have to go and be so nice? I grabbed my bag and put it under my arm and punched it.

'Fit?' he said, appearing in the mirror, dimly shadowed, and dangerous in the candlelight.

To burst, I thought, as we went out into the howling night.

*   *   *

We didn't talk for a while, apart from my initial, 'I've got a Renault too. They're very good, aren't they?'

To which he said, 'I suppose so. I'm not into cars. They just get you from A to B. Where exactly is B, by the way?'

So I told him and we drove in silence.

There was quite enough to look at in the streets. Trees blown down or leaning dangerously. Quite often we had to take detours because whole roads were blocked. Fire engines were out, police were in abundance and once or twice we saw that trees had fallen through roofs. Putney Common looked devastated with great up-ended trunks lying around, roots skywards, like giants brought low.

'Oh, God,' I said, suddenly remembering my role in life. 'I hope Rachel's all right.'

'Your daughter?'

'My daughter.'

'I'm sure she will be. Where is she?'

'Staying with friends for the night.'

'Really?' he said. 'So you *don't* have to get back for the babysitter?'

'I never said I did.'

'You told Gertrude you did.'

'How do you know that?'

'Because she suggested I take you home.'

'Oh, did she?'

Silence.

'Why you?'

He took his hands off the wheel momentarily in a gesture of not knowing and looked at me out of the corner of his eye.

'Don't ask me,' he said. 'I'm only the piano player . . .'

I refused to laugh.

We drove through Barnes which looked less windblown. 'Seems to have died down a little around here,' he said. 'Still worried about your daughter?'

'You never cease to worry about your children,' I said crisply. 'As you will discover soon enough yourself.'

'Really?' He negotiated a branch in the road. 'Thank you for the warning.'

'Don't mention it.'

'Tell me about her.'

'Who?'

'Your daughter.'

'Well, she's, er . . .' I began. And then, annoyingly, I couldn't think of much to say. So I sort of shrugged and said, 'Well . . . she's just

217

. . . well . . . a lovely person . . .'

And he, if you please, had the gall to say, 'Like her mother?'

So that I snapped my mouth shut.

When we got to Mortlake I reconstituted my mouth to direct him homewards.

'Please,' I said, 'can we drive past my friend's house? Just to see that it's in one piece?'

'Certainly we can.'

And it was. It was dark, whole and, apart from the rose bushes looking a bit buffeted, quite as it should be.

'And now for yours?' He cocked an enquiring eye at me.

'Yes,' I said tersely, thinking, Don't ask him in, whatever you do *don't* ask him in.

Florizel Street had one small tree down which we drove round but at my end it was more or less untouched. The bare wisteria branches were down outside and hanging limply across the front door and the broken trellis was going rat-a-tat against the bay window. He pulled into the Webbs' vacant space, in front of my car and turned off the engine.

'No need to do that,' I squeaked. 'I'll just nip out.'

'Which one is it?' he said.

'That one,' I pointed to the branch-strewn porch. He got out, undid my door, and I attempted to get out too—but still with my

218

seatbelt on. It being an inertia-reel thing I was sort of twanged back in. He laughed.

'I thought you were rather up on technology,' he said, and leaned across me to release it. I mean, right across me. So that I could smell his hair. I shrank back in the seat to avoid contact. And the seatbelt recoiled itself. He gave me his hand, which I accepted as lightly as I could while still using its help, and out I stumbled.

'Well, thank you ever so much,' I said, side-stepping and shaking the hand which was still in mine.

'Not at all,' he said, and moved across to open my gate.

'Good bye,' I said positively, which was slightly marred by the fact that he was on my pathway and I was still on the pavement.

'You'll need to get this pinned back up.' He was at the front door now, pushing at the branches. 'I don't think it's snapped though.'

'Oh, good,' I said breezily and fumbled for my keys.

'Could I use your lavatory?' he said.

'What?' I froze.

'Lav-a-tory,' he said.

'What?' I was still fumbling in my bag though I had found the keys. They were rattling in my fingers in a passing imitation of my teeth which also seemed to be joggling about.

'I need a pee,' he said. 'Do you mind?'

'Eek,' I went. The heart, shameful organ, did what they say in books and turned over. Ruth, I thought to myself. Ruth. Ruth. Ruth.

'You pee a lot when you're pregnant,' I said.

That shook him, as indeed it was meant to do.

'Uh,' he said. 'I expect you do.'

'Oh, come on then.' I opened the door and switched on the light very quickly. It didn't work. I realised that no one in the street was showing a light and that the street itself was also unlit. What illumination we had came from the moon. On a blowy night the moon does seem to exult in itself.

'I've got a torch in the car,' he said, and returned with it a second or two later while I was still standing lost for what to do in the hallway.

'Up there, first on the left,' I said.

I walked through to the kitchen automatically switching on the non-existent light. I heard Brian grunt—his usual greeting—in the darkness. And against my better judgement I felt around for some matches and took them through to the dining room where my old oil lamp, dear brassy thing, lived. I used to use it at dinner parties and it still had a bit of oil left in it from Rachel's Hallowe'en party. I say against my better judgement because the glass bowl, being pink, sheds a beautiful soft light which is much conducive to romance and not at *all* conducive

220

to saying good bye to someone as pretty as he. Even if he was someone else's husband, someone else who was pregnant's husband . . .

I kept my coat on and lit the wick. Sure enough it bathed everything in a gentle aura of rosiness. I heard the flush of the cistern and saw the flickering of his torch on the stairs and then he came into the room.

'How pretty,' he said, a deal too softly.

I looked about at the walls and the curtains and things like that. 'Isn't it?' I said.

'I don't mean that,' he said.

'Eek,' I went again.

I thought of many things. I thought of developing hiccups. I thought of vomiting on his feet. I thought of other even worse things by which to defend myself. And as I thought of all these ghastly projections he walked over to me, put his hand on my shoulders, said, 'I'm going to do something I've wanted to do all night.'

And as I went 'Eek' for the umpteenth time, he kissed me. With a good deal too much tongue about it. Or not enough. I was quite uncertain which.

'Ruth,' I murmured in among all the gobbling.

'Ruth-less,' he managed back.

I had no muscles left again. And my eyelids had become glued together. So that I had the merest silly thought that while I kept up the kiss with them closed it was quite all right and wasn't really happening. Only if I opened them would it become a reality. So I jolly well kept them tight shut for a very long time. And then I felt a very soft, warm rubbing around the back of my legs and I wondered, from some far-off faint brain sense, how he was also managing that. It went on for quite a long time (as did the kiss) when I realised that it had a sort of furry quality to it which was not exactly in keeping with male, human. More in keeping, I slowly, slowly realised, with male, dog. It was bloody Brian, in effervescent mood, for him, going round and round our legs and whimpering slightly. I pulled away—very sadly actually—and gasped. 'It's the dog.'

'I know,' he breathed, and I felt him give Brian a delicate but positive push with his foot. I still didn't open my eyes. Having made the bond with myself that once I did open them this sort of thing had to stop, I didn't see why I should rush the undertaking. When I opened my eyes he would be a married man with a baby on the way. With them closed he was a purely sensual delight. So we went on kissing for a considerable time before he eventually stopped and I just *had* to unglue my lids.

'Mmm,' he said holding on to the tops of my arms and grimacing down at the floor. 'Woman's best friend seems to have something for you.'

Still, I felt certain, with the glaze of undeniable arousal in my eyes, I looked downwards too. And if I had eeked a bit in the past it was nothing to the blood-curdling eek I let out now. Blood-curdling being the operative word. For there was Brian, almost as lacklustre as usual, with only the modest difference that his tail curled upwards instead of hanging resolutely downwards. And the reason for this pertness was hanging out of his jaws.

Bulstrode, dead as the proverbial dodo, hung limp and filmy-eyed from Brian's dribbling mouth.

Bulstrode!

CHAPTER FIFTEEN

So this was how God punished adulterers.

I sat down and wept. What with the dead Bulstrode at my feet, all those astonished hormones suddenly forced into life, and Roland saying (from very far off, it seemed to me), 'It's only a rabbit. Don't take on so.' And then, quite funnily really, but in a genuine aside to himself he said, 'This! Over a rabbit! What on earth is she like over *people* for God's sake?'

So I stopped weeping and removed my hands from my face and said, 'They will have Brian shot now.'

'What? For killing a rabbit? No chance.'

'Oh, you don't know the redoubtable Webbs,' I said. 'I think she's a magistrate for a start, or a local councillor, or perhaps just related to royalty, or—who knows—perhaps all three? Anyway, there is no doubt in my mind that she is a woman of influence, and that that—' I pointed to the recumbent and peaceful one '—is a passed-on rabbit. Their passed-on rabbit. Their much adored, pampered, despicable only daughter's passed-on rabbit. For which he—' I pointed at Brian who had the brass nerve to give the faintest suggestion of a wag of his tail and it seemed to me he winked, though I had had rather a lot of the burgundy and another, more recent betrayer of my sanity, so perhaps I imagined that bit '—will have to make the ultimate sacrifice.'

Roland sat down opposite me at the dining table, put his hand under his chin and gave me a look that was a good deal too amused in the circumstances. 'Let me tell you an apocryphal tale,' he said.

I blew my nose. 'No, thank you.'

'No, listen,' he said, and put out his hand to hold mine. Since it had my snotty tissue in it and he did not flinch I had to give him full marks and concede.

'Very well,' I said. I was too miserable to care.

'Once upon a time,' he began, 'there was a family with a dog who lived next door to another family who had a rabbit. And one night the family with the dog opened their back door to let him in and guess what?'

'Oh,' I said wearily. 'I can guess. He'd done a Brian.'

'Absolutely right. He'd done a Brian.'

We both looked down at he whose name had been spoken, who immediately dropped the *cadaver* cuniculus and slopped himself flat on the floor, his head between his paws in characteristically despairing fashion.

'So?' I asked.

'So the lady of the house, practical as all females are, scooped up the dead rabbit, which was looking not unlike this one—' we both looked down again, this time at the grubby mangled furry lump '—and she shampooed it.'

'She *what!*' I shrieked.

'She shampooed it. And then she dried it with a hair dryer, and she combed it until it looked pristine again. Dead—but pristine.'

'What on earth for?' Irritation rose and overtook misery. A shaggy rabbit story was all I needed.

'To make it look as if it died of natural causes.' He grinned delightedly. 'And then she popped it back into its hutch for the owners to find the next morning. One extinct rabbit, dead of natural causes.' He raised his free hand. 'Presto! End of problem.'

I removed my tissued fist from his reach. 'Are you suggesting that I do the same with . . .

that?'

'Why not?'

'For a start Bulstrode didn't live in a hutch—'

'*Bulstrode!?*'

'I didn't name the fucking thing.'

'Calm down,' he said, still looking amused. The mental bucket came off Lydia's head and on to his. 'It doesn't matter. Just let's get it cleaned up—I'll do it if you like—and then we can put him back wherever he came from.'

'But he's probably got bite marks and blood and t-t-torn f-f-flesh.' I couldn't quite keep the tears away.

'I doubt it,' he said and knelt down to examine the body. 'None at all. I think the dog just broke its neck—or it died of fright. It'll clean up lovely. What does it live in if it's not in a hutch?'

'A run. A big wooden and wire thing they made.'

'Well, that's fine,' he said, scooping up the remains. 'We can collapse it a bit on top of him. It'll look like the wind brought it down. Bring the lamp. Where's the kitchen?'

And off we trundled, me in front with the oil lamp, alternating between feeling I was living in a Warhol movie and being Anna Neagle as Florence Nightingale. 'This is ridiculous,' I said. 'Plain ridiculous. No one will believe it. They'll *know*.'

'Well,' he said setting Bulstrode down on

226

the draining board and running water into the bowl. 'They'll have to prove it, won't they? Even if they do suspect, the *prima facie* evidence will be against them. And unless they go for an autopsy—'

'Nothing,' I said darkly, 'would surprise me.'

'Unlikely, though. Bring the lamp here.'

I did, setting it down next to the body. Brian shuffled past us and got into his basket with all the vigour of an earthworm. How could he have come to life enough to do this? It occurred to me that if he was called to give evidence in court no one would believe he was capable, which was a cheering thought.

'Washing-up liquid,' said my descendant of Burke and Hare.

I handed it to him.

He did the whole thing very well and minute observation of the body by him proved to show nothing more than bruising. And while he gave *that* particular body its minute observation, I— I am sorry to say—was giving *his* body mine. Getting the hots for someone during such a pantomime as this was totally unacceptable. So, totally unacceptable I was.

'Hair dryer,' he said, all surgeon-like. 'Take the torch.'

I ran upstairs to my bedroom and—God help me—as well as getting the requisite appliance I gave my hitherto singular domain the quick once-over, straightening the duvet, stuffing used tissues into the basket, kicking my vest under the bed and, worse, putting a quick burst of Givenchy behind my ears. What *was* I doing? I threw off my coat and skeetered down again quite mortified at my own duality.

'You've put scent on,' he said as I handed him the dryer and plugged it in.

'To cover the smell of death,' I replied, quick as ninepence. And was quite glad of the rosy glow which hid my blushes, or I hoped it did.

Of course the dryer didn't work because there was no electricity. He had to towel him dry, which he did most tenderly in the circumstances and at the end of it all Bulstrode looked extremely well. Dead but well, if you can imagine it. He even closed the poor creature's eyes. Then he brushed the fur all smooth, picked him up and said, *'Voilà,* madame. Natural causes, I think.'

'Could we build up a little to putting him back?' I said. I really was quite frightened at the whole idea of consummating this achievement.

He replaced him on the draining board. 'Well, we can't have coffee,' he said.

'How about a brandy?'

'That would make an acceptable alternative,' and he pulled off my pink rubber gloves with a flourish. It was so extraordinarily like a surgical situation that I couldn't help saying so. At which point he reached out and took my face in his hands and said, 'We could do a by-pass on the brandy and play Doctors and Nurses . . .' At that I went very weak and wobbly and did another 'eek' and grabbed the lamp hurriedly, using it rather like a crucifix against a vampire. I didn't *want* to do that, it just happened that way. Years of conditioning about not getting seduced, I suppose, dammit.

'I think a brandy,' I said, thinking of Ruth and her little pea-sized foetus.

Back in the dining room, on opposite sides of the table, it was easier. Though I did still feel dreadfully turned on.

'You'll need wellingtons,' he said, which threw me completely since I was thinking of things other than Bulstrode's return.

We sipped our brandies.

'How clever of you to come up with such a good way out,' I said. 'Is that story true? Where did you hear it?'

'Oh, Ruth told me, I think.'

How could he do that? How could he just mention her name so easily? Given the circumstances and everything. I hardened my heart and all the other bits that were going woggly about him.

'Really?' I said, with more fond imaginings of being coolly relaxed.

'But it's apocryphal, like I said. And the ending is quite funny.'

'Tell me,' I said, through gritted brandy glass.

'Well, in the story, and don't read anything

into it so far as this situation is concerned—'

'I have no intention of reading anything into anything,' I said bluntly, thinking I had made my point rather well. 'Go on.'

'We left the lady of the house stuffing the newly refurbished, though dead, rabbit back into its hutch, yes?'

I nodded.

'And the next morning, while she was pegging out her clothes—'

'A cheerful domestic scene—'

'A cheerful domestic scene.' He nodded. 'She heard, not at all surprisingly, the wail of a child who has just discovered that its rabbit— like the parrot of "and-now-for-something-completely-different" fame—was a deceased rabbit . . .'

'Yes?'

'So, she of the clothes pegs pops her head over the fence to compound her felony of deceit and says, "What's up, dearie?" To which the distraught child, clutching the freshly shampooed cadaver, says tearfully, "Well, my rabbit died yesterday, and I buried him at the bottom of the garden, and now he's back h-h-here in his hu-hu-hutch!"'

Roland was holding his sides with the mirth of it. And I was trying very hard to remain unmoved. But really, despite everything, it was so funny that I couldn't remain unbending after all and I gave in to the kind of laughter that makes you sob it is so evil and wild. I went

230

at it like a cackling hen out of hell until I remembered, quite suddenly, that the fount of this tale was his wife. That stopped me instantly.

'We'd better get it over with,' I said firmly. And picking up the lamp I led the way back to the kitchen.

Mortifyingly he fitted into my wellingtons, if a little tightly, and even if—as I couldn't help myself saying—they were jolly loose on me and needed two pairs of socks for total comfort. I squashed into Rachel's which were much too large for her, as I felt I had to say (I didn't want him thinking there was anything wrong with my daughter—why?), though I couldn't get my heels down into them properly and had to stagger rather than walk as we made our torchlit sortie, with the pristinely deceased Bulstrode, across the garden, through the fence gap (revealed again by the stormy wind, thanks to the cowboy outfit I had employed to renovate it) and into the Webbs' back garden.

Happily most of our work was already done for us in that the wooden run was half down anyway, though whether by the elements or by Brian's assault I couldn't say. Roland knelt while I held the torch, and he placed the body very gently on the ground and then stacked the half collapsed timbers all over it. It looked rather convincing in the pool of light from my torch. Indeed, I was just saying that when the

231

noise of a door stage left stopped my eulogies and another pool of light, not from my hands, came flickering through the darkness. And a strangled voice, sounding somewhat like the Queen might sound if one of her corgis copped it, said,

'Bulstrode! Bulstrode! Are you all right?'

And I just about had time to catch Roland's breathy muttering of, 'It'd serve you right if he said yes—' when Penelope hove into view and elbowed me and *my* torch into oblivion.

*　　　*　　　*

I forgot all thoughts of horseplay. I forgot all power of speech. I also forgot that my heels were in several-sizes-too-small boots.

When I took a step back in true cartoon aghast fashion I promptly fell over, or rather back, into Penelope Webb's mahonia.

Horticulturists among you will know that such shrubs boast prickly leaves. Very prickly leaves. Prickly leaves which are second only to holly in their ability to puncture sensitive skin, which mine most certainly was. It occurred to me as I went down that mahonia was perfectly suited to the Penelope Webb type. Lots of bright appealing berries but watch out if you try to touch. A long metaphorical consideration, but then, I did have quite a long and complicated way to fall. Mahonia never was, nor ever would be, a favourite of mine.

And I remember thinking a further two things as I went down. One was that I would swap all this, verily all this, and go back to being Mrs Murray living with Gordon Murray, I truly did. And the other was that what the leaves were managing to do so cruelly to all my exposed bits (backs of knees, arms and wrists, neck and ears) would, in any event, unquestionably put paid to horseplay— thoughts of which had, even as I tumbled like Lucifer, begun to resurface.

My (or rather Roland's) torch went out and as I finished falling it occurred to me that I might just stay down there for ever. It was certainly better than emerging and facing what would require to be faced. I closed my eyes and prepared to give myself up to remaining inanimate. At last I knew what it felt like to be Brian.

CHAPTER FIFTEEN

People just will *not* leave you alone. You try to die quietly and peacefully by sticking your head in your gas oven and the milkman decides to call for payment and hauls you out; you convince yourself that you look good in red (though mother always said you didn't) so some kind friend takes up the maternal refrain and tells you you look like an open wound.

233

Similarly, much as I would have happily gone on lying there, it was not to be. Roland hauled me out. And Penelope Webb stood by, ill-lit by torchlight, and looking a deal more proud than the fair Titania.

Speech was called for.

'I'm so sorry about Bulstrode,' I began. And then, 'Ouch!' For Roland had given my upper arm an unhorse-play-like squeeze.

'Mrs Murray saw something was wrong,' he said. 'And that's why we came over here.' And he squeezed hard again just as I took breath to speak I know not what. He then went on at some length about the storm, the collapse of the run, and made an astonishingly ambivalent series of statements, which ended up with the incontestable, 'And I am afraid that he was already dead . . .'

Penelope Webb shrank. Titania gave way to harassed motherhood for which I felt mostly relief and just a little sympathy. She ran her fingers through her hair putting the hairband at a most comical angle and said, 'It's her birthday this weekend. I only came back because she was worried about the ruddy thing—' I warmed to her '—and now I've got to go back and tell her *this*. Oh, it's too much, it really is.' She stamped her foot and I saw at once where Alison got some of her characteristics. 'And Rex will be livid. He spent ages building this bloody thing.' She gave the tumbled run a kick.

Warmer and warmer . . .

'Shall I bury him?' asked Roland.

'Shouldn't she see the body—to grieve over it or something?' I added, calling up some vestige of child psychology and feeling rather pleased with myself. 'Ouch!'

Roland had my arm in that grip again.

'I think we ought to get it buried,' he said positively, with just a hint of warning in his voice.

'Oh, I *see*,' says I. 'Yes, yes. Straight away, if not sooner—' And I saw in the mingled moonlight and torchbeam that he looked at me far less indulgently than I would have liked. Men can switch from the romantic ideal to pragmatic coolness very swiftly, a phenomenon I had noticed before but had forgotten until then. Women on the other hand go on feeling the romance of the thing until it occurs to them how one-sided it has become and they stop too. Then men say, 'Don't you love me any more?' But I digress . . .

*   *   *

'Then what?' said Lydia the following day when I went to collect Rachel. We were in her kitchen, electricity restored and the girls were playing upstairs.

'Well, while he buried the evidence I took La Webb indoors and gave her a brandy. She's all right really, in an uptight sort of way. She told me quite a lot about herself while Bulstrode was being laid to rest—she's had two miscarriages and a hysterectomy and she's only thirty-eight and her husband—'

'Pat!' Lydia yelled. 'I don't mean *then*. I mean *later*, with *him*.'

'Oh, *that*,' I said as nonchalantly as I could. 'Well, he went home.'

'Before that . . . ?'

'He was extremely insulting about Julian and Mrs Protheroe.'

'What was she doing there?' (Lydia's Paula went to the same school as Rachel.)

'I mean the lions in the front room.'

'Oh, for God's sake . . .' She put her head in her hands and shook it in pure frustration. I felt I had paid her back enough for all that stuff about my boring men at parties. She gave me a very direct look, the kind that brooks no more nonsense, and said, 'I mean, did anything *happen?*'

'Of course it didn't. He's a married man. With his first baby on the way. What sort of a woman do you think I am?'

'Well,' she said, 'a very self-controlled one.'

'I know,' I said miserably.

'Didn't he try anything?'

'What, with Penelope Webb sitting there in the lamplight?'

'Didn't he *say* anything then?'

'He tried to kiss me at the door, but I didn't let him. I thanked him a lot, of course. I kept on and on saying thank you, and he kept saying "Don't mention it," and shuffling about a bit on the step and then he said, "Can I ring you?" And I said, "No, I don't think so." I said that I'd got a bit carried away with the burgundy et cetera, laughed gaily and off he went.'

'Well done,' she said, but she didn't sound completely convinced. As, indeed, I was not.

And then Rachel and Paula came into the kitchen and they both went on and on about the storm and how exciting it was and I tried to join in, but what with the late night and all the excesses and everything I just felt ruffled and tetchy.

'Is Brian all right?' asked my daughter with fervour.

And I very nearly said something back to her that I shouldn't regarding Brian and what he could do with himself.

*   *   *

Things did not improve over the next couple of weeks. I was still tetchy and irritable and it was impossible to settle back into my hitherto cosy slot. I couldn't even bob about on my own to Rod Stewart because it made me feel more bad-tempered than ever.

Going to the supermarket, which I used to enjoy—especially when the shopping trolley hadn't been vandalised and the wheels ran straight (a small thing to the Universe but quite a joyful event in my low-key lifestyle)— no longer made me feel busy and fulfilled and I began to see that the scarlet polka-dot sneakers and the so-what image was a bit less exciting than I had thought. Have some dignity, for Christ's sake, I said to myself as I caught my reflection bending over the ice-cream cabinet. It is true what they say about the face of a woman over forty: if she has any sense she won't be caught bending her sagging jowls over the eyes of someone she wants to impress. What I caught sight of in the shining chromework of the freezer was very depressing. Not least because, up to that point, I had looked upon the ageing process as something to celebrate. Another step further on towards Mrs Pomfretship and all those dear little grandchildren crowding round my knee. Pendant over the additive-free vanilla, these pleasures to come seemed less desirable and I was more concerned, in an abstract way of course, with the thought that if it ever came to it I had best stick with the missionary position.

I walked Brian much more briskly than usual in the mornings so that he was actually moved to whimper a couple of times—an unknown development of protest for him—and I was so preoccupied with being out of sorts that I forgot, once, to take the pooper-scooper. Brian deposited what was required of him with his usual military precision to the side of the path and there was nothing I could do but leave it where it was and pretend it wasn't there. As I marched off there was a terrible howl of rage, a human howl, from behind me, and the red-haired woman descended, waving her tennis racquet about and calling me all the names I would have called myself had I been her. The trouble was, I was ready for a fight—well, verbally anyway—and instead of doing the wise thing of letting her finish and then explaining, I let rip back.

She called me dirty. I called her insane. She said she would get the police. I said try it. She said people like me should be made to scrub the streets (something I always thought about dog owners, it bringing out the Fascist in my breast) and I told her to boil her head. Then he of the chip-pan hair and shades sauntered over and joined in, defending me in his Roy Orbison sort of a way—very cool he was—and then all the others trickled over and took up my cause too. Very fiercely. Suddenly I became one of them, a sister-in-shit, so that I got very confused about where I stood at all. The Hilary person patted Brian and then me (in much the same way) and said how awful people were about doggies' natural functions and just where *were* they supposed to go? And weren't they also God's creations and part of His great pattern? I looked down at Brian, who had brightened up considerably at all the attention and was deeply immersed in the Alsatian's bum, and I thought, no, I don't think so. So while they all went on and on at each other I just melted away, dragging him with me. He kept looking over his shoulder with regret and I found myself saying out loud that if *I* couldn't have myself some carnal pleasures then I was damned if he could . . .

And Mr Harris's nose-hairs had lost their fascination too. I even felt unmoved at the expenses routine.

'You seem out of sorts, Mrs Murray,' he said one morning. 'I hope you are not going down with anything. If you feel that you are I should take a day or two off. You wouldn't want to go spreading it around, now would you?'

I was about to say that what I suffered from was not catching but checked myself. I was weary, *really* weary suddenly and the thought of taking a day or two off and just being at home was immensely tempting. Anyway, Christmas loomed. I had to begin on that. Rachel wanted a bike and Gordon and I were going to buy it together. I ought, at least, to go and do some homework on the wretched thing. And I had to sort out with Gordon which part of the holiday she was going to spend with him. I hadn't liked to think about it up until now because, really, I wanted to have her for the whole time. Now, strangely, it didn't matter so much. I don't mean that I didn't care, because I did, it was only a feeling that the days apart from her, whichever they were, were not really symbolic of anything. If he wanted—and if *she* wanted—Rachel could go to him for Christmas Day this time. Why not? I thought. After all, I get all the best bits, the biggest chunks of time. Why not stop resenting his rights as a father? I felt rather proud of myself for working this out. I had defused myself somewhere along the line and could be generous. I went home early that day—it was a Wednesday—at Mr Harris's insistence. 'Take the rest of the week,' he said firmly. 'And make sure you are *quite* better for Monday.' And as I walked past his desk to collect my coat off the hook, he actually recoiled as if I breathed death.

I left a message on Gordon's answerphone when I got in, suggesting that he might like to come over that evening for a meal. It was the first invitation I had ever issued to him and I found myself wanting him to come very much indeed. I pushed aside a little voice that said, 'You are lonely,' and told it to put itself where the monkey put the nuts. Lonely? Me? I had loads of friends, just loads. And to prove it I rang Wanda.

I hadn't seen her for a couple of months. The last time was when she came up to town to go to a hairdressing convention or something and we had lunch at her hotel. She was bigger and bronzer than ever and spoke in her loud unselfconscious way about life near

Cambridge. Apparently she was the only person for miles around with anything but Anglo-Saxon skin and it gave her entrée and cachet wherever she went. 'I wouldn't give you twopence for London,' she said. 'Everyone falling over themselves to be nice and liberal about *colour*. Down where we are they just treat you as an alien and give you the respect they'd accord a visitor from Mars. Hell, I don't *want* to be integrated, thank you very much. I prefer being special. Why don't you come down and stay. Mike'd do your hair for free. And like I said we've got some *lovely* men, just *lo-ver-ly.*' Her laugh had rung out and I'd winced as usual and said maybe, sometime, perhaps, and changed the subject. Now I decided to accept.

'Well, *hi!*' she screamed down the phone. 'I was just thinking about you the other day. How are things?'

'I think I'm a little under the weather,' I said.

'Under *who?*' she screamed again.

Could I handle a weekend of this? In the past her raunchiness had always been infectious since it was tempered with a quick wit. Today I just felt irritated. But I had made up my mind to go if I could: anything was better, suddenly, than staying here. So I said, 'Were you serious when you asked me down?'

'Sure,' she said. 'Come now. Put a toothbrush in a bag and get driving, girl.'

'Well, I can't do that. Rachel's still at school. But I thought I might haul her out early on Friday and set off then. How does that sound? I expect we'd reach you about six.'

'Sounds fine.'

'Would it be possible to bring Brian too?'

It was as if a rocket had gone off down the phone. Extraordinary wheezings and grunts hit the line before they were condensed into proper language.

'Have you got a man at last?'

Oh God, I thought, not Wanda too.

'No,' I said coldly. 'I'm talking about our dog.'

'Oh,' she said with reasonable amelioration. 'Well, fine. Bring him too.'

*   *   *

I felt better after that and took Brian with me when I collected Rachel from school. She was delighted and knelt down and patted him like she'd been away for a month instead of a day.

'How come?' she said as we walked home. I usually came straight from work and dogless.

I told her and also that I hoped Gordon was coming for a meal that night.

'Oh, that's smashing,' she said, and I felt very proud of myself until she added, 'And I expect he'll be bringing Miranda too.' Then I felt not so proud of myself. It had never occurred to me that he might do that.

'Oh, I shouldn't think so,' I said, annoyed at how disappointed she looked. 'He'll want to come on his own and see you.'

He would, wouldn't he?

He bloody would not.

When we got back the telephone was ringing and Rachel rushed to it.

'It's Daddy,' she mouthed at me. And then to her father, 'Oh, *good*. About seven o'clock I should think.' She looked at me for approval and I nodded. Then she listened, smiled and said, 'Yes, I thought so. I'll tell Mum.' And she put down the phone.

'He's coming,' she said, and tossed over her shoulder en route for the kitchen the palsy-effecting statement. 'And Miranda is coming. I said she would.'

*   *   *

There is very little point in trying to be conformist in this life. Look at Penelope Webb, still foot-stamping at thirty-eight, for all her outward respectability. I have no doubt that it would have shocked her to the core to know that on the other side of her walls a woman was preparing lentil soup and roast lamb for her ex-husband and his lover. I, on the other hand, having once overcome the idea that social mores were based on humanity, found the whole thing quite simple. I mean, there was absolutely no logical or emotional reason why Miranda should not come to dine. And—*entre nous*—I was rather interested to meet her. Well, to be accurate to see what she looked like. Anyway, the projected excitement helped alleviate some of my grumpy tetchiness so in a way I was grateful to her and Gordon.

Rachel opened the front door to them while I was in the kitchen sieving the soup. I had on my mumsy pinny and jeans and a sweatshirt, which was my way of saying that I felt terrifically relaxed (which I didn't) and also of showing how harmoniously I fitted into my calm, unruffled domesticity *à deux*, or *à deux avec chien*. I was showing what a happy and uncomplicated single mother I was (which at that precise point I was not). Rimsky-Korsakov's *Scheherezade*, playing sweet and low, completed the picture. On reflection, as I reflected into the sieve, the musical choice was very apt: what a tall story *I* was weaving for them here.

Gordon came breezing into the kitchen rubbing his hands and bringing that cold smell of a frosty night in with him. He had the brass nerve to pat my bottom and peck me on the cheek with his cold lips and beardy stubble, just like the husband in an Oxo advertisement. Talk about *déjà vu*. And then he turned and pulled Miranda towards me, as if she were a slave in a market, and for a moment I was sorely tempted to ask her to open her mouth while I inspected her teeth.

They say love is blind, do they not? Well, maybe unlove is blind also. Maybe Miranda really was 'gorgeous', 'a lovely girl', 'terrific looker', and all those other things that Gordon had rapturised about to me, but from where I stood—bepinnied ex-wife—she looked, well, rather *plain*. Which was perfectly all right, of course, only not what I had been expecting, given all the descriptive build-up during the last four months. What I had anticipated was a cross between the young Marilyn and a vamp. And even despite 'unlove', by no stretch of the imagination was she like either of those. She was quite *big*, in a chunky sort of way, as tall as Gordon and, if anything, broader in the chest (of which there was rather a lot but which was worn more like a shelf than twin spheres of ultimate desire). She had a very open smile from a very large mouth (I found myself wondering as one will—or I will at any rate— how Gordon managed to cover it with his own very little one) and small brown eyes that almost disappeared when she mobilised her face. Her hair was dark and cut in a long pageboy with a too-short (in my opinion) fringe so that she had an air of permanent surprise. And she wore almost exactly what I was wearing, bar the pinny of course. If someone had told me that she had come straight off the Russian steppes I would not have been at all surprised.

'Welcome,' I said, extending my hand.

She giggled and put a bunch of freesias into it. 'Thank you for asking me,' she managed.

Perhaps it was all in the voice. For it was low and musical and I could quite understand someone being seduced by its sound.

'Thank you for the flowers,' I said.

And then Rachel, coming up from behind, put her hand into Miranda's and said to her, 'See. I told you.'

'Told you what?' I asked.

'That you wouldn't bite.'

'Did you think I would then?'

'No,' said Miranda, looking at Gordon who was really enjoying all this, 'But he did.'

I turned to put the flowers in the sink and said, 'I know I did many things to you in my time, Gordon, but I never bit you, did I?'

And I thought, as I ran the water on to the stems, that there *had* been a time when I bit him. And not in anger either. Had I really been a woman like that once? Driven to bite and scratch in surrender and ecstasy? Would I ever be like that again? I shook my head at the gushing water. I doubted it. I doubted it very much. And how I envied Gordon at that moment, how I envied Jo at that moment, despite the fact that she butterflied from bed to bed, how I envied, God help me, *Miranda* at that moment. Ah well. There was but one certainty in all this. I turned back from the sink and looked at it. There was absolutely not the remotest possibility that I could do such things with Gordon ever again.

CHAPTER SEVENTEEN

I played Brahms's *German Requiem* rather a lot over the next couple of days. I was at home, quite legitimately, and that was nice in a way, though I had sorrow and grumpiness as companions. Well, at least there were things to do; sorrow and grumpiness and me worked our way through all the chores and bits that I had so far left undone.

Phillida came down from the bathroom and was replaced by something altogether more soothing and plain. I finished off my bedroom curtains, the pattern of which (sob sob) no man would ever see. And I thought once or twice (be honest, be honest, many more times that *that*) of Roland's chest, and his humour, and his quite nauseatingly apparent rightness in terms of attraction. The curtains hung lopsidedly. Well, that didn't matter. They were done, and up, so something had been achieved.

Vanessa rang and asked me out for lunch but I declined. 'I'm off sick,' I said, which was the truth. She accepted this and threw out an invitation to go there for Christmas, which I also declined. I wanted to spend that time here at Florizel Street, dug in, with Rachel and

Brian and my first New Age Christmas tree. Despite my grand mental gesture, Gordon did not want Rachel with him for the holiday. He and Miranda were going to Barbados.

Bar fucking-bados.

And it wasn't the right place to take a kid of ten, now was it? I didn't really mind. Well, I did and I didn't. But really, what could I say? Lovers need space, I found myself thinking. And I wondered where, suddenly, all this understanding and well-behaved me had sprung from. I suppose I was aware of how grateful I should be that Gordon had fallen so happily and uncomplicatedly in love. What could have been a disastrously stressful four months for our daughter had actually proved to be made easy by this liaison. Somewhere along the line I had shed a skin of obtusity. I was down to the balance level. I'd rather Miranda and Gordon were happy together because it helped us to be. Therefore, Barbadian delights while I was dealing with cold turkey here were a very small price.

Rachel had pouted a bit at this piece of news but Miranda tickled her chin and said, 'If Mummy doesn't mind we'll take you away somewhere at Easter.'

'Where?' she said with that childish directness that is so unnerving.

Certainly Gordon was unnerved. He began to huff and puff again, just as he used to, but Miranda only said, 'Oh, Gor!' (*Gor*? Why

249

hadn't I ever thought of such an awful abbreviation?) 'We've already *talked* about this. If you're going to do that thing in Barcelona why can't Rachel come too? She'd keep me company and it'd be lovely. Wouldn't it, Pat?'

Ah me! The enthusiasm of youth. I, suddenly, could think of other companions than my daughter in such a place.

'Where is Barcelona?' said Rachel.

'Spain,' said Miranda, giving Gor a very positive look.

'What about it?' he said to me. I could read him like the proverbial. How he wanted me to say no.

'That,' I said, 'sounds wonderful. Cheese anybody?'

Brian sauntered out from his lair and both Rachel and Miranda fed him surreptitious scraps, smiling knowingly at each other as they did so. 'What a smashing dog,' said my husband's lover. 'Pleased to meet you.' And the wretched animal finalised a trick that Rachel had been trying to teach him since he first arrived: he sat back on his miserable haunches and held up a paw. 'Ah,' said Miranda. 'Are we friends then?'

Amen to that, I thought. I suppose we are.

Later, while Gordon and I sat, curiously, side by side and more relaxed than I could remember, on the settee with our brandies, I watched Rachel (now in her nightdress) and

Miranda (who was drinking Coke quite as happily as our daughter and, I thought, more happily than she had sipped her Chianti) playing Pass the Pigs. They argued, laughed, tried to cheat, while the two of us gazed on fondly like a pair of doting parents on a pair of delightful children.

'She *is* a lovely girl,' I whispered to him.

'I know,' he said, almost wet-eyed. 'She's gorgeous.'

I could see it now. And ouch! I felt bruised with envy.

After they left I slept fitfully. Too much booze or not enough. Somewhere inside me I ached and no matter where I turned on the mattress the aching was not relieved. Thank heavens for the weekend and Wanda. Something to look forward to. I had not felt the need for something to look forward to so much since we moved. Maybe I would try out Wanda's lo-ver-ly fenmen. I dozed off uncomfortably. I felt too hot though the weather was frosty, and when Rachel crept beneath the duvet at seven o'clock with her atlas and began talking enthusiastically about Barcelona it took a great deal of control to be enthusiastic back.

'You won't ever marry again, will you?' she said as she idly traced a finger over the Pyrenees.

I was about to say, 'No, not ever. Certainly not . . .' when out came, 'You never know about the future.'

Her finger stopped and she looked at me with alarm, 'But I thought it would just be the two of us and Brian.'

'Well,' I stroked her hair. 'It probably will.'

'Only probably?'

'None of us can look into the future. But I shouldn't think so. Why, would it worry you?'

'Mary Clark's got a new daddy and he's horrible. He makes her go to bed at *eight* and he sleeps in the same bed as Carol all the time.' She looked around her and patted my duvet. 'I wouldn't like that.'

'One day,' I said, 'you'll leave here and have a home of your own.'

Big eyes met mine, widened with indignation. 'I'd *never* do that,' she said. 'I'll always stay here with you.'

'Well, we'll see . . .' How many times have we all vowed not to use that stock parental phrase?

After a moment she said, 'Well, I suppose it might be all right. At least you would choose somebody nice.'

'I hope so. *If* it ever happens. And anyway, one thing's for sure: you only have one daddy and that is Gordon. He will always be your father and nobody else will. OK?'

She nodded and smiled more comfortably. 'I hope he marries Miranda though,' she said cheerfully. 'He needs looking after and she's ever so nice.'

It occurred to me, and not for the first time, that men still hold the aces. I bridled. 'If you don't mind him marrying again then it's not fair to say I can't, is it?'

She thought about this, struggled with it, and then the childish sense of fair play surfaced. 'I suppose so,' she said. 'But he's got to like dogs. And not be too old.'

'Too old for what?' I was genuinely interested.

'Too old for *you*, of course. Do you really think you will?' And while I was getting ready to say something well-adjusted and psychologically sound, she added, 'And do you think there'll be a swimming pool in Barcelona?'

'Don't know. And don't know,' I said. I surprised myself yet again. Surely the answer to the first should have been a straight No?

* * *

During the two days' grace from computers Mr Harris rang a few times. I could almost feel the hair-twiddling down the phone as he asked me what I felt were irrelevancies. Where was this? Had I done that? Could I remember if . . . ? They were not real enquiries but symbols of his power. He worked in a hotbed of activity, he was desperately executive; *ergo* he needed to keep his finger on every pulse, which meant making important phone calls to

253

his absent employee. In a way I was grateful to him for making me feel relevant somewhere. Inside myself I felt a bit lost, as if the air had gone out of my system or I had been fighting something for a very long time and now the battle was over. Only it was a Pyrrhic victory. Yes, yes, we had come through, Rachel, Gordon and me. But somehow only they were happy in the victory. I, hunched over my curtain hemming, was as miserable as sin. Sin, I thought. Why didn't I just give in to it when I had the chance? I think it was at that point that the line of the curtaining went amok.

*   *   *

Wanda was thrilled when we arrived, and her delight was infectious. She piled chocolates into Rachel's lap (such things do childless people do) and rolled on the carpet with a most surprised Brian who attempted to keep up a modicum of death-wish restraint but failed. He actually barked. And Wanda barked back at him. He tried it again, seemed to like it and actually had to be made to shut up.

Their house was even more bizarrely furnished than I remembered it. Lots of white leather and black shiny cushions fringed with gold. And Wanda had set up a proper bar in the front room, with a tap atop and mirrors and stools surrounding an engraved (highly!) glass bar top. Rachel was fascinated by the myriad bottles that were reflected and reflected and reflected again and Wanda fixed her an enormous bowl of sticky something or other that she *said* was scarcely alcoholic but which, from the way my daughter's cheeks grew flushed, and from the way she went so willingly to bed half an hour later, made me very suspicious.

'Kids drink that all the time at home,' said Wanda, after I had made a passing attempt to clean Rachel's teeth, while she kept complaining that she didn't feel tired at *all*, and got her into bed where she promptly began snoring.

'If she wakes up with a hangover,' I said, 'I'll never forgive you.'

'It will be as mother's milk,' she said, holding up her hands in mock honesty. 'Anyway, she can't have a hangover because we're going to the village Christmas fair tomorrow. She'll be fine. You mark my words.'

If there is anything more annoying than being told by someone without the experience of parenthood that they *know* how children will react, then I have yet to find it. Or possibly there *is*. It is when those same uninitiated souls are proved *right*. Which the fulsome Wanda was.

She and I had spent the previous night very quietly. Michael was out until late. 'He's been meaning to spend an evening with the salon girls before Christmas so this seemed a good opportunity,' said Wanda.

'You mean you kicked him out,' I said (I was on my second something or other, less sticky and more fiery than Rachel's and its effect unlikely, I thought cheerfully, to be entirely overridden by Ditchling's festive extravaganza on the morrow).

'Ye-es and no-o,' she said. 'I just want to know what's been happening, that's all. You can't talk about sex and stuff with a man around. They get horny.'

'But I don't want to talk about sex and stuff,' I said. 'I haven't anything to say on the subject. Nothing at all, actually.'

'Don't you miss it?' she said, brown eyes widening.

'Wanda,' I said, resuming, I hoped, a sober air, 'I never had it! You know Gordon and I never slept together for years.'

'Oh, I know that,' she said dismissively. 'You crazy pair. But haven't you met anyone? Anyone at all?' She leaned forward and pressed her hand on to my pubic bone. 'I mean, anyone who does anything to you *down there*?'

'Get off,' I said, quite enjoying the sensation, though I wasn't going to tell her that. 'Get your witch's touch off my privates.'

'Rats,' she said, leaning back in her chair again. 'Don't kid me.'

'I am *not* kidding you. It's the truth.'

She looked at me. I looked at her. We both

256

took a sip from our glasses. I could smell the meal that was simmering away in the kitchen. What I was going to say was that I felt hungry. Instead I suddenly burst into tears—I mean half-laughing half-crying sort of tears.

'Oh Wanda,' I said, choking a bit. 'You really are delicious. And awful.'

And then I told her.

All about Roland and the shirt and Rod Stewart and everything.

'Huh,' she said at the end of it. 'Forget him. You need those sorts of complications like I need a perm.' She tickled her fingers through her tight black curls.

'I know,' I said sadly. 'But all the same, all the same . . .'

'All the same *nothing*,' she said. 'You wait till tomorrow night. We've got a few people coming here who might make you change your mind.'

'Lo-ver-ly fenmen?' I said, suddenly feeling very warm and easy (tight in retrospect. Why fight? One is quite the opposite after a cocktail or two).

'Sure,' she said. 'See how the shoe fits.' She rolled her eyes and then stood up. 'Sex,' she said, 'is a very wonderful thing.' And she stopped rolling to wink. 'And now, let's eat.'

When Mike came in, all blond and flushed from, no doubt, an awful lot of boss-type flirtation, it was quite clear that they couldn't wait to get into bed together. I suddenly felt intensely superfluous and hied myself off to my room hoping the sounds of their humping wouldn't reach its walls. And I thought again how foolish (and blessed, of course) we are to have children. Look at those two, I thought, as squeaks and rumbles began to erupt and as I tried to concentrate on my Margaret Drabble, both for one and both for each. And at it all night very probably, if the tune-up was anything to go by.

*   *   *

The village looked really pretty and Christmassy decked out in the frosty morning air. Festoons of red and green hung from the flat pink walls of ancient houses, and on the village green they had erected a huge red and white marquee that was full of slightly batty old ladies serving tea, nervous spinsters, a vicar, several stoutly brogued women with sensible hair and a hotchpotch of enthusiastic, pink-cheeked youth. I felt indecently ordinary as I fed my way in and out of the stalls. Time seemed to have stood still in this little corner of Suffolk and although there must have been some straight-looking people there, I didn't notice them. It could have been thirty years ago, even down to the tea urn and home-made buns. Rachel, un hung over, took off with her purse to do her gift shopping, while I, hung over slightly, wove my way through it all with

Wanda. 'Why aren't you behind a stall?' I said.

'Because Mike's doing haircuts and I'll help him later.'

I looked at her. Around her head she was wearing a fluffy white shawl with silver tassels and she looked so beautiful—not at all frazzled after what I knew had been a long and active night.

'How on earth do you stay so fresh?' I said irritably.

'Giving in to pleasure whenever I can,' she said, and gave me a look.

I decided that everybody could have home-made jam, or chutney, or preserves, or scented pillows and suchlike for Christmas. So I bought most of my presents there that morning. There is nothing quite like the feeling of having more or less done your Yuletide shopping—you feel quite superior, or I did—and knowing that you have contributed to a good cause (rebuilding the tower of the little Norman church) at the same time adds another dimension of supremacy. Rachel returned to my side about half an hour later with her own amazing collection of tiny things: egg cosies (*does* anybody actually use them?), herb sachets and the like. She was clutching among this lot a large, slightly squashed cake.

'Give us a bite,' I said, swooping my mouth down to get at it, but she held it away indignantly 'It's for *Brian*,' she said and, dumping everything (save the doggy treat) into my already overspilling arms, she took it outside to where he was tethered.

One day mothers will *really* rebel. Not all that bra-burning, consciousness-raising stuff, but a true overthrow of the system. They will not collate socks, wipe baths, care for the offsprings' pets and generally turn the universe for them. They will rise above it all and strike a blow for the death of parental serfdom. They will say, 'Enough is enough. Clear up your own messes, deal with your own difficulties, fly your own kite and pick up your knickers yourself . . .' In the meantime I stood there, weighted down with this plethora of her purchases and mine, and tried to think how best to attempt movement. Through the tent flap I could see her bending lovingly over our morose hound, feeding him as if he were a much loved sick relative. I nearly called her back. I nearly let the rebel strike out—but failed. Had we been at home, among the like-minded of the metropolis, I think I would have. The time had come to assert myself and not feel guilty any more. Only there, among all those jolly ladies and tweed-clad menfolk, I lost my bottle. 'Later,' I muttered to myself. 'Later, my girl. Just you wait.' And I jiggled and woggled my way across to Mike and Wanda as best I could, hangover and irritation making me feel quite wild inside.

'Wow!' said Wanda, who was standing by with comb and mirror as Mike snipped and caressed at a sedentary male's head. 'You look sparky.'

'I'm bloody cross,' I said. 'I feel like I'm my daughter's dump bucket. Just look at all this stuff—' I made the mistake of moving my arms slightly and a shower of nonsenses rained down on the sedentary figure's head.

'Ouch!' he said and groped to recover a wooden pencil box that had lodged near his neck. And then came another, much more feeling, ouch, as Mike's scissors engaged his ear-lobe. Blood came spurting out, fortunately on to the towel that was draped round his shoulders, and not surprisingly, he stood up sharpish.

'Well,' said Wanda. 'I hadn't quite expected to introduce you two so early in the day—'

'Jesus, Mike!' said a strangled voice, belonging to the ear which was now being held by a hand and through which blood coursed. 'What the hell are you *doing* to me?'

'Sorry,' said Mike. 'But you moved.'

'Of course I moved. Something hit me.'

'Oh God,' I muttered, dropping a few more things for good measure. 'It's all my daughter's fault.'

'Really?' said the voice again, a little icily and with some animosity. 'I thought I saw *you* drop it.'

'Well, yes,' I said, irritation resurfacing. 'But she shouldn't have put it there in the first place.'

'Right—well—I'll go and ask her to say sorry in that case, shall I? I mean, it'd be nice to get an apology from *somebody*.'

'There's no need to be so rude—'

'Just look at me!' he expostulated, indicating his ear.

I looked at him. He was quite pleasant-looking really, in an angry, blood-soaked way. He had a round face with crinkly button eyes and a big—half-cut—thatch of black hair on top of it. He could have been younger or older than me but at that moment he most certainly couldn't have been crosser. And probably the crinkles were normally laughter lines. At that moment, however, they were anything but.

'Calm down, Steve,' Mike said. 'It's only your ear, not your goolies. Ears always bleed a lot.' And he began to clean it with a tissue, pinching the lobe between finger and thumb. 'It'll soon stop.'

'Look at my jacket,' said the bleeder. 'Just look at it.'

There were a few drops of blood on the sleeve of his not-altogether-pristine anorak.

'I'll pay for the cleaning,' I said, thinking as I did so that this really was a case of *déjà vu.* 'And, sorry—' I added defiantly.

'Well, there we are,' said Wanda. 'She's apologised. And you can put that in the washing machine. It won't stain if you do it quickly. You go off now and do it right away. Besides, it could do with a wash.'

'Yes,' I said, wishing I hadn't, but things do come out.

He gave me a really acid look.

'I'll pay for the washing powder and the electricity,' I added, thinking that I might as well be hung for the proverbial sheep.

'Very big of you,' he said. 'This actually hurts, you know.' He clasped his ear which was now blessed with a little piece of tissue to hold off further gouts.

'Aah,' I said with a little more sarcasm than I really meant.

And if looks could kill Rachel would have been made motherless.

'See you tonight?' called Wanda as he stomped off.

And then Mike doubled up with laughter. 'I'd better go after him,' he said. 'I don't think he realises that he's only half cut.' And snapping the air with his scissors he followed the earholder out of the tent.

'Well!' said Wanda with what could best be described as a straight look. 'You certainly blew that.'

'What a twerp,' I said. 'What a priggish twerp.'

'Oh, come on. Be fair. He did have quite a slice taken out of him.'

'Why are men such babies?'

'Because their mothers suckle them longer. Anyway, he'll be all right by tonight, I expect. He's lovely really. I know you'll like him.' She gave me another of those looks. 'At least, I thought you might—'

'Is he—'

'He was—'

'Well, shove that,' I said firmly.

'But he's perfect. Just perfect! If you put him in a book no one would believe you.' She began counting on her fingers. 'One, he's the same age as you. Two, he's the editor of *Eastern News*, so he's *interesting*. Three, his girlfriend went off to Honk Kong'

'I'm not surprised.'

She ignored this.

'So he's not gay. And four, he's not poor either.'

'And five, I don't like him.'

'Well, girl, that's as may be. We'll see tonight when he's recovered. And when Mike balances him up a bit.' She let out another of her loud laughs that, I swear, caused the tea cups to rattle. 'And *six* . . .'

'Yes?'

'It was only his ear and not his—'

'Oh, shut up,' I said, weary suddenly. 'Can I go back and put this lot indoors? I am extremely pissed off with looking like Santa's little helper.'

Rachel had made a friend. A boy of about her own age. And they were talking dog as I tottered past. 'You might help your mother,' I said.

'But Luke's going to show me his puppies.'

I looked at Luke across my awkward armful. Rebellion rose. 'Why don't you *both* give me a hand and then—'

Rebellion died again. A woman, presumably Luke's mother, whose well-worn cagoul and stout green wellingtons denoted a real woman-of-the-country, said, 'You're staying with Wanda and Michael, aren't you? Well, we're only a few houses away. Perhaps your daughter could stay for lunch? I'll see her back. Is that all right?'

Rachel was nodding enthusiastically—even Brian was on his feet. What could I say? It was back to before bra-burning after all.

'Go on then,' I said. 'I'll manage this lot on my own.'

If I had hoped for something to penetrate the dense undergrowth of child, it did not.

'Great,' she said, without a backward glance. Little runt.

The woman turned and beamed. 'Lucy Turner,' she said, holding out her hand which I, of course, could not take. 'I expect we'll meet again tonight?'

'I expect we will,' I said through gritted teeth.

For some reason I wanted to scream.

*　　　*　　　*

The reason became apparent that evening as I shook out the folds of my white satin blouse

265

and placed it next to my black silk skirt on the bed. I had pinned a lot of hope on Wanda's fenmen—since I was alone in my bedroom with no one to observe me I could let the truth surface—and if that had been the best of them, that one with the pig-stuck ear, then the satin and silk I had packed so hopefully were like sackcloth to me now. There was absolutely no chance of my kindling any romantic interest with him—even if he suffered a revision and arrived that night with the hots for me there was still no chance. He wouldn't, anyway. A woman knows, I thought as I dabbed scent in my cleavage. He will make some unpleasant little aside about this morning, and move to the other side of the room. And I will be left with Wanda's reserve, the poultry man from just outside Norwich, who—as she insisted on telling me—was a leading light in the amateur dramatic society and a part-time poet to boot. Very fascinating.

I went in to see Rachel on the way downstairs. She was sitting up in bed looking fresh-aired and cheerful and reading a *Beano* annual. 'Luke lent me this,' she said. 'He's great. I said we might be able to have one of his puppies.'

'No,' I said firmly.

'Couldn't *we* live in the country?'

'No, we could *not.*'

'Why?' she said, with the wide-eyed wonder of one who is seldom denied anything.

266

'Because . . . because I've got my job in London.'

'You could get a job here. Luke's mother breeds dogs. You could do that. I wouldn't mind if you got married again if we could live in the country.'

The look on her face as she said this was akin to the look she manages when she's trying to strike a chores-for-pocket-money bargain. It called for firm handling and never mind the sensitive psychology and the guilt.

'I am not going to live in the country. I am not going to marry again—'

'You said you could never be sure,' she said with almost adult celerity.

'*And* I hate dogs,' I said.

There, it was out. I waited for the burning attrition.

'Don't be silly,' she said, turning no hair, no hair at all. 'You love Brian, don't you?' Brian, suddenly it seemed attuned to his name, cocked his head. Coming to life after all this time? That was a bit thick.

Be honest with your children, I remembered reading in Ms Leach, or Dr Spock or somesuch. I reached out and scratched the least offensive of his two moth-eaten ears. 'Oh sure, I love him,' I said. I got up off the bed and smoothed my skirt. I was near to tears again, which was perfectly ridiculous. It had to be hormonal. 'But *only* him,' I said with feeling. 'Light out in half an hour now.' And I went slowly down the stairs.

*   *   *

I was absolutely right.

Steve said, 'I think I'll keep away from you' soon after he arrived. And he did. For which I was truly grateful. The poultry man from Norwich was short and burly and had obviously been apprised of my availability by Wanda. He cleaved to me for a considerable time and kept sloshing wine into my glass. I tipped some of it on to the yucca plant—every time he had his back turned to grab another handful of cheese straws, stuffed eggs or a sausage on a stick (it was that sort of catering—Wanda clearly knew her territory) I slugged the plant pot.

'My,' he said rapturously. 'You can certainly drink.'

He had terrible halitosis. I kept wondering how his opposite lead in *Cinderella* (they were doing a panto and he was the prince) managed to get by without aid of a clothes peg. Maybe he'd just eaten something, but I didn't think so—it was the kind of breath that is used to being bad, an overactive gut or something. Anyway, as soon as I could I excused myself and went over to Lucy Turner, with whom I spent an excruciating rest-of-party discussing dogs and children (in that order) and yearning with all my heart for Margaret Drabble and

268

bed.

*　　　*　　　*

So, home we came. My heart (though Wanda tried to persuade me otherwise) completely unengaged with anything from there—and Rachel's quite the opposite. Luke and she made a nice little charade of saying goodbye through the car window, and he said he would write. She said she would too and I thought, I bet you don't. I bet you only write if I remind you. But I was wrong. As soon as we entered our house she was asking for writing paper and up in her room, closely watched by Brian, beavering away with a pen that fairly sparked. That seemed such a cruel irony that I couldn't even take pleasure in the fact that she had done something quite independently and off her own bat. I unpacked, put the blouse out for the cleaners and hung the skirt back on its rail, sorted out our two lots of Christmas purchases, and went and had a bath. I tried not to think of anything as I soaked in it. I certainly tried not to think of Roland and his shirt-smell. But it was very hard. Not even invoking the memory of the poultry man's breath managed to even the score. I put my head under the water and blew bubbles. At least I could go back to work tomorrow. At least I had a niche somewhere. When I went in to tell Rachel to get ready for bed she already

269

was, tickling Brian's ear and re-reading what she had written.

'May I see?' I asked, sitting down beside her.

'Certainly *not*,' she said, in a voice she had copied well from me. 'I don't ask you about your personal life, do I?'

Just as well that you don't, I thought dejectedly, as I went back downstairs and poured myself a drink, since I hadn't got one . . .

I put on the German Requiem again, which seemed just too perfect, and I sat hunched up and miserable for quite a long time before giving up and going to bed. The only letter I had to write was my thank you note to Wanda, but I didn't feel much like writing it then. The truth was, and I confessed it to myself as I slid under the duvet, there was a definite void in my life. Though whether it required filling from a general source, or from a particular one, I couldn't quite be sure . . .

CHAPTER EIGHTEEN

The blues remained throughout most of December, though I tried to snap out of them by immersing myself in all the preparations for Christmas. The trouble with Christmas is that it is a wonderful time (no, really). Despite the fact that one lot of parents vies with the other for the grandchildren and everybody always goes down with whatever virus—cold, influenza, stomach bug—doing the rounds just in time for the big day, it *is* a wonderful time. If nothing has upset your emotional equilibrium.

I didn't have to deal with the parent thing. Mine were alive and well and living in Australia near my younger sister Julia, so any invitation they might deliver could only be for form's sake. They would ring, as usual, on Christmas Day, check if the presents had arrived, amaze Rachel with their tales of barbecued turkey on the beach, say for the umpteenth time 'You must come over, Pat,' to which I would say, 'I'll start saving now shall I?' and that would be that for another year. I had never been particularly close to them so there was no real heart-wrenching, and they had only seen Rachel when she was a babe-in-arms, so there was nothing much except photographs and the names Granny and Grandad to link her with them.

And the viral ghost of Marley did not appear for either me or Rachel. Poor Mr Harris went down with a something, for which he blamed me. I longed to tell him that his diagnosis of my out-of-sortedness had been wrong and that what I had been suffering from was not infectious, but that would have involved confessing to taking time off under

271

false pretences. All in all it seemed better to accept full responsibility so I sent him some fruit (so good for the heart) and rang him a couple of times for advice that I did not strictly need. I thought he would like to go on feeling Executive while he lay in his bed. In traditional fashion he was overtaken by his bug just a couple of days before the office closed so there was scarcely anything to do. I rather wished there had been.

I rather wished there had been because on the emotional equilibrium front I was not doing too well. I put away the German Requiem and the Rod Stewart but that didn't seem to raise my spirits much. And I went at the festive preparations with gusto—paper chains, snow on the windows, ceiling-high tree, the lot—watched by an astonished Brian who was so moved by the sight of the tree that he went and peed up against it. I had to smack him for that, which caused an argument between me and Rachel. 'He's only doing what is natural,' she said, and I thought with disgust that I had bred an infant Hilary. I sent her up to her room for being cheeky, which she didn't really deserve, sent Brian back into his coffin in the kitchen, from which he eyed me hollowly as I poured myself too much brandy and sat down with a theatrical flop of despair. This is no good, I said to myself, this is no good at all. You must snap out of it. For Rachel's sake. And then I thought, slugging away at the brandy (which, I decided, was far too good for burning on top of the pudding anyway), hell's bells, never mind snapping out of it for *her*—what about *me?*

*   *   *

Gordon and I went out to buy Rachel's bicycle together. I was not looking forward to this. I had never shopped for anything with him if I could avoid it. A terrible melancholy would descend on him as he looked at the price of things, and he would declaim in loud tones to powerless shop assistants that all the prices were inflated, the quality lousy, and what had happened to value for money in this day and age? Meanwhile I used to stand in the background, usually shifting from foot to foot and trying to look like he was just some crank passing through. I was interested, however, to see how his relationship with Miranda had changed him. If he was going to Barbados with her—and presumably paying—then perhaps we could go for the five-star model and all the trimmings, instead of the basic frame and two wheels my conditioning had led me to expect. My research said there was a difference of half as much again for this 'ace machine'; my research also said that it was the one that Rachel desired without expectation. It would be nice to surprise her. *That* might lift the spirits a bit.

The day began rather well. Gordon called for me at the house and we drove off to the best place for bicycles that I knew, according to my extensive research. It was only ten minutes' drive away and we chatted amiably enough. He looked a bit pink, I thought, so I said conversationally, 'You look a bit flushed. I hope you aren't going down with something before your holiday.'

He had begun humming a carol, very prettily, up until I said that. And then he stopped. 'Thank you,' he said crossly. 'As a matter of fact I've been using the sunbed.'

'Oh,' I said. 'Sorry.'

And we drove on in silence. If he wanted to launch himself on a Barbadian beach already looking like a lobster that was his business. But it had somewhat diminished the amiability between us.

At the shop he was still frosty and he blew the usual fuse at the prices. We ended up back outside, on the pavement, having a row and it was *plus ça change* all over again.

'All right,' I said. 'If you know so much, take me where you can find better value.'

'I certainly will,' he said, and we drove off to a shop in Clapham which was down a horrible litter-strewn side-street. I should have known, I should have guessed. The place sold second-hand, reconditioned bikes, some of which looked as though they had been used to tootle between the lines during World War I.

Back on the pavement again I said, 'You can't—you simply can't—be so mean.'

'It's not mean,' he said. 'It's practical. What does she need all those fancy extras for? Rachel wants a bike that will get her from one place to another, not a showpiece.'

'A showpiece is precisely what she *does* want,' I said. 'Haven't you ever heard of a child's need to be the same as its peers? Can you imagine how she'll feel turning up at the cycle club with one of those bone-shakers?'

'But they're about three times the price!' he exploded.

And then it was out. I said, 'If you can take Miranda to Barbados you can pay half the cost of a decent bicycle for your daughter.'

And *he* said, with pride if you please, 'I'm not taking Miranda to Barbados, she's taking herself.'

'You mean she's paying?'

'Of course. She's quite rich. Her father's a banker. I thought you knew.'

I might have guessed. No wonder he was so plus-perfectly happy.

'You *bastard!*' I roared at him, there on the pavement. 'You absolute one-hundred-per-cent *shit!*'

Which was not really fair since it was probably not of his seeking that she had money, but I had had enough by then. Rage, envy, my own miseries all welled up and spilled over. He grinned at me which, frankly, did it.

And I punched him on the nose. God knows what well of violence that gesture came out of. I did temper the punch a little during the motion so that by the time it engaged with its target it was fairly harmless, but I didn't manage to stop it altogether. I remembered how he had once done just the same to me. Perhaps I had been waiting for vengeance all these years. Fortunately the results of my violence were not so messy as his had been. He only reeled a bit and blood did not pour from the assaulted organ as he held it gingerly.

And then, from behind me came the toot of a car horn, and I looked round to see who was interfering with the perfectly normal event of an estranged couple scrapping on the pavement. It was Roland's car, passing slowly by in the stream of traffic bent on entering the main road, and he waved from its shadows. Unsurprisingly, it was a tentative wave. I just turned my back on it—one for shame, two for despair, the latter because my heart went bump at the sight of him, and bump again when I saw he was alone. No newly pregnant, sexually rampant wife sat in proper state by his side. I could have been in that car, if not legitimately then in authorised illicitude.

'Damn you!' I screamed at Gordon. 'Take me back to the other place *now*. I'm going to buy the thing even if you *won't!*'

'Apologise,' he said nasally. 'Apologise or I won't take you anywhere.'

'Apologise yourself!' I said.

'Then you—' he took his hand off his nose long enough to point a quivering finger at me '—can make your own sodding way.'

'Right.' I tossed my head, an apocryphal gesture hitherto, but now rather a pleasant reality, and off I strode without so much as looking back once.

'Patricia!' he called with an attempt to be commanding, which was quite undone by the nasal tone.

I walked on. It would be easy to get a train back and, buoyed with my successful sortie into violence, I stepped out towards the station, head held high. If a party of muggers had met me coming along the way they would have had short shrift. That, at any rate, was how I felt. When I got back home I would buy the best bicycle on offer, hang the expense, and make quite sure that the gift tag said in large lettering 'with love from Mummy' only. Gordon could present her with a puncture repair kit, or a saddle-bag (not leather, of course), or even one of those nice little water bottles you can fit on the front, anything so long as it was under five pounds and made a biggish parcel. That was his mark and always would be . . .

I was just turning off the street and into the station entrance when a car tooted again: same car, same toot, same owner. I knew this without even looking round. I rearranged my face from its 'Let's-have-you,-you-muggers-out-there' savagery, to an expression as near to blankness-about-to-be-surprised as I could, and turned.

'Friend of yours back there?' said Roland, leaning across the empty passenger seat to speak through the open window.

'My ex-husband . . .'

'Are you all right? Or do you want a lift?'

'I'm all right actually.'

'I'm going your way.' He gave a grin which did not produce the same effect at all as Gordon's. *'Actually.'*

'Well . . .' I said, hoping it carried a tone of warning. 'Thank you very much.'

And I got in. After all, I thought, it would be singularly ungracious not to.

*　　*　　*

'What happened back there?' he said, after we had driven a short way in silence. 'Or would you prefer not to say?'

So I told him. All about the bicycle and Gordon's meanness and why, suddenly, I had been moved to hit out. I ended up by adding, as an afterthought really, that I owed Gordon a punch on the nose and I described that bitter scene of ten years ago. Roland patted my hand which made me feel very cared-for suddenly and dangerously close to tears, self-pity being difficult enough without the benefit of someone else entering into it too, so I changed the subject.

'What do you do for a living?' I asked.

For some reason he found this amusing. 'How formal,' he said, removing his hand. 'Well, I'm a vet.'

I remembered Bulstrode and all that. No wonder he had dealt with it so well.

'What?'

'A vet. You know, ministering to animals, that kind of thing. A pet doctor.'

I had never in all my wildest imaginings, and I confess that there *had* been some, thought of him as one of those. It didn't have quite the ring of stylish excitement to it. Perhaps he was joking. I gave him a quick sideways look but he didn't look like a man who had just invented a rather silly profession for himself.

'But you can't be,' I said. 'You hate dogs. You said so.'

'I hate Mondays too,' he said mildly. 'But I have to deal with them in order to participate in the rest of life. Anyway, it's more their owners and what they let them get up to than the animals themselves.'

'Thank you,' I said.

He didn't seem much perturbed. All he said was, 'Oh, I forgot. You love the things and you've got one, a killer too. Ah well. I suppose some owners are more tolerable than others.' And then he gave *me* a sideways look so that I couldn't help but laugh.

'As a matter of fact,' I said, 'I don't like dogs and I can't *stand* their owners. I got Brian for Rachel.'

'I didn't put you down as a doggy-type person.'

I was longing to ask him what sort of person he did put me down as but forbore. Instead I told him all about Crap Green and the assorted characters which made him laugh and we were back at the High Road and near to the bicycle shop before I realised.

'You could drop me here,' I said.

'Oh?' He seemed a little startled. 'I can take you to your door. It's no trouble . . .'

I was tempted. Oh, *wasn't* I tempted. And I could imagine the 'would you like to come in for a cup of tea?' and the acceptance of the offer—and all sorts of other things too. But good sense surfaced. It would be a dead end, an exercise riddled with guilt, an absolute no-hoper. I just wasn't cut out to be the Other Woman. Not even with someone like him. So I just said, 'No, thanks. I've got to go to that shop down there—' I pointed and buy this bloody bike. But thank you.' And as he pulled in I remembered to get the seatbelt undone this time and was quite smoothly and swiftly out of the car before any further hooks could weaken the resolve.

As I was closing the door he gave me a really meaningful look, the sort that makes you squeak internally, and said, 'I'd really like to see you again.'

'I'm sure we'll meet up somewhere,' I said gaily.

'About the other night—' he said, with just an edge of what? Exasperation? Desperation?

'Oh, forget it,' I said. 'Don't apologise.'

He opened those extraordinary nice eyes of his very wide, 'I wasn't going to.'

'Well, anyway . . .' And just before I closed the door I added, 'By the way, how's Ruth?'

'Fine,' he said. 'She seems fine . . . Look—' He reached over to impede the closing process.

I increased the pressure. 'Well, give her my best wishes.'

And click, I shut him away sharpish.

I don't know how I managed to buy a bicycle after that. All I can say is that mothers are made of very stern stuff. Because I did, even though one of us, either the assistant or me, was floating in a fuzzy haze of unreality, and not a little tinged with melancholy too. What a fiasco! I had been so looking forward to making this purchase, so full of the thrill it would bring to Rachel's face on Christmas morning. And now, well, it had all got lost in some other kind of emotion and the face I kept thinking about was not very often hers. Silly woman, I told myself, but that didn't seem to stop it very much.

＊   ＊   ＊

I rang Gordon to apologise. He accepted the apology quite gracefully but I had to put my hand over the telephone to hide my laughter when he said, 'My nose is still swollen, you know. It'll still be up when I go away.' The thought of him lying like a glistening lobster with glacé cherry decoration was enormously cheering. And because of that I managed to redouble my penitence.

'I don't know *what* came over me,' I said.

'You're probably menopausal,' he said acidly. 'You want to watch it or you'll be shop-lifting next. Happy Christmas.' And he rang off.

What with that piece of man-reasoning shoved up my jumper and permanent recall on the sight of Roland, it certainly gave the festivities an edge. But at least now I was both miserable *and* angry, the latter being a much more positive emotion to bear. It made me quite hysterical at times. So much so that when Rachel (having oohed and aahed and done exactly the right things over her bicycle) opened her present from her father and it proved to be a saddle-bag (nice and waterproof and plastic) I fell about laughing for several uncontrollable minutes. Until Brian, who suddenly remembered what he had learned with Wanda, began barking. An event perfectly designed to calm me down with the wonder of it.

With determined optimism I sang very loudly around the piano at Lydia's little soirée on Christmas Eve so that Rachel winced and asked me, discreetly, to stop. Which I refused to do. And Jo and her children (who came to me for Christmas Day) left us saying how much they had enjoyed everything *especially* the game of hide and seek which had exhausted all of us. It involved a great deal of running up and down stairs and shrieking, in which I can honourably say I participated with true leadership skills.

This was, after all, my first Christmas of freedom. The festival, the moment on the calendar to which I had looked forward as a watershed, the time when those ties cut loose could show how atrophied they had become. It was to be the supreme period of happiness, true independence, guiltless celebration. Well, it proved to be only some of those things. I had to invent the rest.

Photographs developed since show me with a very bright smile stamped on my face and a swathe of tinsel in my hair. There is even one of me fondling Brian's ears, which are also similarly decked, while he looks up at me with yearning love and desire, as if I were perhaps some distant memory of Bulstrode . . . Apart from the tinsel I definitely detected shades of Mrs Pomfret in that picture. Which should, if I were true to my oft-spoke hopes, have been cheering.

It was not.

And in the photograph I noticed lines on my face that certainly had not been there before. I held the picture under the electric light and scanned it anxiously and the results of such scanning meant that I spent a good deal less time in front of the mirror than I used to. I even managed to put on my make-up without really looking (this can be done) and went to the extravagant lengths of buying some extremely expensive anti-wrinkle cream from one of those Barbie-doll beauty girls in a department store. I took the precaution of taking the label off the jar before leaving it around. I might be suffering the pangs of age but I certainly didn't want anyone to think I cared . . . Doing this made me feel faintly mad. Perhaps I was menopausal. I didn't want to be, though until then I had looked forward to it as a pleasant milestone towards calm old age. Sod Gordon. I hoped he would get bitten by sand-flies or drown in those balmy turquoise seas . . . and I hoped the sun would bake his nose an even crisper hue. Wherever he was I hoped that battered organ hurt like *hell.*

*　　　*　　　*

New Year's Eve was fine. I spent it with Vanessa and Max in London. They gave one of their hotel parties complete with band and I went with fire in my heart and a very positive

284

notion of dancing all night. Ru-Randolph was *not* there. I was a bit miffed at this since, with an arrogance borne of a determination to do *something* mould-breaking, I had decided it might be helpful to have a fling with him after all. Using some soft-focus imagination, his funny hair and dullish face had become quite appealing and—to be blunt—I concentrated on his being wealthy too. That, as they say, concentrated the mind wonderfully, especially the mind of a woman weaned into adulthood with Gordon as wet-nurse. I planned to be dashing and amusing and desirable (it all worked beautifully in my mind) and to say yes to whatever the outcome might be. So it was quite a blow when I arrived there to find him absent. Apparently he had gone to Barbados too, which at least tempered the disappointment with some amusing side-thoughts: perhaps he would meet up with Gordon and Miranda—anything was possible after all—and Gordon, still nursing his damaged conk, would declaim about his vicious wife, neither of them ever knowing of the common mutuality. I indulged myself with this comic possibility, which helped considerably. Indeed, I decided to find everything amusing that night. I was determined to find everything amusing. When things *didn't* begin to be amusing I grabbed Max, and later a chap called Anthony who looked a bit like a hippopotamus, and went off whirling around the room. I had on the yellow frock and the shoes (bad cess to unfashionability) and hugely enjoyed them this time. And me and Anthony hit it off terrifically well—*terrifically well.* I could see Vanessa looking pleased about that.

So *terrifically* well did we hit it off that I was moved to say so to him during one of the less manic numbers. He was trying to go as slow as the music said and hold me to him a bit but I didn't feel like sticking my nose in his dress suit lapel *just* yet, so I woggled around and smiled up at him and said, 'We do seem to be hitting it off, don't we?'

And he smiled back (just a little nervously) and said, 'Yes.'

And I then said—more to myself than to him, and in some wonder—'Considering how very much you remind me of a hippopotamus. Ha ha.' And then he wasn't smiling much any more and there were no further attempts to get my nose back into the smooch position, and that was the last dance I ever had with him.

Back I came to Florizel Street, singing to the taxi man who remarked, as I tumbled out on to the pavement, that he had seen it all before . . . And there we were, with a new year before us. Me, Rachel and our dear little ball of crap, Brian. A new year and a new life as a threesome. How lovely. That was all I had asked of the future, now wasn't it? But all I had on the first day of this new-year life was a blister on my heel and a hangover. Ah me!

The days afterwards were rather flat.

*   *   *

I did all the right things. I took everything very seriously at work and Mr Harris gave me a salary increase. So thrilling. And I filled the house with the happy sound of children's laughter inviting all and sundry back for tea after school—the more the merrier—until Rachel said wistfully one day, 'I wouldn't mind going to someone else's house for a change . . .' This scuppered the cosy Victorian vision I had created, rather neatly. Anyway, there is also something quite melancholy about the sound of children's laughter if you are not quite feeling up to it. When Rachel wasn't there I found myself talking to the bloody dog, who had the grace to look as if he had a glimmering of reciprocation somewhere inside his flat head. But I found the sense of loneliness frightening. Phillida had warned me about it. She had said that there would be a reckoning, a crunch time, and I guessed that this was it. Up to a point you can surround yourself with your friends, and up to a point you can go out and do things. But home is home, after all, and most of your time must be spent there. Florizel Street began to feel oppressive, like a prison for my singularity and

287

I didn't want to tell anyone I felt like that about it because I knew it would sound pathetic. Lydia would no doubt require a very large bucket over her head to stop all the told-you-sos that would be flying about.

It took a great deal of control not to cleave to my daughter during all this, but I had to let her go freely. What with the cycle club, her friends and the Gordon weekends that loomed, she was quite often spoken for. I took a little comfort, but not much, from the fact that one of us was doing all right.

The prospect of people talking kindly behind my back, saying things like 'We've got to look after poor old Pat' and then turning up brightly with 'things to do', was perfectly appalling. I was sorry, in retrospect, that I had said that thing about hippos to Anthony. I was sorry that, in my arrogance, I had refused to let Ru-Randolph take me home when I had the chance. I was even sorry, God help me, that I had bounced the pencil box off Steve. I couldn't *quite* be sorry about tipping the vino into the plant with Prince Charming. There were some things, I decided with relief, that even I could not countenance. And to avoid some interesting imaginings wherein Brian became dangerously ill (in the middle of the night) and I just *had* to get hold of a veterinary chap (skating over the fact that I had no clue as to where to reach the one I had in mind) I bought myself some tapestry work to do.

Tapestry! Me? And settled down with it and the television to see the long, dark winter through.

Peace and love, I told the peach-bottomed Cupid in my lap as I stabbed at his nether regions with my needle. Peace and love. Well, peace anyway.

Work was going well. Boring, but well. And the cold weather made the ground much harder, which made the pooper-scooper much easier, so there were benefits all around me. Gordon brought Rachel back a little pack of playing cards which said Barbados on them and a miniature bottle of rum for me, over which I made such profuse and glowing thanks that even he began to look suspicious of its authenticity. And life ground on.

I told myself that the thing was to keep my head down, look forward to the spring which (like Mondays?) had to come eventually. When I wasn't doing the tapestry I played Patience with the Barbadian cards and I took heart from the fact—as an indicator of my unsinful goodness—that I never cheated myself *once*.

And then, out of the midnight-blue velvet, came Burns Night.

CHAPTER NINETEEN

It occurred on a Gordon weekend or I very probably would not have gone. Apart from the venue reminding me of forfeited delights, I was weary of playing the party game. Christmas and New Year provide a false account of real life: bonhomie abounds, social gatherings fall thick and plenty and you are lulled into a sense of heightened living which tails off dramatically as grotty old February approaches. What I had to do was come to terms (oh, dreadful phrase) with day-to-day living *sans*-hype. I fancied that I was doing that quite nicely when Gertrude rang.

'I'm giving a Bums Night for Alec,' she said, 'and I should like you to come.'

'Do you know,' I said, 'I don't feel up to it. Can I pass?'

'It's not going to be large,' she said, 'and I'm not attempting further interference in your love life. Do say you will. I ought to make it up to you after last time. I just got carried away. I apologise. Do come.'

Dear Gertrude.

And what, really, had I to look forward to if I didn't? A whole weekend of Brian, who didn't like Rachel being away at all, my tapestry, my cards at which I couldn't even cheat and perhaps—if I was really lucky—a re-run of *The Maltese Falcon* on Channel 4.

'Come on,' she wheedled. 'You can always slip off early. An independent woman like you. It'll be a free dinner. You can eat and run, if you like.'

'Do you mean that?'

'Of course. But I hope you won't have to.'

'And no fiddling with fate?'

'Cross my heart.'

'Then thank you, Gertrude, I'd love to come. Do we have to dress up like Flora MacDonald or what?'

'Not at all. Alec will be in his kilt but I shouldn't let that worry you. Good. I'm glad you can come. Do you want to bring Rachel and bed her down here?'

'She's with Gordon this weekend.'

'And how is all that working out?'

'Very well, really.'

'You sound a bit low.'

'Yes, well, we can't all be love's young dream, can we?'

'Ouch,' she said. 'I did offend you, didn't I?'

'Oh, I'm sorry. To be truthful it gets a bit lonely here sometimes.'

'I bet it does. Perhaps you should go out more?'

'It's not that kind of loneliness. Anyway, I have been going out so don't be patronising—'

'Matronising,' she said drily.

'Well, anyway. Thank you for thinking of me. I'll look forward to it. Shall I bring a haggis or something?'

Gertrude forgot her repentant style and was suitably terse about this. 'Are you suggesting bringing food *here?* What do you think I've been slaving over sheep's innards all week for?'

Well, *quite.*

It was funny, really. When Gordon came to collect Rachel he asked me quite casually if I was doing anything that night and when I said I was going to a Burns party he looked very put out. He didn't wear his Scottishness as some do, forever singing 'Scotland the Brave' and leaping into battle but I could see it annoyed him that a mere southerner was taking pleasure out of something that was nothing whatsoever to do with her.

'Where?' he said peremptorily.

I told him.

'She's English,' he said indignantly.

'I know, but her new lover is Scottish.'

'What?' he said, looking shocked.

'Gertrude. Has a lover. He is Scottish.' I enunciated all this as if for an idiot.

'Gertrude?' he said. 'Gertrude has a *lover?*'

'Quite a dashing one too,' I said with pride.

'Well, well,' he retorted, with an evil little smile. And just as he turned down the path with Rachel he added, 'Even someone as old as her, eh? Looks like everyone's got themselves someone except you, Patsy. I wonder why?'

I wasn't quick enough to say what I should have said, which was, 'Because after you, dear, I wouldn't dare to risk it.'

And anyway, it wasn't really the truth. Even if it had been once.

*   *   *

I thought about going in Rachel's kilt but decided that, whilst it was all right for a forty-year-old woman to show her knees, it was probably not all right for her to show her family jewels, even among friends. It was a pretty short piece of clothing even on its owner. On the other hand, I was not going to get called nun-like again so I went completely over the top and wore the yellow dress. It was probably about the last time I could wear it, these things, as Vanessa so often said, being so *unfashionable* after a season. Anyway, that was one of several excuses I made to myself for the grandeur of my toilette. I practised saying, 'I have always *loved* Robbie Burns. All those lilting laments and sardonic verses,' and hoped, if I ever had to use the phrase, no one would pursue it. I only knew 'The Flea' and 'Tam o'Shanter' and while I guessed they were perfectly acceptable north of the border, down here in southern Clapham country only the more *sensitive* works would be of interest.

I didn't add a bow to my hair, which I contemplated doing. I remembered, just in

293

time, the Christmas photograph and the tinsel and knew that fairymania could be taken too far. I compromised by pinching some of Rachel's gold glitter dust. It was supposed to go on my hair but quite a lot got stuck to my cheeks too. Oh, well, I thought darkly as I waited for the taxi, no nun of woman born ever went to a party looking like an ancient sparkler.

At least this time there were no high winds nor stormy skies, and now that Bulstrode was rotting in his grave, Brian could be trusted. I gave him a good solid pat and was astonished when he suddenly leapt out of his comatosia and licked my face. The gesture didn't last long and he was soon slumped back again. Indeed, if it were not for the wetness on my cheek and the liberal sprinkling of fairy dust that adhered to his nose, I might almost have imagined it. Well, well, I thought, they say that every little doggy has his day. Perhaps Brian had discovered his. Or perhaps he had finally realised who paid the food bills. Whatever the cause, I was quite touched by the gesture. Maybe Lassie had finally Come Home after all. When I came back from Gertrude's I might sit and tell Brian all about it. He'd like that, foolish hound, and I could maybe sneak some haggis back for him too. Stick with your trusted ally, I told myself, even if it is just a half-baked hound.

'Perhaps you can warm my bed for me

tonight,' I said, giving him an affectionate pat. Such indulgence would take him to ecstasy since it was what he always wanted when Rachel was away. And why not? It was a cold night and he could sleep on my feet. They were always chilly nowadays. He looked up at me, wet-eyed and yearningly I gave him another stroke and released another shower of the gold-dust.

'Later,' I said. 'You are going to be one happy dog.'

He yawned. Perhaps he was thinking that he had heard all that before. The glitter rather suited him. And as I stood up I had a sudden and shocking thought which was, if he deigned to lick it off, he might get quite badly ill in the night. So I wiped him down with a damp piece of kitchen towel, just to be sure he wouldn't, and felt immensely positive at my resolve. This may sound quite insane to outsiders, but it all seemed perfectly acceptable to me.

I did feel quite spirited as I stepped out into the night and even the taxi driver was moved to comment on the spring in my heel and the spangle of my face. I think he was the same one who had brought me home from Vanessa and Max's do. I rather hoped he was. I quite liked the idea of appearing to be the Gay Socialite.

* * *

I was still feeling pleased with this GS aspect of myself as Gertrude, whose approval was warm and strong, ushered me into that same old room.

'I love your tam-o'-shanter,' I was just saying to her, and was about to go on about Burn's poem of the same name by way of appearing *au fait*, when I couldn't speak any more. Across the room, over by the french windows, was the stomach-turning sight, *literally* stomach-turning sight, of Roland the Shirt and a tall, black-haired elegant creature (female, disgustingly female), whose mien declared very positively that I want this man, I will have this man, I will sleep with this man later, and sleep was a pretty euphemistic piece of vocabulary. This was a fine time for me to discover a latent understanding of body language. Nor was this female, I was sure, the kind of female who would mind one jot about wives and pregnancy and silly stuff like that. He was entertaining her with some tale or other, moving his hands about in front of him by way of describing something (not that she had left much space between them for explanatory gesture), while she, just the right height to look up adoringly, had her large dark eyes fixed on his face in unqualified rapture. Talk about a mouse to a cat . . . She had feline whiskers all over her.

'Who is that?' I hissed to Gertrude.

'Why, that's Roland,' she said with a hint of

wonder. 'You met him before.'

'No,' I said. 'I don't mean him. I mean the *woman*.' And then I remembered myself enough to stop sounding so dramatic. 'I mean,' (lightly now, don't arouse suspicion) 'she looks familiar.' (Ho ho. Apposite choice of words.) 'Who is she?'

Gertrude looked. 'That's Elinor,' she said. 'Elinor Shaw. She's my editor. She's just got divorced so you've got something in common. Come over and I'll introduce you ...'

I jumped back and landed on her toe. Fortunately, the apologies and confusion stopped her proposal. There is much to be said for being clumsy sometimes.

'Is Ruth here?' I whispered when Gertrude's tartaned ear had righted itself.

'No,' said Gertrude. 'And you are a darned sight heavier than you look.'

'Sorry,' I said abstractedly.

'You might sound as if you mean it.'

I took my eyes away from those dark and yielding ones.

'I'm hungry,' I said.

'Well, we'll be eating soon. Now, come over and let me introduce you.'

And she prepared to move off.

Just for a split second my eyes and his met. He made a gesture of punching himself on the nose, raised an amused eyebrow and I, completely stomachless by now and with the added difficulty of no joints left in my knees,

297

was out of the door, down the stairs and into the kitchen, before you could say Robbie, let alone Burns. Gertrude followed, puffingly, in hot pursuit.

The table was not laid for a buffet, it was laid for dinner. I had hoped to grab a handful of something to chew by way of explanation for the Seb Coe exit.

'For heaven's sake,' she said. 'Have you got worms?'

'Well, you're such a good cook. And I really am starving.' I looked around me wildly for anything to grab. My stomach said no, my need for subterfuge said yes.

Gertrude, looking a bit flustered but accepting the statement as a good cook will, said, 'I know I am, dear girl, but there's no need to be quite so desperate. I've never let anyone go hungry yet, I hope.'

'No you haven't,' I said cajolingly. 'But I forgot lunch. Mustn't drink on an empty stomach. *Please* give me something to eat.'

Was Oliver Twist more needy? Absolutely not.

So she busied herself around a couple of dishes and handed me an oatcake with a dollop of something on it. Herring, I think it was, though it might have been strawberry jam for all I noticed or cared.

'Oh, *thanks*,' I said greedily, and damn nearly choked trying to swallow it whole. 'Tell me about—' I tried to think of a gambit to keep us there for ever, '—tell me about, um . . .' I looked around for inspiration and was about to ask the safest thing of all, which was about the meal tonight, when I remembered that it was haggis. The thought of Gertrude regaling me—as she would, oh she would—about the preparation of those minced disgustings was too much for my tactics of despair. So I ended up by sounding quite dotty. '*Alec!*' I said, through an unchewable mouthful of baked grain. Have you noticed how hard oats are to masticate? Well, just try it when your mouth has gone dry and your stomach has been on a journey and is now back in unreceptive mood . . .'Yes, *yes*. Where is Alec?'

'Well,' she said, slightly puzzled, which was fair enough, 'he's upstairs. In his kilt. And he's brought his accordion. Why don't we go up and you can talk to him yourself? And have a drink—' she looked at me critically '—once you've got that inside you. I must say you certainly look as if you need one—'

'No!' I said, spraying a load of crumbs at her. 'I mean, tell me more about Alec and the, um, you know . . .' It must have come out leeringly because she smiled with coy questioning.

'No,' she said. 'I'm not sure what you're on about. Do you mean sex over sixty?'

I squeaked a bit at that. 'Certainly not. Well, not if you don't want to. That is, well . . . yes.'

Anything to keep us down there.

She patted my shoulder. 'Oh, does *that* worry you?' she said kindly.

'What?' She raised a springy grey eyebrow. 'Sex?' I squeaked through the oatcake.

'You tell me. I don't know what's going on. You came in looking so bright and now you're all over the place.' She brushed a few crumbs off my velvet chest. 'Come on, now. Be brave. Let's go upstairs and have a drink. And calm down. People aren't going to bite you, you know. And you look absolutely splendid.'

With which she marched away so that I could only follow.

Looking absolutely splendid, I thought ruefully, doesn't mean you feel it.

Just before she opened the door upstairs again I said, 'Why isn't Ruth here?'

Gertrude turned to me, already twisting the handle. 'I didn't ask her,' she said simply.

'Why ever not?'

'Well, I don't *always*,' she said, quite matter-of-factly.

'But—' I hissed, and poked my finger at the door panel '—you've asked Roland.'

'Yes,' she said puzzled. 'He's here.'

'Well, isn't that a bit odd?'

'Odd? Why odd?'

'Well, I mean, I know you're a nonconformist and all that, but husbands and wives usually go together. Especially when one of them is pregnant.'

'Yes, they do,' she said. 'I didn't ask Victor either.'

With that she pushed open the door, put her large warm hand on the small of my back and with a neat little shove pushed me in.

'Alec,' she called. 'Here's Pat. Come and talk to her will you. I must go and look at the pans.'

There was a terrible moment when I thought I was going to be hysterical. First because of Alec's outfit and the knees and the little swinging sporran that looked so obscene, and second because about a million and a half pennies had just dropped to where my rotating stomach refused to accept them.

'Alec,' I said, cutting across what I think was some fulsome praise for my outfit. 'Is Victor married to Ruth?'

He looked at me, mouth open, previous sentence unfinished.

'Well, he was when I saw him last week,' he said, and laughed.

'Then who . . .' I glanced millisecondly across to the french windows. They were still standing there, though now with their backs to us, looking out and horribly close to each other, practically entwined like ivy '. . . is Roland?'

'Well,' said Alec, a deal too loudly, and he began to turn to indicate where Roland was.

'No, no,' I hissed. Hissing had become part of my persona suddenly. 'I mean, what is his

301

relationship to Ruth?'

'Her brother,' he said.

Than which, I declare, there could be no shorter nor more powerful sentence in the history of my conversational exchanges.

I am quite sure all of you knew this a long time since. I am quite sure all of you will be thinking, Oh, come now, surely you cannot pretend that you did not know . . . Well, so it was. When one is at the centre of the vortex, one's vision becomes distorted. Everyone else, watching from the periphery, is likely to have twenty-twenty. Metaphorically speaking, Alec had just given me a pair of glasses and the clarity was astounding. Indeed, it took some moments for air to return to my windpipe. Meanwhile I gave a faithful impersonation of a guppy and squeezed his elbow to maintain contact with earthly matters. It really was as bad as that.

'Her *brother!*' Strangulation remained.

'People do have them you know,' he said kindly. 'And now come and have a drink. I expect you'd like one?'

Swinging his kilt he led me, lock, stock, empty of stomach and quite devoid of knee joints, across to where the drinks, and Roland-plus-one, were standing.

I don't know if there is a female version of working your balls off. Breasts don't have the same ring of virility and everything else is nice and neatly tucked away. Perhaps some inspired feminist could let me know. In the meantime, that apparently solely masculine activity must suffice to indicate how hard I worked to win Roland back into my fold. What I did not do as we sat down to dine would scarcely fill a nun's dance shoe. He was diagonally opposite me. And black hair, with her sultry eyes and long white hands, was some way down from me to the right. Good old Gertrude for sticking rigidly to her seating plan. I could see that Elinor Thing was jolly cross about it, and there was a little altercation as she attempted to seat herself next to him, but Gertrude wasn't having any.

'Elinor,' she called commandingly. 'Come and sit here. I want you to meet . . .'

Who cares *who* she wanted her to meet? It could have been William Hurt or Robert Redford (and that *is* saying something). If I had been grateful for this rigidity in the past in terms of being seated away from Gordon, I was immeasurably grateful for it on Burns Night. We were close enough to do each other a lot of psychological damage, which is precisely what I intended to do. What was the point of holding back? There would be no further opportunities and there was no time for subtlety. Vamping is not second nature to me, but I had a go at it. I could think of little else.

I began at once, taking a leaf out of Lauren Bacall's come-hither notebook. It seemed to me that it was best to have a role model in mind and I had just finished reading her autobiography which Wanda (trust her) had lent me, so I was quite into the concept. And not only that but if I began to feel faint-hearted or embarrassed (which, to be frank, I did—I mean, these things do not sit easy on an ordinary woman) I could simply pretend that I *was* Lauren Bacall and not me, and therefore feel free to pursue it. Under the circumstances, and having to eat haggis while attempting this feat of switched persona and seduction (and having to ignore those itsy-bitsy pieces of gristle that you would so love to remove from the cracks in your teeth) I think it looked quite seductive. Though I was so busy doing it I didn't sort of look at the result. But it seemed to work. Good grief, I thought at one point as I looked across the table and focused for a moment, it *has to* . . .

And I redoubled my efforts.

I even managed, with some careful peeking under the tablecloth to make sure I got the right limb (there was a young poetess from Wanstead directly opposite me and it would have been bad form to have upset her meal) to touch his foot with mine (I have never, ever, ever played footsy with anyone before). When he looked up, having first looked under, and then into my eyes, I gave him the benefit (I hoped) of a terrifically wanton wink. It brought me out in a cold sweat to do it, but, really, I had no option, had I? And then he put his hand under his chin and leaned across the tablecloth slightly and said at last, 'Just what is going on?' with, I was relieved to see, more amusement than recoil.

So I put my hand on my chin and said through half-closed eyes (*just* like Ms Bacall, I hoped—only I didn't have the dangling cigarette mouth-cornerwards), 'I thought you were married to Ruth. I *am* glad that you are not.'

And he had the grace to remove his hand from his chin and stretch out his arms across the table in a sort of easing-of-tension way and say, 'Well, well. Did you now?' and laugh a bit.

But really, it was only when Alec came wafting around with the brandy bottle and Roland declined to have any, while reciprocating the footsy under the table, and saying, 'Better not, thanks, Alec. I think I may be calling in for a nightcap somewhere later,' and giving me a very dangerous and quizzing sort of look, that I ventured to hope the balls-off routine had worked. I was a bit regretful about relinquishing it, really. Though some men say the role of hunter is onerous, I didn't find it so. Not having much experience of taking my destiny in my own hands, it proved to be rather satisfactory and appealing. Especially when Lauren B had to take the responsibility instead of me. But for the time being, the old roles resumed and I went back to a modicum of coyness. I gave a little flutter of approval to his veiled enquiry (Oh yuk!), and that, really, was that. I took a peep at old sultryness further down the table and decided (in conscience) that she would easily find someone else, her being so lovely. And anyway, if she was only *just* divorced then I had seniority of claim over her; I had been in the dog days far longer than she had, even if I hadn't realised it. So with that sisterly thought I put her out of my mind and concentrated on thoughts of a far nicer, more personal, more pressing nature.

That was probably the longest Burns Night known to woman. Even with the most intimate, liberal of friendships, it is not on to leave the dinner table (potential seductresses take note) immediately the food is finished. Decency required at least half an hour's post-prandial conversation despite Gertrude's suggestion that I could eat and run if I wanted. I couldn't be that rude, not when I was so *happy*, now could I? And anyway, there were Alec's accordion-accompanied renderings of some (far, far too many) of Burns's songs and other Scottish bardship. The only thing that kept me halfway towards coping was the humour of it all. Catching Roland's eye became too dangerous and there was certainly no question of any more footsy. One more pressing of my naked instep and I would have had to be peeled off the ceiling.

306

Retrospectively, I am astonished that no one read the charge in the air because it was fairly crackling by the time—quite suddenly and programmed, apparently, without any conscious thought—I stood up and said that I had to be going.

'Is anyone driving towards . . . ?' I began.

And before I had finished the sentence Roland was also on his feet saying, 'Yes, I am. I'll give you a lift.' But I don't think anyone noticed that I had left out the name of my destination. Not that it mattered. Not that anything much mattered after that, except a series of convoluted thoughts (which took on a peculiarly consuming importance) about whether Brian had behaved himself and whether I would have time to check that my vests and used tissues were well out of sight, and whether there was still some oil left in the pink lamp. Earth-turning stuff like that. And even *they* became irrelevant once we were outside Gertrude's house, breathing the cold night air, the vapour of our laughter swirling between us.

*   *   *

Poor Brian. He had no chance with my feet that night. Not that—I could see by his face— he had really expected the promise of a night spent with me to come true. He accepted his defeat quite characteristically with just a grunt

307

and a relocation of his world-weary head before closing his eyes to it all. If Roland's presence gave him any happy memory of Bulstrode and a night of abandonment, he kept it to himself. There was no flicker of recognition as he gave himself up to the self-flailing joys of acute loneliness. He *liked* the dog days. He, comfortably, mourned the absent Rachel. I, quite suddenly, did neither. To each their own. Well, for the time being anyway. And as I turned out the light in the kitchen and left him to snore in his comatose darkness it felt very much as if I, too, had been claimed from some sort of halfway pound. Though, without doubt, I had no intention of being so unaroused by the circumstance as he. There are some corollaries that leave each other at the station. Brian could have his pleasurable death-wish and he was welcome to it. I was going for the 'life' side of things, than which, very probably, and just at that moment especially (though who knows what the future might bring? For there are, after all, no absolute story endings, happy or otherwise, only continuations unto the grave), there seemed no better method than that simple, eternal relationship known, to we foolish romantics, as love.

We hope you have enjoyed this Large Print book. Other Chivers Press or Thorndike Press Large Print books are available at your library or directly from the publishers.

For more information about current and forthcoming titles, please call or write, without obligation, to:

Chivers Large Print
published by BBC Audiobooks Ltd
St James House, The Square
Lower Bristol Road
Bath BA2 3BH
UK
email: bbcaudiobooks@bbc.co.uk
www.bbcaudiobooks.co.uk

OR

Thorndike Press
295 Kennedy Memorial Drive
Waterville
Maine 04901
USA
www.gale.com/thorndike
www.gale.com/wheeler

All our Large Print titles are designed for easy reading, and all our books are made to last.